DEAD IN OXFORD

A gripping crime thriller full of twists

Doug Mullen Book 3

To David,

Peter Tickler

PETER TICKLER

JOFFE BOOKS

First published 2020
Joffe Books, London
www.joffebooks.com

ISBN 978-1-78931-435-9

PART 1

THE FIRE

CHAPTER 1

Becca Baines would kill him. Not literally of course. Becca was a tough cookie, but killing a man because he had stood her up on a supper date was a step too far, even for her. A volley of verbals almost certainly. A refusal to see him ever again. Possibly even a jab in the ribs with her forefinger, though Doug Mullen doubted it. She was a woman who had no need to resort to physical violence. Her tongue was sufficient.

Mullen cursed himself. How could he have been so stupid? His mobile had been on the verge of disaster for days, the battery regularly running down to nothing within a few hours of being charged, but he had never quite got around to doing anything about it. And now here he was, running hopelessly late with a dud mobile, no car charger in the car — *duh!* — and no other means to tell her that he wasn't going to be home to welcome her into the house for the meal he had planned. He tried to dredge his memory for her mobile number, but of course he couldn't remember it. It was stored in his contact list on his dead phone. Who memorised numbers these days? What was the point?

For times like these? The voice in his head wasn't going to be silenced but Mullen tried to ignore it and swore again.

At least she would have been able to let herself into the house. Thank God he had taken Rex the Westiepoodle with him, or there would have been something very nasty to clear up behind the sofa — the dog's favourite spot. He pressed the accelerator down hard as his battered Ford Focus laboured its way up East Ilsey Hill. What would Professor Moody think about him leaving a key under a plant pot for visitors? When she had taken up a temporary fellowship in the USA and signed him up to babysit her house and dog, she had left him a long list of rules. Do this, don't do that. Stay out of her bedroom, for example. Sex on the Afghan rug was banned, too (though not, apparently, on any others). There had been copious notes on how to run the garden. But there had been no pronouncement on the leaving of keys under plant pots where any half-smart burglar would find it. Actually, as he assured himself, the key was well-hidden and it was only Becca and his neighbour, Karen, who knew about it. So what harm was there in that?

Isn't that the first place a burglar would look? Under a plant pot? The accusing voice in his head still hadn't given up. Mullen switched on the radio and turned up the volume. The music drowned out his thoughts. He would be home in twenty minutes and then he would explain to Becca what had happened — *if* she was still there and didn't brain him first.

The first hint of trouble was a police car which roared past him as he headed up Cumnor Hill. But Mullen didn't connect the blaring siren and flashing lights with himself. Why should he? That would be paranoia. Besides, his thoughts had now returned to Becca. It was only as he turned into his road and saw not just the police car but a fire engine outside his house that panic bazookaed him. He pressed his accelerator and then a few moments later hit the brake pedal, screeching to a halt behind the emergency vehicles like a stunt driver.

He jumped out and rushed forward, forgetful of the dog. Flames and smoke belched out of the house from both the downstairs and upstairs windows.

'Becca!' he screamed.

'Stop!' someone shouted. He ignored the call and ran towards the side gate that led into the back garden. He could see that entry from the front was out of the question, but maybe he could get in via the patio doors at the back. He had keys for both in his pocket and he scrabbled for them with one hand as he hurtled forward, crashing open the flimsy wooden gate and ignoring the repeated calls for him to stop.

He reached the patio doors and tried to fit the key into the lock. He couldn't see any flames, but the kitchen was thick with dense black smoke. The key turned and Mullen wrenched hard at the handle. Once, twice and then a third time. When the door finally gave way and slid open, a ferocious torrent of heat and flame blew him backwards.

He forced himself to his feet. He had to try again. 'Becca!' He lowered his head like a bull and prepared to charge forward into the inferno. But he never crossed the threshold. Strong arms grabbed him and held him firm.

'You bloody fool!' It was that same Mancunian voice that had shouted at him to stop, but this time it was right by his ear. 'What the hell are you trying to do?'

Mullen wanted to answer, but he was already being frogmarched away. And in his heart, he knew that he was too late.

It was only when the paramedics took charge of him that the pain hit him. He was shivering and the left side of his face felt like it had had the skin ripped clean off. 'Becca's in there . . . Becca's in there.' He kept repeating the words like a mantra. Fear had taken hold of him and was twisting hard.

'If she's in there, they'll get her out,' someone said.

'Of course they will,' someone else said.

But Mullen didn't believe either of them. No one could have survived that.

There was a yap. A familiar yap. Rex. 'Is this your dog?' A policeman held him. 'Followed you round the back. Stupid as you are.'

Mullen curled his fingers around Rex's collar. 'My girlfriend, Becca . . .' *Girlfriend.* He had never called her that before, never before thought of her as that. 'She's in there.'

There was a silence, the sort of silence that brought panic.

'You'd better get him to hospital.'

'You're sure?' a female paramedic said.

The policeman leaned closer to her, dropping his voice, but not so as Mullen couldn't hear. 'One body inside, but she's beyond help.'

Mullen opened his mouth to say something, but the pain seared down his face again. He felt a prick in his arm. *Morphine* he thought to himself. *I hope to God it's morphine.* And then he felt himself beginning to cry.

PART 2

BEFORE THE FIRE

CHAPTER 2

It all began with the midday mail delivery. There was the clang of the letterbox plate heralding its arrival and Doug Mullen, who was having a dull, slow day, got up from the kitchen table and padded through to the front hall. He picked up the small pile of mail from the floor and went back to his seat. He looked through it without enthusiasm. 'Mail' was barely the right word: the first three items were just leaflets advertising a local Indian takeaway, a special pizza deal and a sofa sale. Only one item could be termed a *bona fide* piece of mail.

Mullen stared at it in surprise. Firstly because it was addressed to him (he rarely got any letters of any sort — they were always for Professor Melissa Moody) and secondly because the envelope was pink. He lifted the envelope to his nose and sniffed. It was an act of hope rather than expectation and the result was exactly as he knew it would be: not even a hint of perfume.

He took a sip from the mug of freshly made coffee that sat on the table in front of him. He savoured for a few moments the prospect of what might be in the envelope then slipped one of Professor Moody's rather fancy knives under the flap and slit it open.

He looked inside and for a moment failed to find anything. Then he saw it, and with a deft pinch of his fingers removed the small scrap of paper. It was a newspaper cutting from the personal columns. It was a notice of a death:

Wright, Linda, mother of Ben, Sandra and Kevin, died on 23 June. Private interment at St Nicholas Church, Badgerhurst, Hampshire 11:00 a.m. on 6 July. No flowers. Donations to St Berenice's Hospice.

Mullen's first reaction was a practical one, to check his phone for the date and time. The sixth of July was today. And it was already 12:44 p.m. Too late to attend even if he had wanted to. In any case, he was pretty sure that 'private interment' meant he would have been neither expected nor wanted. In fact, if he was certain of anything, it was that his turning up at the funeral like a ghost would have been extremely unwelcome.

These thoughts were followed by a tsunami of memories that he had long tried to bury deep within his subconscious. They hit him like a series of flashbacks.

And then, very suddenly, Mullen was on his feet and dashing to the downstairs loo where he collapsed onto his knees and was violently sick.

When he made his way back into the kitchen some five minutes later, it was to discover a ring tone coming from the middle of the table. *Skype*, he thought. *Oh shit!* He grabbed his tablet and opened it up.

It was Professor Moody. That was no surprise, largely because she was the only person who ever called him via Skype. A girlfriend called Philippa had Skyped him a few times, but he had only just got used to it when she had concluded that Mullen was a dead loss and given up all contact.

'Hello, Professor!' He tried to sound much more upbeat than he felt. She had initially told him that he could call her 'Mel' though '*not* Melissa!' but Mullen had preferred 'Professor' — it seemed more professional. She hadn't mentioned it again, so he reckoned that secretly she liked it.

'Where is Rex?' she said.

Right on cue, the black Westiepoodle came waddling across the floor. Mullen scooped him up and sat him on his knee, positioning the iPad so that she could see him properly.

'How's my little Rexie?'

Rex didn't reply (obviously), but he did sniff at the iPad. Mullen scrabbled in his shirt pocket for a dog treat and gave it to him, knowing the procedure.

'Mummy will be home soon. Don't you worry, darling.' For a high-flying professor, Moody could be remarkably soppy. 'Maybe sooner than you know.'

If, like Rex, Mullen's ears had been capable of it, they would have pricked up. He wasn't expecting her back for a couple of months.

'Don't you worry, Douglas.' The professor seemed to sense his alarm from across the Atlantic. 'I won't throw you out on the street. It will only be for a few days. Then I'll be gone again. It all depends.'

Rex had apparently had enough. He extracted himself from Mullen's gentle grip and flopped down onto the floor.

'Anyway . . .' The professor shifted from soppy mode into business mode. 'Show me the kitchen.'

Mullen never knew when the professor was going to call. That was because the main reason for the calls was to check up — not just on Rex's wellbeing, but also on Mullen's housekeeping.

Mullen stood up and dutifully gave her a sweep of the kitchen. There were two sinks and two draining boards and an expanse of slate work surface. All were immaculately clean and clear of debris. The need to keep things smart and tidy, ready at any moment for a general inspection, had been one aspect of his army life that was currently standing him in very good stead.

'Hmm! Now how about my bedroom?'

This took Mullen by surprise. Her bedroom was out of bounds. She had made that clear at the very beginning. It would, he felt sure, be dusty, even though he had kept the door firmly shut. He tramped obediently up the stairs and opened the door. He stood there and scanned the camera slowly around the room.

'Good,' she said. 'But maybe you could give it a spring clean.'

'Of course.'

'Back to the kitchen, then. I've time for a little chat, but I'm being picked up in twenty minutes, so not too long.'

Picked up by whom? Mullen was human enough to be curious. A taxi? A boyfriend. A girlfriend? He suspected she was gay but wouldn't have bet his mortgage on it — if he had one.

Back at the kitchen table, Mullen sipped at his now lukewarm coffee. He guessed she wanted to talk about some aspect of the house, but instead she asked him how he was. Mullen was surprised. That wasn't how their conversations usually worked.

'OK,' he said.

'You've got breakfast down your T-shirt.'

'Have I?' The breakfast was regurgitated and smelly, but he wasn't going to admit to that. He would change as soon as the call ended.

'You look tired. And stressed. Or maybe like a man who's seen a ghost.'

He nodded, not sure how else to react.

'So Douglas, I'll repeat my question. How are you?'

Doug Mullen, now that he had been given permission, told her — rather, he began to tell her — about the death notice and who Linda, Ben and the others were and why it was such a bolt out of the blue. But he didn't get to the nastier memories because, like an old-fashioned traffic police officer, she held up her hand. *Stop!*

'I think you need to talk to someone, Douglas. Face to face and not over Skype. So I am going to get in touch with a therapist I know. Kazia Ciesla. And she will contact you and you will tell her all about it and I will pay the bill. OK?'

Mullen nodded dumbly. He wasn't sure how he felt about therapy. Right now, it was as if he was in a crazy dream.

Maybe he would wake up from it and everything would be back to normal. Maybe after a day or two he would get some perspective on it all and things would suddenly make sense. Or maybe not.

'Well?'

'That's very kind of you.'

'Now I really must go.' The professor brought him back down to earth with a bump. 'Wait for Kazia to contact you and don't let me down, Douglas. In the meantime, you can always talk to the dog. But don't scare him.'

She terminated the Skype call abruptly, leaving Mullen feeling strangely bereft. He would have liked to have talked to her longer. There was so much he could have told her.

Rex, who had retreated to his basket, gave a whine. A whine of sympathy? Mullen liked to think so. But talk to the dog? Rex might be a good companion, but he wasn't the sounding board that Mullen needed. No doubt the dog wanted to walk, not talk.

Pull yourself together, lad! Mullen stood up and stripped off his T-shirt and then, for good measure, his shorts. He couldn't take the dog out reeking of vomit.

* * *

Mullen was running late. It had been a third wretched night, one of intermittent wakefulness and nightmarish dreams. Of course, in the end he had fallen into a deep sleep, shortly after five o'clock and after a second cup of night-time tea in the kitchen. As a consequence he had slept through the alarm on his mobile phone and only woken when Rex had jumped up on the bed and licked his face. It had taken Mullen a few moments to come to and remember with horror that he had an appointment with Becca Baines that morning.

He had pushed Rex out into the garden with his breakfast, showered, eaten two bits of toast, locked the dog in the house and headed for town. He had been lucky that he had got to the bus stop just as a number four pulled up. Even so, a glance at his watch told him that he would be lucky to get to the Ashmolean Museum on time.

He sat upright in his seat and tried to relax. He was tired and his stomach was churning and the bus was stopping and starting with an irregularity that seemed designed to keep its passengers constantly on edge. By the time he got to the centre and off the bus, he was running very late. He hurried as fast as he could past the numerous tourists who thronged Oxford, but his bowels were giving him grief. He should have gone to the loo, but now wasn't the time. He jogged between the traffic in Beaumont Street and found himself in front of the museum.

One, two, three, four, five and he was up the steps. To any casual observer, he would have appeared the epitome of a man in a hurry, but despite that he stopped dead and stood rock still for several seconds as he looked up the tall classical columns that framed the entrance to the Ashmolean. It may have been the oldest university museum in the world — he knew that because he had looked it up on Wikipedia the previous evening — but despite having lived in the Oxford area for nearly two years, he had never set foot inside it.

Indeed he wouldn't have been going there on this particular morning if he hadn't been asked to do so. Rightly or wrongly, he lumped the Ashmolean alongside the Bodleian and all the imposing stone-faced colleges that dominated the centre of the medieval city. Visually they were impressive, he acknowledged that, but they were also the icons of privilege and learning: architecturally grand, but emotionally they left him cold. They were all part of a world from which he felt utterly excluded.

But this wasn't the only reason why Mullen hesitated. His bowels were gripped with pain again. Why the hell hadn't he gone to the loo at home? He looked at his mobile phone. He was surprised that he hadn't received an irritated text from Becca Baines to ask him where the heck he had got to. That was something. He felt annoyed with himself. If there was one thing the army had drummed into his skull, it was the importance of being on time. Yet here he was running late for a meeting with someone who might — or might not — put some work his way.

He knew Becca but hadn't seen or heard from her for over a year. Her phone call the previous evening had been something of a relief. It had come immediately after Kazia Ciesla had phoned to arrange a first meeting, and Mullen had felt the pleasure of being a man in demand. But Becca had been extremely cagey about why she wanted to see him. She had hinted at needing his professional (ha!) skills. He only hoped she wasn't going to ask him to provide them as a favour 'for old time's sake'. He really needed the money.

He ignored the pain in his gut and marched across the courtyard and in through the rotating glass doors. He had discovered that there were two places to eat or have a coffee in the Ashmolean: one in the basement and the other up four flights of stairs. Becca had unfortunately chosen the latter. Mullen kept himself pretty fit, but in his current state he felt anything but, and by the time he had reached the top floor he felt even worse. He pushed through the door into the restaurant and scanned the area. Only three tables were occupied: a pair of middle-aged women just in front of him, a bearded man glued to his newspaper and, in the far corner, Becca Baines.

He wended his way through the tables. 'I'm sorry, Becca. The traffic was awful.'

She looked up at him, a half-smile on her face. 'How are you, Doug?'

'Fine.' He pulled off his leather jacket, draped it over the back of his chair and sat down. 'How about you?'

'Good, thanks.'

She didn't look it. There were dark bags under her eyes. Long shifts at the hospital, he guessed. And he remembered her as a woman who played hard as well as worked hard. He waited for her to start things off. During their brief friendship, she had always had something to say for herself, but not this morning. They sat in uncertain silence.

There was a cough and a waitress materialised to Mullen's left. 'Can I get you something, sir?'

'Americano,' he said. 'With milk. And a glass of tap water.' Actually, he would have preferred a pain-numbing depth charge to sort out his gut, but he doubted if anything like that would be on the menu.

The waitress withdrew.

He smiled across the table at Becca, trying to keep it light, trying to ignore the urge to rush to the loo. 'Is this a date?'

'Bit late for that, Doug.' Her face cracked into laughter. She stood up and turned so he could see her in profile. She had been a big woman when Mullen had last seen her, but she was a lot bigger now. 'Twenty-nine weeks too late, in point of fact.'

'Blimey.'

'Don't you dare say you thought I had just put on a bit of weight or I'll clock you one.'

'No, of course not. I just . . .' He stumbled to a halt then made a clumsy recovery. 'Congratulations . . .' It seemed the least that he should be saying. 'Who's the lucky guy?'

She slumped down heavily into her chair. 'The lucky guy has pissed off into the ether. Domesticity and fatherhood are not, it seems, his cup of tea.'

'I'm sorry.'

'As you may recall, Doug, I never was very good at picking men.'

He took a sip at his coffee, remembering how he had first seen her, through the lens of a camera kissing his client's husband. Despite that, he had liked Becca. She'd been fun and crude and blunt and they'd had had a moment when their lives had collided. Mullen pulled himself back to the present. 'So why did you contact me, Becca?'

She shrugged.

'You want me to help in some way?'

'You probably can't.'

He pondered this. When a woman called him to a meeting and then told him he probably couldn't help her, it was a sure-fire way of getting his interest. He was a sucker for a damsel in distress, even when the damsel came with as much baggage as Becca.

'Try me.'

'I can't afford to pay you lots of money, Doug, and nor can my friend.'

Mullen wasn't surprised. Becca was a nurse. Pregnant. No bloke. She wanted him to do something for free. Or as near as dammit.

'Does your friend have a name?'

'Marie. She lives next door to me.'

'So what's the problem?'

'Her husband killed himself.'

Mullen waited. What was there to say?

Becca continued. 'He rang her up to say he was sorry and then, while she was on the phone, he blew out his brains.'

'God!' It was as if an incendiary device had gone off inside his head. 'Sorry!' He held up his right hand in apology. 'I need to go to the loo. Just wait here and I'll be back.'

It took him just over four minutes to do what he needed to do and get back out into the restaurant. He was trying at the same time to get his brain and emotions unscrambled. After the funeral announcement in the pink envelope had hurtled him back to the trauma of his mate's death, now out of the blue he was being asked to investigate a man blowing his brains out. Back to the past, and back to the present. He didn't know what to think. What was he letting himself in for?

He was so preoccupied that he was halfway across the restaurant heading for their table before he realised that Becca wasn't there. He looked around. The two old ladies were still at their post but their eyes were directed towards the door. The man with the newspaper was still engrossed in it, almost hidden by it. Mullen looked around, wondering if perhaps Becca had decided to move to another more private part of the restaurant, but he couldn't see her anywhere. He reached the table. Her cup was half empty. Her handbag had gone and so had her mobile phone. Had she gone to the loo, too? He looked around for the waitress. He would ask her. Maybe she would know where Becca had gone.

At this point the two old women, as if controlled by a puppeteer, stood up sharply and hurried towards the exit door. That was the first sign — or rather the first sign that Mullen picked up on — that something had happened. He followed them. They stopped at the top of the stairs just outside the restaurant door. Mullen caught up and peered over their shoulders down the stairs. Alarm and consternation swirled around like leaves in an autumn squall. A small crowd of people was on the lower stairwell. They must have been coming up but had come to a halt. Hands were on mouths and whispers were exchanged. One of them had a mobile phone against his ear.

The centre of everyone's attention was at the bottom of the first tier of stairs, which twisted left a full hundred and eighty degrees before continuing downwards. This was where Mullen saw his waitress talking into a mobile phone. Beyond her, another woman was on her knees, leaning over a prone figure. She appeared to have medical training because she was checking for signs of life. The woman looked up and said something to the waitress, who began to wave her left hand, making patterns in the air. She moved forwards, motioning the onlookers to move back down to the floor below. Mullen wiped the cold sweat off his forehead and plunged down the stairs. He had good view of the body now. As he had feared, it was Becca Baines.

'Is she all right? I just went to the toilet. She's pregnant. What about the baby?' The words tumbled forth from his mouth. Normally a man who stayed calm in a crisis, Mullen knew he was a barely coherent mess.

'I think so,' the woman said. She spoke with a mid-European accent and a trace of annoyance. 'I would like you to stay calm, sir. As you see, she's had a fall — a fainting spell on the stairs, it seems. We have summoned an ambulance.' Her hand was on Becca's left wrist, checking the pulse. She said something in Polish that Mullen failed to understand and then adjusted the coat that she had folded under Becca's head. Only then did she look up and focus her attention on Mullen. 'I must now look after the lady until the ambulance comes.' These were words of dismissal. Mullen, still on his haunches, leaned back against the wall. He didn't mind the fact that the woman had taken control. He didn't mind if she was a bit bossy. But he sure as hell wasn't going to leave Becca.

He rode with her in the ambulance. She was semi-conscious by now and had a large swelling on her forehead. He remained silent.

Once at the John Radcliffe Hospital, he found himself being told to stay in the waiting area while she was assessed. Perhaps if he had lied when asked if he was the father of the child, he would have been admitted to the inner sanctum, but he hadn't and he wasn't.

He had, however, taken charge of her handbag. He unzipped it and located her mobile phone. To his surprise it wasn't PIN protected. *Careless*, he thought. He scrolled through the list of contacts. He felt a slight pang of guilt, but the fact was, he needed to contact someone. There was no *Mum* or *Dad* but there was a *Marie*. No surname. Just Marie. *The* Marie? He rang her.

A woman answered on the second ring.

'Hi, Becs.'

'I'm not Becca. I'm an old friend of hers . . . Doug.'

'So why are you ringing me from her phone? Has she left it with you by mistake?'

'No.' He took a breath to calm himself. 'She's in hospital. She fell down the stairs in the Ashmolean in Oxford and—'

'Oh my God! Is she all right? And the baby? What about the baby?'

Two hours later, Mullen and Marie Dench were sitting side by side on plastic chairs at Becca's bedside. They had relapsed into silence. A tall doctor with floppy hair and an upper-class accent had declared that the baby was fine and that Becca was too. All she needed was rest, he said, before departing with the air of a man with a train to catch and no interest in allowing his monologue to become a conversation.

'I need a coffee,' Marie said suddenly, 'and the toilet.' She upped and went before Mullen could get his brain together to respond.

He found sitting in silence with Becca much more relaxing than sitting in silence with Marie and Becca. Marie was an encumbrance. A mean thing to think, perhaps, but that was how he felt. Now, for a few minutes, he was free to concentrate wholly on Becca. He sat there, alert and anxious, willing her to wake up. And then, much to his surprise, she opened her eyes. Just opened them. She didn't look around or turn her head, let alone acknowledge him or show any sign of speaking. Then, as if obeying the orders of the doctor, she slipped back into the oblivion of sleep.

When Marie reappeared with two cups of coffee, Mullen wondered whether he should ask her about her husband, but he quickly dismissed the thought. It was hardly the right time. In any case, Marie seemed to know nothing about him. Maybe Becca hadn't actually told her of her intentions to call on his help as a private detective.

So they sat there, talking rather awkwardly and sipping their coffees. Marie was French. Her English was immaculate and softly spoken, but her accent gave her origins away. Mostly she spoke about Becca and her own son, James. 'We are neighbours. Becca is a good neighbour.' When she did ask Mullen about himself, he concentrated on the army background and then the fact that he was house-sitting for a professor who had taken a temporary academic post in the USA. It seemed safer to ignore the private detective angle.

A nurse came in. 'Becca needs rest,' she announced, a pointed and polite way of telling them they really should have left some time ago. 'We'll keep her in for observation overnight. Who should we contact in the morning?'

'Me!' Marie was quicker on the draw than Mullen.

Even so, they both handed over mobile numbers, Marie as main contact and Mullen as backup, and then they left.

It was raining outside and a cool wind was blowing, but Marie didn't seem to notice as she lit up a cigarette. She blew out a trail of smoke that flew carelessly over Mullen's right shoulder. 'So you and Becca are good friends?' She tossed the question out with deceptive casualness.

'Yes, I guess we are,' he replied.

'So how come she has never mentioned you?' Not so much a question as a grenade.

He looked at his watch. 'Look, Marie, I have to get home and let the dog out or he'll be ringing the RSPCA and reporting me.'

'Are you the father of her baby, Doug?' The grenade exploded.

'No!' The word came out faster and harsher than he had intended.

'Because that would explain it, would it not — why she has never told me about you?'

'That's not it.'

'So what are you not telling me?' Behind her softly spoken English was a Professor Moody-like incisiveness.

Mullen sighed. 'Becca and I met the year before last. But we are not lovers. Never have been. I'm a private detective and I first came across her during an investigation.'

'Merde!' Marie took a final vicious pull on her cigarette, dropped it on the pavement and stamped on it. 'You are a detective? A private eye?'

'She told me about your husband.'

'She should not have.'

'She's worried about you.'

Marie felt in her pockets and lit up another cigarette.

'I'm sorry for your loss,' Mullen said, trying to make amends.

Her eyes blazed. 'You are sorry? You did not know him.'

Mullen said nothing, merely watched as she enveloped herself in more swirling smoke.

'What did she tell you?' she hissed.

'Not much. We didn't finish our conversation. She told me that your husband had shot himself. Then I had to go to the loo. And when I returned, she had fallen down the stairs.'

Marie said something in French. More swearing, Mullen guessed. Anger was bubbling out of her like molten lava. She stabbed a finger at his chest.

'Becca should not have involved you. My husband is dead. Suicide. There is nothing to investigate. Now, if you do not mind, I must go and pick my child up from school.'

Mullen watched her stride across the car park beyond the bus stop. There was an X13 waiting there and he hurried across, getting on just before the driver closed the doors. Up on the top deck, he scanned the car park, but Marie was nowhere to be seen. He leaned back and shut his eyes as the bus began its bumpy trip across Oxford.

Nothing to investigate. The words resonated round his head. Why had Marie Dench been so insistent about that?

CHAPTER 3

Mullen got the phone call at eight thirty a.m. It was Becca, asking him to rescue her. 'They want my bed,' she told him. 'Marie thought she had this morning off, but she's been called into work today. And anyway, she's pretty pissed off with me for contacting you.'

So Mullen, ever the gallant knight, picked Becca up. But she didn't want to go home. 'Any chance of a nice brunch at yours, Doug? The hospital food was lousy.'

Becca still looked tired, with dark rings round red eyes and one heck of a bruise on her forehead, but otherwise she was much as Mullen remembered. 'A fancy house and a cute little doggie!' she exclaimed on meeting Rex in the enormous kitchen. 'You've fallen on your feet and no mistake.'

'How would you like your egg?'

'Poached, please. Two, if that's not pushing my luck.' She knelt down on the floor and began to fondle Rex. 'What is she?'

'She's a he. Name of Rex. A Westiepoodle. They're usually white, not black.'

'Ah, bless!' She cradled Rex against her capacious bosom.

Twenty minutes later, Mullen and Becca were both sitting at the table. Mullen was feeling rather pleased with himself for conjuring up such a spread at short notice — eggs, bacon, chipolatas, mushrooms, tomatoes and baked beans, plus brown toast. Normally he settled for muesli or else toast and marmalade. After all, who wanted to cook a full English breakfast for one?

'So how do you know Marie?'

Becca didn't answer for three mouthfuls. Then she held her fork in the air and waved it in Mullen's direction. 'I met her in the hospital. She's a nurse, but now she works out in the community, part-time. I live next door to her. I got fed up with my flat in Wood Farm and she told me about the cottage next to hers. It's in the middle of nowhere, the sort of place an estate agent would describe as "full of potential," which all adds up to a nice cheap rent.' She skewered a mushroom and piece of sausage and resumed her meal.

Mullen took a sip of tea. He watched her continue to demolish her plate of food. He liked having company. Sometimes he pretended to himself that he was at heart a loner and that Rex was enough of a companion, but it wasn't true. The conversation with Professor Moody had unsettled him. Of course, he had already been unsettled by the death notice and all the memories that it had disturbed. But the professor's hint that she might return for a fleeting visit had underlined the fact that in the autumn she would be back for good, and he would have to move out and start over again somewhere else. He wasn't so much a loner as lonely.

Becca leaned back in her chair and belched. Mullen was only halfway through his food, but her plate was bare except for half a sausage.

'Do you mind if I give this to Rex?'

'I don't feed him from the table. It might get him into bad habits.'

Becca picked up the piece of sausage. There was a gleam in her eye. 'Rules are made to be broken.' She tossed the sausage to Rex, who grabbed it triumphantly and withdrew to his basket. 'He's been ever so good. I think he deserves a little treat.'

Mullen didn't agree. But he didn't argue either. It wouldn't have done any good if he had. Instead, he said, 'It's good to see you again, Becca.'

'Likewise, Doug.' She smiled. 'Do you mind if I crash upstairs for a while? I can't face going home just yet.'

'Be my guest.'

It was almost one p.m when Becca stumped down the stairs and into the kitchen. Mullen was ironing.

She laughed. 'Well, would you Adam and Eve it? Mr Mullen, the domestic god!'

Mullen pretended not to care, but the sheets were linen and the professor's return was no longer a distant mirage. A spring clean of her room ought to include fresh bedding, he reckoned. 'Feeling better?' he said.

She moved towards him until she was up close. She smelled of perfume. Had she been rooting through the professor's things? She whispered in his ear. 'Maybe you could come and keep house for me, Doug.' Then another laugh, cruder this time.

He couldn't help smiling.

'Actually, Doug, I've just had a phone call from Marie. She's calmed down. Says she's sorry if she was rude to you yesterday. But if you could run me home now, she'd like to talk to you before she has to collect her son from school.'

* * *

Marie didn't seem to know how to start. She had made each of them a mug of tea, but now that they were sitting down — she and Becca next to each other on the sofa and Mullen opposite on the matching armchair — nothing was happening. Becca patted her encouragingly on the shoulder but that merely caused tears to run down her cheeks. She pulled a handkerchief from the sleeve of her cardigan and dabbed at her face.

'When you're ready,' Mullen said calmly. 'There's no rush.' In another life, he would have made a good therapist.

Marie sucked in a deep breath and let it out slowly. In . . . Out . . . In . . . Out . . . In . . . Out.

Finally, she spoke. 'It was just after nine o'clock. I know that because I had been listening to the radio. When he is home, he likes to watch the TV, but I like to listen to the radio. BBC Radio Four, mostly. News, documentaries, dramas. I love a good drama.

'I was worried. He was late. Sometimes he works late if Amanda has arranged for a private party in the evening. But normally he is home by seven p.m. He always tells me if he is going to be late. He warns me. Like a man should.

'I ring him twice. I leave voice messages on his phone. I send texts. *Rien.* Nothing. No reply. I think I hear his car. I pull the curtain to the side and look out of the window.'

Marie stood up and walked over to the front window, where she mimicked what she had done. 'Like this. But it is another car driving past, not his. My car is there. A red Ford Ka. Parked to the left. To the right, *rien.*

'I am fussing. That is what I tell myself. *Cut him some slack, Marie,* as you English would say. Maybe he is having a drink with a friend. But he should not drink and drive. I pour myself a gin and tonic. If he is drinking, why shouldn't I?' Marie looked out of the window for several seconds more before moving back across the room and slumping down on the sofa.

'When my phone rang, when I saw it was him, I was cross. I am not a saint. I do not pretend to be perfect. I get angry like anyone else. "Where are you?" I demand. "Why did you not ring earlier?"

'"Sorry," he says — as if it is enough just to say sorry.

'"I sent you two texts", I say. "Two!"' Marie stabbed the air with her forefinger twice, underlining her point.

'"Yes," he says.

'I say, "You did not reply."

'"No," he says. It is always the same with him . . . "*Yes . . . No . . . Sorry*" — always waiting until the storm has blown itself out. Pah!'

Mullen wasn't sure if this was another French word or not, but there was no mistaking the venom with which she spat it out.

'Then I ask him if he is with Amanda.' Marie turned her full gaze on Mullen. 'Amanda is his boss. She runs the café. He cooks. She tells him what to do and he does it. And Amanda is "*buxom*". That is his word for her. Buxom. He likes buxom.'

Mullen didn't comment. Whatever else Marie was, that wasn't a word that could be applied to her. *Skinny*, *thin as a rake* was more like it.

There was a long pause as Marie gathered her breath and her thoughts. 'Then I say — God forgive me — I say, "Have you been fucking Amanda?"

'"I'm not with Amanda," he says. "I promise. I'm not with Amanda."

'It is the way he says it. Suddenly, I know something is wrong. My anger goes. Just like that.' Marie clicked her fingers.

'I listen. I hear only his breathing. Heavy and slow, as if he has been climbing up some mountain and has been compelled to stop. "Robert," I say. "Where are you?"

'"I'm sorry, *ma cherie*."

'I do not know what to think. He is not with Amanda. He is with someone else. He is leaving me for someone else. Who?'

It was Marie who was breathing heavily now. Mullen wondered if she was going to hyperventilate. Her face was red, her eyes bulbous.

'"What are you talking about?" I say.

'"This is for the best," he says. "I am so sorry."

'"What are you talking about?" I say. But he says nothing. I hear only his heavy breathing and then a noise. A terrible noise, like a branch being broken by a pair of giant hands. Crack! And then — nothing.'

Marie stood up. It was as if some internal switch in her brain had been flicked. Off went the emotional upheaval and on went the practical coping mechanism.

'I must go. I need to collect James from school.' She spoke in short, controlled phrases. Almost robotic. 'It is his music lesson today. I always meet him so that he doesn't have to carry the violin on the bus. Thank you for coming, Mr Mullen. I appreciate your concern, but there is nothing that can be done. My husband killed himself. That is a fact. I am still angry with him. I hope you will not judge me for that. But I cannot change facts. Nor can anyone else.'

'It's my fault,' said Becca. 'I thought Doug might be able to help — maybe find out something that the police couldn't. Maybe find out why Robert . . .'

'Why he killed himself? What does it matter? And what good will it do if Mr Mullen does find out? Will it bring Robert back from the dead? Will it make everything all right for James? Of course it will not!'

Marie bent down and picked up both Becca's and Mullen's mugs. She brandished them in the air, one in each hand, as if they were cymbals she was going to smack together and make some cacophonous din.

Her arms froze. Her eyes focused on some horizon visible only to her. And when she spoke it was in a ghostly whisper. 'It would have been better if Robert had been killed in a car accident.' Her hands dropped slowly to her sides. 'It would have been kinder to us who have been left behind. Whatever compelled him to do it, he took the coward's way out. And for that I will never forgive him. Never!'

* * *

Becca's house was a tiny cottage a short walk along the lane. Despite a sudden downpour, Mullen left his car outside Marie's and walked with Becca because he was curious to see where she lived but also because he had a question for her. He waited until he was inside.

'Fancy another cup of tea?' she said.

Mullen checked his watch. 'Actually I need to get to Headington for a meeting.'

‘A meeting? In a dingy pub, you mean? With brown envelopes stuffed with used fivers being passed surreptitiously under dirty tables? How very mysterious.’

‘Not exactly.’ He didn’t feel ready to tell her that he was having to see a therapist. ‘But I do want to ask you something.’

‘As long as it has nothing to do with my sex life, you can ask away.’ She emitted another of her throaty laughs.

‘Becca, why did you get in touch with me when Marie and the police and the coroner all agree that it’s a case of suicide?’

She faced him. ‘Because Robert had no reason to kill himself.’

‘How can you possibly know that?’

She grabbed him by the arm of his jacket and pulled on it hard. ‘Two weeks before he died, Robert told me he was planning to take Marie and James away on a surprise holiday abroad. He asked me for advice on where would be a good place. I don’t think he had ever been abroad in his life. Now why on earth would he have done that if he had been feeling suicidal?’

Mullen nodded. It was a fair point, and yet . . . ‘People’s moods can swing. Or perhaps something happened to change things.’

Becca released her grip on his jacket. ‘Hoorah! Got it in one, Doug. Maybe something changed. And if it did, I want to know what it was and then I want you to tell me and then we’ll decide together whether we should tell Marie.’

* * *

It was a strange place to give therapy. That was Mullen’s initial assessment. ‘Use the side gate and follow the path down to the building at the bottom of the garden’ were Kazia Ciesla’s instructions and he followed them to the letter until he reached a shed. Not a shed as in the ones you often saw on allotments or your average back garden. It was more of a high-class, oversized Wendy house painted duck egg blue with white-framed windows either side of a door, which stood ajar. Mullen paused, uncertain how to proceed. A cat appeared at that moment, slipping out past his feet, apparently unconcerned by his presence. Then, from inside, came a voice. 'Do come in.'

Mullen took a deep breath and entered Kazia Ciesla's lair.

The shed consisted of a single room. A large green, brown and beige Persian-style rug covered most of the floor. A plainer tapestry in similar colours was draped across the rear wall. A low, glass-topped coffee table and two armchairs were the only pieces of furniture. In the left-hand chair sat Kazia Ciesla. She gestured to the other armchair. 'Shut the door and do take a seat.'

Mullen closed the door behind him and sat down. He wiped his hands on his jeans, conscious of the sweat on his palms. It was warmer inside than it had been out. There was a glass of water on the table in front of him. He picked it up and drank half of it.

'Do you prefer Douglas or Doug?'

'Doug.'

'Well, Doug, why have you come to see me?' She sat very still, her hands folded on her lap. She was dressed in a plain green dress, as if trying to tone in with her surroundings. Her short russet hair was cut like a helmet, long silver earrings hung like leaves above an unadorned neck. Early forties was Mullen's guess.

'Professor Moody suggested it.'

She said nothing, though he recognised the flicker of disappointment in her face. It lasted for barely a moment before her professionalism reasserted itself. She continued to say nothing. She was waiting.

Mullen felt himself squirm like a child at primary school who had gravely disappointed his teacher. Of course, that wasn't what she'd been asking. Professor Moody had set it all up.

'I received a notice of death in the post.'

Kazia gave a barely perceptible nod, but one that signified approval and encouragement — or that was how Mullen interpreted it.

'It had been cut out of a newspaper. It was in a pink envelope. A white address label, but handwritten. Nothing else inside.' It was easier to talk about these details. But somehow he knew Kazia wanted him to dig deeper. Why would she be interested in the colour of the envelope? She could have said *'Come on Doug. Let's not skirt around things. Who was the dead person?'*. She was almost certainly thinking that. But Kazia Ciesla remained silent and unmoving in her chair, her hands in her lap, one on top of the other, inscrutable as the Mona Lisa.

Mullen wiped his brow. He took off his jacket and scrabbled in the inside pocket, pulling out the newspaper cutting in its envelope. He read it to her, a word or two at a time, as if he was a primary school child struggling to read, though in fact he could have recited it from memory.

'Wright, Linda, mother of Ben, Sandra and Kevin, died on 23 June. Private interment at St Nicholas Church, Badgerhurst, Hampshire 11:00 a.m. on 6 July. No flowers. Donations to St Berenice's Hospice.'

He paused, conscious that his heart was hammering like crazy. He took three or four deep breaths, waiting until he felt able to continue.

'Linda Wright was the mother of my mate, Ben. I only met her twice. But Ben and I did our army training together. Ben was a nice guy, easy to talk to. He chummed up with me on the first day, and that was how it was until the day he died.'

More palpitations. Another long pause. He looked up at Kazia. She was sitting absolutely still. She might have been a statue were it not for the rise and fall of her breast and the occasional flicker of her intense, watchful eyes. He looked down again, unable to face her or the demons that she was placidly summoning up. It was so much easier to keep it all locked away.

'Receiving that notice of her death,' she said at last, 'and receiving it so unexpectedly, may have awakened memories you would rather have kept buried.' She reverted to silence and more waiting. But Mullen's brain and body had gone into lockdown. The silence expanded into a yawning chasm of nothingness, more awkward with every passing minute until, unexpectedly, Kazia broke it. 'Doug . . . if you feel able, I want you to tell me what happened to Ben.'

Mullen closed his eyes and immediately regretted it. It was like switching on a clip from a horror video. There was a man in army fatigues slumped over a table. A single bright light. It was Ben, of course. Who else could it have been? And there was a terrible smell of blood and burnt flesh that wrenched Mullen back twenty years. The ghastly figure sat up suddenly and then slowly, oh so slowly, twisted around to look at Mullen. His mouth wasn't a mouth, but a hole out of which blood was pouring. The eyes were black sockets. There was a yell. Someone was yelling. Mullen jerked his eyes wide open and realised that it was him.

'Doug!' Kazia's voice was raised, but steady. She gave no sign of being alarmed. He felt like he was about to explode. 'Doug?'

He breathed heavily but he plunged in, desperate to get it all over. 'Ben shot himself. Simple as that. We had been on a three-day exercise. We came home. A group of us went to pub and had a few drinks. When I came back, I noticed Ben's door was shut. There was light coming out from under the door, so I thought I'd go and see him. I knocked and didn't wait for a reply — just barged in. I was a bit drunk. He was slumped over his desk. He had this anglepoise lamp. He had painted it red, white and blue, like the Union Jack, and it shone a pool of light down onto the table. I walked over to slap him on the shoulder — wake him up and give him a scare. But when I reached the table I realised there was blood all over it. His head was on its side and half his face was blown away. God, it was terrible.'

He shut his eyes and he was instantly back there that night, in that small room with the stench of death all around him, and the nausea came flooding though his body. He jumped to his feet, knocking his water flying as he did so, and headed for the door. He managed to pull it open just before he vomited.

* * *

Sitting at his desk in what had once been a bedroom but was now his study, Leo Francombe couldn't help noticing the fact that Kazia's client had been sick all over the path just outside her studio. He swore. Kazia did not normally reduce people to such a state. But he felt little sympathy for the man doubled over the rather expensive paving. His thoughts were devoid of charity. Rather he was wondering which of them, Kazia or her wretched patient, would clean it up and swab it all down. Because one of them would most certainly have to. Otherwise he would have to say something.

Leo straightened up. Kazia appeared at the door behind her client. She laid a hand on his shoulder, exchanged a few words and then walked him towards the side gate. Leo frowned. The man looked familiar. He had seen him somewhere. He rubbed at his chin. He prided himself on his ability to remember faces and names. Of course . . . the hospital! The man had been in Becca's room the other day, along with Marie Dench. And now he was seeing Kazia. He'd be keeping an eye on this man.

CHAPTER 4

Mullen got up at five thirty the next morning. He'd had a surprisingly good night and, after the previous evening's fun and games, he was hungry. So he ate a quick breakfast and drank a milky cup of tea before bundling himself and Rex into the car. Within five minutes he was on the A34 and heading north.

He tried to push Ben to the back of his head. He had slept better than he had feared. It was as if the daytime flashback at Kazia Ciesla's had, temporarily at least, put a stop to the disturbing nightmares. Furthermore, he had decided to set his mind on the present, on what he had promised Becca he would do, rather than dwell on the past. So he focused on Robert Dench. Various questions were whizzing around inside his skull. His destination was some twenty miles away. He wondered idly why Robert had chosen that particular wood to kill himself — if indeed he *had* killed himself. Why not Bagley Wood or Wytham Wood? But, more importantly, who was the dog walker who had found the body?

After returning home from Kazia's, he'd thrown all his clothes into the washing machine before padding upstairs and taking a very long shower, which he'd only stopped when the hot water had run out. He'd then made himself a mug of strong tea and slumped on one of the armchairs. Rex had jumped up onto his lap and there they had sat, dog comforting human and human stroking dog until, with a sudden pang of guilt, Mullen had realised that he hadn't fed Rex his supper.

Only later, after a short walk round the block with the dog, had Mullen finally felt ready to open up his iPad. Then, with Rex again on his lap, he had read all the media reports he could find concerning Robert Dench's death. They had all been very similar and none of them had named the man who had found the body. He had apparently been walking his dog at six thirty in the morning and that was why Mullen had got up long before the dawn chorus today in the hope that his potential witness was a man of rigorous habits. Anyone who walked their dog that early did so for a reason — a dog that demanded it, the need to get to work on time, or just the habit of always waking up early. Mullen reckoned that bumping into him at six thirty that morning really wasn't such a long shot — or at least that was what he kept telling himself as he drove north up the A34.

When he reached the wood in which Robert had died, he parked his long-suffering Ford Focus on the side of the road near a pedestrian gate. There were plenty of tyre marks to tell him that other people did that too — though no other cars were there as early as this today. There were also public footpath signs and well-worn tracks that made it clear that this was the way that inhabitants of the village would enter the wood. As he zipped up his leather jacket, Mullen assured himself that he had shortened the odds of meeting this guy as much as he possibly could.

He kept Rex on the lead, which didn't much please the dog as he snuffled out the delights of this unexplored territory. Mullen walked slowly along the main path into the wood. The cloudless sky meant it was cold, but not as dark as it might easily have been.

Then, about fifteen minutes later, he heard sounds. A large dog came trundling up the path towards him, followed more slowly by a man in a flat cap. Mullen tightened the lead on Rex, ready to drag the little chap out of any trouble. But the golden retriever, which skidded to a halt by Rex, was only interested in playing with Mullen's toy dog, not in eating it.

'Hello. Not seen you around here before.' The man looked at least seventy and nothing like the commuter that Mullen had conjured up in his imagination.

Mullen held up the spray of flowers that he held in his free hand. 'I knew Robert Dench — the man who committed suicide here a few weeks ago? I'm on my way to visit my mother and thought I'd stop off and leave a little tribute. But of course, it's a big wood and I've no idea exactly where he died. Robert and I . . . well, I'm ashamed to say we fell out and I wanted to say sorry.'

The man looked him up and down before nodding. 'I'll show you.' He trudged on past Mullen, up the gradual slope to the top before forking left down a narrower track. 'There.' He pointed to a small pile of stones.

Mullen knelt down and laid the flowers there. 'It must be a terrible thing, to find a man dead.'

It was a stab in the dark. He'd expected all the regulars would know where the dead man had been found, but it was a witness he really wanted. For all Mullen knew, he was going to have to repeat this routine several times, but this was his lucky morning.

'It was.' The man took his cap off in a sudden act of respect. 'Never seen the bloke before. It would have been worse if he had been someone I knew from the village. Even so . . . it was the last thing I was expecting. The problem is that now I expect to find a corpse every time I walk the dog.'

'I gather he shot himself.'

'His head was a mess.' The man shook his head as he relived the memory. 'God only knows what drives a man to do that to himself.'

Mullen had been thinking that too, but he hadn't come up with an answer either. 'So you just stumbled across him?'

'Not me. It was the dog who found him. Bounding off in front of me like he had spotted a rabbit. We don't normally take this route, but he must have smelled him.'

'The blood, you mean.'

'Not just the blood . . . the urine, too.'

'Urine?'

'Yes. When I caught up with the dog, he was sniffing and licking at the man's crotch. I had to pull him off by the collar. That was when I smelled it. It had pretty much dried, but by God, his trousers stank. The poor guy must have pissed all down himself.'

* * *

Becca arrived at their agreed rendezvous point dead on one fifteen, just as she had promised. They were meeting in Headington, although Mullen had rung her as soon as he'd got home and had already given her a brief update over the phone.

'He wet himself?' Becca had said. 'As in . . . he was scared?'

'I guess so.'

'Do people normally wet themselves before they blow their brains out?'

'Possibly not. I don't really know.' *Had Ben wet himself?* The question popped unbidden into his head.

'Well, the alternative is that someone else blew his brains out. Made him ring Marie and then — *bang!*'

Mullen had been coming to that conclusion too, but he wasn't sure.

'That makes much more sense,' Becca had said, plunging on. 'He was planning a big holiday. He was happy. It makes no sense that he killed himself.'

'So who might have wanted him dead?'

She had given one of her trademark raucous laughs. 'Hell, Doug, you're the private eye. But I do have an idea. So let's meet for lunch.'

Becca was still working at the hospital but, in her pregnant state, had been given largely administrative duties in the ward and offered some leeway on her hours. So she turned up, somewhat to Mullen's surprise, bang on time and led him straight into Amanda's Café.

'This looks nice,' he said as they settled into their chairs.

She leaned forward and waited for him to do the same. 'I haven't brought you here because it's nice. This is where Robert worked.'

A woman approached them, businesslike and slightly red in the face. 'Welcome to our little café.' She gave them each a small menu. 'How are you, my dear? Can't be long now.' She was addressing Becca, but she swept a welcoming grin round to include Mullen. 'I'll give you both a couple of minutes to decide what you want, then I'll be back.'

'I've not got a lot of time,' Becca said. I'll have the soup of the day, followed by an ice cream sundae.'

'The same for me.' Mullen reckoned it was easier that way, despite a gut feeling that he was making a big dietary mistake. 'And a glass of water.'

'That's Amanda,' Becca whispered, as the woman moved away.

Mullen watched her while pretending not to. Dyed blonde hair cut into a tidy bob, forties, somewhat thickset. And buxom. That had been Marie's caustic description.

'Do you know her?' he asked.

'Not really. Only by repute.'

He glanced across at Amanda again. She spoke to a skinny, red-haired woman before disappearing into what he assumed was the kitchen.

'Marie used to talk about her. She seemed worried that Robert and her might be getting on a bit too well in the heat of the kitchen.'

'Seriously?'

'I came here once to scout her out. I didn't tell Marie, of course, but I was really curious.'

The redhead meandered across the room between the tables and delivered two iced waters. 'Hi, I'm Carly,' she said, robotically, and placed the glasses on the table.

'Thank you, Carly.'

She hovered there, as if waiting for something. Then 'Thank *you!'* she said, before making her way back to the counter.

'And?' Mullen said.

'And they certainly had a lively relationship. One minute she would be all over him, congratulating him on some dish, the next she'd be tearing strips off him like he was the biggest plonker in the world.'

Mullen wondered what to make of that. Amanda had reappeared behind the servery with a tray in her hands. She said something to Carly before she herself headed over towards them. It was their soup and rolls.

'I was sorry to hear about your chef,' Becca said.

Caught off balance, Amanda hesitated then proceeded to unload the tray. She straightened herself, looked carefully at Becca, then shrugged. 'You never know what's going on inside people's heads, do you? He came in to work, did his shift as normal, and then went off and killed himself.' She stood there for several moments, slipping the empty tray under her arm as if marking the man's death with a brief silence. 'A terrible thing,' she said, before turning away.

* * *

DI Susan Holden had finished work on time for a change and her mind was focused on what she might do to make the most of her evening. Her mother? No. The gym? Definitely not! A film? That was more like it. She'd ring round some of her friends and see if anyone was free. Maybe take in a cocktail or two on the top floor of the Westgate Centre first – pretend she was a tourist. Why not?

She pulled off Abingdon Road, down Edith Road and was surprised to find a parking space waiting ever so politely right outside her front door. It felt like a good omen. She inserted her car first time and gave herself a mental pat on the back. As she got out, a scruffy blue Ford Focus pulled past. She noticed it only in the sense that it wasn't immediately recognisable, not one of the cars that parked regularly at her end of Chilswell Road, but her mind was already on whom she might ring. She crossed the road, went up the short path to her front door and let herself in. It was musty and warm. She went through to the kitchen-diner and opened first the back door and then the window over the sink. She hung up her jacket in the corridor and set about making a cup of tea.

She had scrolled through her mobile phone contacts and had decided to ring first Karen and then Rachel when the bell rang. She cursed — '*Not very ladylike*' her mother would have said, had she been in earshot — and tramped towards the front door. She peered through the spyhole and her heart sank. She put her hand on the lock and held it there in indecision. Should she or shouldn't she? The man on the other side of the door probably spelled trouble. But that wasn't the reason she felt a surge of irritation. She could ignore him or she could deal with him and, Holden being Holden, she twisted the lock and pulled the door open.

'Hi!' His greeting was wary, as if sensing her mood. 'I hope you don't mind . . . '

'Of course I mind.' Her mouth snapped like a crocodile's. 'That's your blue Ford Focus isn't it?' She waited for a response.

He nodded.

'You followed me home.'

Another, even more reluctant nod.

'You don't come to my house. You don't come and bother me in my private time. You go to the station.'

'Of course. I do understand. And in normal circumstances, that is exactly what I'd do, but . . .' He gave her a little boy lost smile. 'I can just go away if that's what you want.'

That was exactly what she wanted. Now that the idea of going to a film had germinated in her head, she really wanted to go and see one. Any one. On the other hand, the detective inside her was curious to know what had brought Doug Mullen to her house. So she relented. 'You'd better come in. But don't even think about making yourself comfortable.'

Again he nodded agreement.

And she, inconsistently, offered him a cup of tea before he reached the kitchen.

* * *

'So what is it?'

They sat either side of a kitchen table, she with a red mug and he with a yellow one. She had already informed him, somewhat sheepishly, that she had won them in a raffle, as if she was afraid he was marking her down as having a lack of taste.

'Robert Dench . . .' he said.

She frowned. 'Suicide,' she said, as the details bubbled to the surface. 'Shot himself in the middle of a wood. Rang his wife just before he did. Not my case, of course, but I like to keep abreast of things.'

Mullen sipped his tea. As she waited for him to speak, her brain was already jumping to conclusions. *Mullen doesn't think it was suicide. Of course he doesn't, or why else would he be here?*

'The clock is ticking, Doug. And there's a blue moon tonight, so I'm going out.'

He straightened himself and looked across at her. 'Robert Dench urinated down his trousers just before he died.'

'Really?' Holden couldn't help but wonder where he had got that information. She hadn't been aware of it, but then why would she have had that level of detail about the case?

'And he was planning a once-in-a-lifetime holiday with his wife, Marie, and son, James.'

'You have been a busy boy.'

Mullen was always like a dog with a bone. 'Somehow, it just doesn't add up. So — and I know this is a big ask — I was hoping you might like to check out the fine details. See if the phone records and witness statements match Marie's account of what happened.'

Holden stood up and walked across to the back door, allowing the breeze to play on her face. 'Is Marie Dench your client?'

Mullen nodded. 'In a manner of speaking.'

'Yet you seem to be suggesting that A, her husband was murdered and B, that she may have been lying and so presumably was involved in that murder. If that was really the case, why on earth would she have hired you?'

'It wasn't her who approached me in the first place. It was her friend. And I think Marie then felt she had no option.'

'Does this friend have a name?'

'Everyone has a name.' He clearly wasn't going to tell her. 'She's a reliable source. Look, I just want to satisfy myself that Marie isn't involved. Then I can look at other options.'

'The case is closed, Doug. The coroner found that Robert's death was suicide. You can't seriously expect me to reopen it.'

'Not reopen it as such. I just want you to do me a favour and see if it all looks kosher.' He stood up and drained his tea, then went over to the sink and rinsed out his mug. He put his business card by the kettle. 'Please!' Again he flashed his winning smile at her. 'I'm one of the good guys, remember?' He made his way to the front door.

Holden followed him and placed her hand on the latch before he could let himself out. 'You never came here and you never spoke to me, Doug.'

'No, of course not.'

'And I am making no promises.'

'Absolutely not.'

'And never come to my house again.'

He made a face but said nothing.

'Promise me that.'

'Not sure I can.'

Holden sighed before removing her hand from the door.

Mullen opened it. He looked her full in the face. 'Have a nice evening.' He gave her a parting smile and then the door clicked shut behind him.

Holden slid the security chain in place and stood there listening. She heard the sound of Mullen's car door slamming shut and then the growl of his engine as he brought his ageing heap of metal to life before driving off.

'Damn you, Doug Mullen,' she said to the empty house.

* * *

As it turned out, both Karen and Rachel were in and very much up for an evening out. 'Absolutely!' Karen had squealed, her voice bubbling with excitement. 'My mother's staying, so she can babysit. Let's start with a cocktail. Or maybe two! I just need a quick shower and time to get my glad rags on, and then it's Oxford, here I come.'

And so, one hour later, the city centre was where Holden was heading to, a hastily consumed sandwich in her stomach. Their rendezvous was a bar on the top floor of the redeveloped Westgate. But as she made her way up Marlborough Road, she extracted her mobile from her bag and made the call that, ever since Mullen had pleaded his case, she had known she would make sooner or later. She might as well make it sooner and then she could go and have a silly and inebriated evening with her friends.

The recently retired Detective Inspector Greg Collins answered immediately. 'Oh, hello. How are you, Susan?'

'Fine, thank you, Greg. Enjoying retirement? Digging the allotment? Redecorating the house?'

'Not a chance. Joined the Aunt Sally team. Taken out a season ticket at the Kassam. That's about it.'

'Not becoming a football hooligan, I hope?'

'Look . . .' There was a sharp change of tone in his voice. 'Enough of the joshing. What is it you want?'

Greg Collins might have been an outmoded, hardcore male, but he wasn't stupid. And he and Holden had never been on best-buddy terms. Cool was the kindest that could have been said about their professional relationship. The fact was that she had disliked him from the first day she had encountered him and nothing had happened in the meantime to alter that. She was glad to get to the point of her call.

'Robert Dench.'

What about him?'

'Any doubts over the suicide verdict?'

There was a brief silence. Holden could imagine the steam coming out of Collins's ears. Then came the brusque reply. 'No.'

'Because someone I know doesn't think he was the suicidal type.'

'Someone you know? And who would that be?'

'My informant seems reliable.'

'Look. The guy's fingerprints were all over the gun. He rang his wife and told her he was sorry just before he pulled the trigger.'

'You've only got his wife's word that that was what he said.'

'We followed up the phone records. It all added up. The time of the call, the duration of the call. There was no reason to doubt anything. A simple case of suicide. Case closed. I don't believe in looking for improbable solutions when the truth is staring me in the face.'

'He was planning to take his wife and daughter on holiday — their first time abroad. Hardly the action of a man planning to kill himself.'

'What the hell is this?' he said. 'Robert Dench killed himself. End of story. We did everything by the book and checked all the avenues. The coroner agreed. So you'd better not start stirring shit up. I'm retired. I've got my pension. I don't need any grief.'

'I just wanted to check things out—'

'I am going to terminate this call, Susan. Let me remind you that I still have friends in the force who'll watch my back — just as I always watched theirs. So goodbye. And don't ring me again. Ever!'

CHAPTER 5

Holden was feeling pretty pleased with herself. Much to her surprise, she was in the office of Detective Superintendent McPherson, and even more to her surprise, he was telling her what a good job she had done over the case of a missing boy. Of course, everyone liked a bit of praise and Holden was no different. He had asked her for a few details and so she had run through it.

Right from the beginning of the case, in which a boy called Alistair had disappeared on his way to school, Holden had sensed that something was wrong. Even now, as she summarised it to McPherson, she wasn't sure what precisely had caused that feeling. There was plenty about the parents that she didn't like: they had all the worst attributes of the middle class — pushy, demanding action, threatening to go to the media, treating her with zero respect.

Like the good professional, she had tried to ignore that. She had known she ought not to be surprised by their behaviour — their only child had gone missing. Those weren't the circumstances in which you saw people at their best. But she had seen something else in them, as she had watched them make a public appeal, as she had witnessed them arguing round the back of the station, as they had sniped about the school and their neighbours and the boy's 'unsuitable' friends. She had observed all this and bitten her tongue and come to the conclusion that the boy had surely done a runner. She would have done so if they had been her parents. But of course she hadn't said as much to anyone, even to DC Benning. Nor had she slackened in her determination to find the boy. She had walked the same roads to school as the boy did, talked to anyone who would talk to her, asked his few friends where he liked to hang out and what he liked to do, and she had noticed that one of them, a girl called Jessica, was more evasive in her answers than the others.

Holden didn't believe in hunches, but this time she had definitely had a hunch. So she had followed Jessica home from school. Twenty minutes later Jessica's mother had arrived, and half an hour after that Jessica had reappeared and walked up the road. Out of sight of the house, she had pulled out her mobile and made a call. Two minutes later a car had pulled up and she had got in. The driver had been old and dark-skinned. Holden had reckoned it was a taxi. She had noted the registration number, just in case, and had followed the car down Woodstock Road, right along Observatory Road and then left into Walton Street where it stopped opposite the Phoenix cinema — all very straightforward. The girl had got out, crossed the road and gone inside. But by the time Holden had parked her car and entered the foyer, there had been no sign of her.

'Just started,' the woman behind the desk had volunteered.

'I don't mind.' Holden had bought a ticket and made her way in. She had selected a seat in the back row. The adverts had finished and people had been advised to switch off their mobiles. Holden had dutifully put hers on silent. It hadn't taken long for her to spot Jessica. Her curly hair was distinctive. She had been sitting next to another girl who, as far as Holden had been able to make out in the light flickering from the screen, had long blonde hair. Holden had settled down to watch the film. There had been no point in wasting her ticket.

The blonde girl had made her mistake as they were exiting, by pausing at the gents before Jessica could grab her by the arm. Holden had followed them outside. She had walked fast, caught them up, had then overtaken them and spun round in front of them. 'Alistair, isn't it?' Holden had said, staring at Jessica's companion.

'When did you work it out?' McPherson was saying.

Holden shrugged.

'Bloody good work. High profile case brought to a successful conclusion. Missing child found alive and well. Very good for Thames Valley Police's profile too.'

'I feel sorry for the boy.'

'Quite. But, in our line of work, feeling sorry is a bit of a luxury.'

Holden nodded. She had suddenly had enough of McPherson. 'Is that all, sir?'

'Not quite.'

Holden waited. What now? She had plenty of paperwork to catch up with and after that she hoped to get home early. She had earned it.

'I bumped into Greg Collins last night.' There was a pause — the lull before the storm. 'Why on earth are you making enquiries into the Robert Dench case?' He didn't wait for an answer. 'It's done and dusted. Suicide. The coroner has pronounced. Case closed. And a damned fine way for Collins to finish his career.'

'An old friend approached me, sir.'

'I don't care if the Queen of Sheba approached you. The case is closed. Haven't you been watching the news recently? There is plenty more real crime out there for us to investigate. So go and get on with it and forget about Robert Dench. Do I make myself clear, Inspector?'

'Yes, sir.'

'Actions have consequences, Inspector. Remember that.'

* * *

'You said last time that you blamed yourself for your friend Ben's death,' Kazia Ciesla said. 'Would you like to tell me why?'

It was late afternoon. Outside, the rush hour was in full flow, except that 'full flow' was not an expression that should ever be used to describe an Oxford rush hour. Mullen had felt its effects as he had crawled along the Eastern Bypass Road. It was only when he finally managed to fork left off the ring road just north of the Mini plant that the traffic speed had crept up to something like fifteen miles per hour. And so it had been a somewhat stressed Mullen who had arrived five minutes late for his second session with Kazia.

She was dressed very differently from their previous meeting. The elegant green dress and carefully chosen accessories had been replaced by a purple top, grey jogging bottoms and white and blue trainers. She wore no earrings this time. It was as if she intended going for a run or a training session at the gym as soon as she got him over and done with. He felt distinctly uncomfortable.

There were no polite preambles, no *'How are you feeling, Doug?'*, no offer of a cup of tea either. Just a glass of water set in front of him on the low table. She had barely allowed him time to sit down and get comfortable before she had fired off her first question. This was a much less serene and a much more businesslike Kazia. Or maybe, Mullen pondered, this was merely a different type of tactic, plotted carefully over her breakfast-time coffee. After the soft-soap of the last session, perhaps she wanted to apply a bit of pressure.

'I wasn't there for him,' he answered.

'Why not?' No long silences today either. No waiting patiently for Mullen. It was straight in with the next question.

'I was out.'

'Out where?'

'At the pub.'

'On your own?'

'No. There were lots of us there.'

'Who do you mean by "us"?'

‘Our mates. Fellow recruits. We’d been on a three-day training exercise. It was a tough one and we reckoned we’d earned a beer or two.’

‘But Ben wasn’t one of “us”?’

‘Yes. No.’ Mullen pulled at his T-shirt. It was warm and humid inside the little room and his clothing stuck uncomfortably to his body. ‘What I mean is, he didn’t come to the pub.’

‘Why didn’t he?’

‘I don’t know.’ Mullen’s voice was raised. He could feel something building inside him as each intrusive question stabbed home. He felt an urge to stand up and leave. If she kept on at him, he would. He’d walk out.

But this time Kazia didn’t hit him with another question. Instead, she picked up her glass and took a sip of water. Even so, not for a single moment did she take her eyes off him. She took a second sip and set her glass back down on the low table between them. She waited. Back to the tactics of the previous session.

Mullen knew he’d have to say something. So eventually he did. ‘He didn’t feel like it, I guess.’

She raised her eyebrows. ‘You can do better than that, Doug.’

Irritation rippled through him. He picked up his glass and took two sips of water. Ben had been softer, kinder and less cocky than the rest of them. He had seemed different, a man standing on the outside looking in. Mullen had found him interesting. And he had instinctively known that he needed protecting.

‘Well?’ Kazia spoke sharply. There was impatience in her voice, as if the desire to get to the gym was proving stronger than the requirement to be endlessly nice to her client.

‘I think he was gay.’

‘I think’ was a lie. The truth was that he had known Ben was gay. Ben had told him so on the second night of that exercise.

‘Was he bullied because of it?’

Mullen nodded. *Of course he was bullied.*

'Did you bully him, Doug?'

Mullen was being to feel like he was on trial in a court of law and that Kazia was a relentless prosecuting barrister. 'Of course I didn't. What the hell sort of man do you think I am? I was his friend. I tried to protect him.'

'You tried?' She spoke very softly but her words were like a bayonet rammed into his stomach.

You tried — and failed. That was what she meant. And she was right. That was what he had always known. And felt. The guilt of letting his mate down so utterly that he killed himself.

'I did my best!' The words were little more than a whisper. They were also a cry for help. 'I tried to be his pal. I tried to keep the others off his case. But he didn't fit in. That was his problem. To be honest, I don't know why he ever opted to join the army.'

Kazia pursed her lips. There were traces of bright red lipstick on them, remnants that she had failed to remove. And they sparked another memory that Mullen had buried deeper than a coal mine.

'There's something I haven't told you,' he said.

She said nothing, allowing him to carry on. She merely waited, as if she already knew the importance of what he wanted to say. She was giving him time, though he was aware that maybe this endless patience and waiting in silence was merely a different way of applying pressure.

'When I found him — dead — he was wearing a dress.' Mullen shuddered at the horror of that memory. But he needed to say more. Now that he had started, he couldn't prevent it from all tumbling out. 'There was a lipstick lying on the table, too. And when I looked at what was left of his mouth, I could see red on it. I was damned nearly sick. I didn't know what to do. I knew I had to report the death but I didn't want him to be found like that. So I cut the dress off him. I hid it in a bag and got rid of it. And I took the lipstick because I didn't want him to be found with it. I didn't want him to be a laughing stock. At least I could do that for him.'

Silence descended like a gentle morning mist in the middle of a heat wave. Mullen felt exhausted, as if he had just completed a ten-mile run with a rucksack on his back. Even Kazia looked in a mild state of shock, as if she had opened Pandora's box and then been surprised by the horrors that had flown out. She licked her lips, but no further probing questions came out.

Mullen picked up his glass and drained the water. He'd had enough.

'Is there anything else you'd like to tell me?' Another question, a gentle one. Or maybe a siren call, summoning Mullen to plunge into the wild seas and swim towards the rocks of self-knowledge and destruction.

'Yes . . .' He surprised himself. 'Yes, there is.'

He had gone to the funeral. Of course he had. It had been a question of duty, of honouring Ben and asking for his forgiveness, of telling him how sorry he was not to have been there in his hour of need. There had been only three other guys in uniform: two had been Mullen's fellow squaddies and the other the sergeant major who revelled in his job of breaking the recruits all down before moulding them into the ways of the army. He, to Mullen's surprise, had seemed genuinely distressed. As for all the civilians, there had been a few more of them, and all but one had been unknown to Mullen. It had seemed a small turnout, surprisingly so. It was as if a young guy blowing his own brains out was a cause for shame. Had they put it down to cowardice? Was it the sort of death that had had everyone reaching for reasons why they couldn't possibly attend the funeral? Had people viewed his suicide as a deadly illness that he might pass on?

Mullen would have preferred to have left straight after the service, but the sergeant major had made it clear that he hadn't come all this way to miss out on a free drink afterwards. 'Besides, we need to toast his memory,' he'd insisted. 'There but for the grace of God . . .'

Mullen had been halfway through his lager when he'd been surprised to spot a woman making her way through the sparse crowd towards him. He had known who she was: Ben's mother. He had met her briefly once before when she had visited the barracks and Ben had introduced her just before they had headed off for a meal out somewhere.

'My best mate, Doug,' he had said. *'And this is my Mum, Linda.'*

She had shaken his hand. *'Ben has told me all about you.'* She had given him a broad smile.

But she hadn't been smiling as she had threaded her way past the rest of the mourners. Her face had been bleak and hard as granite. She had stopped in front of him.

'I'm so sorry for your loss.' The trite words had come unbidden from Mullen's lips. What else do you say to a grieving mother?

'You're not welcome here.' The savagery of her words had been like a whiplash, had taken Mullen completely by surprise. 'Where the hell were you when he needed you? In the pub, I expect. Getting drunk while he blew his brains out.'

'I . . . I . . .'

'Mates are meant to look after each other. Every time he rang home, he talked about you. I knew he wasn't happy. But I thought as long as he had a best mate, he'd be OK. How wrong I was!'

Mullen had searched for words, searched in vain for something to say that might help.

'I hope you rot in hell!' she had snarled. And she'd spat full in Mullen's face.

Mullen told Kazia all of this, and at the end he sat in silence and wondered if now the bad dreams would finally stop. Was that all it took to reach a place of peace? Was Kazia the absolver of wrongs committed? Was she the layperson's equivalent of a Roman Catholic priest, who heard your confession and then absolved you of all sin? He wished it was as simple as that but he knew it wasn't. It was Ben's forgiveness he needed or Linda's, and that would never be forthcoming.

'Thank you, Doug, for being so open.' He was only barely conscious of Kazia speaking. He should have done more for Ben, that was the bottom line. *A sin of omission.* Wasn't that what a priest would call it? But it was more than that. He *had* gone out drinking and *had* left Ben behind to fight his demons on his own. He didn't think he could forgive himself for that.

He began to rock in his chair. Somewhere deep within pulsed a memory of himself sitting on his mother's lap as she soothed him to sleep in a rocking chair. He felt tears run softly down his cheeks.

'The session is over, I'm afraid,' Kazia broke in. Mullen looked at his watch. It felt like he had been there only a few minutes. 'I have another appointment. But I don't want you going away and beating yourself up about it. It sounds as though you were a good friend to Ben. Maybe others weren't.'

He wiped his face with his bare arm and stood up. He couldn't wait to get out of the tiny room and into the fresh air.

'Feel free to ring me. Any time of day or night. Leave me a message and I will ring you back as soon as I can. And of course I'd like us to meet again — if you so wish.'

* * *

The second session of therapy had ended much more successfully for Mullen than the first. How could it not have after the vomiting episode? But that didn't mean all was suddenly right in his inner world. *'Talking to someone about a trauma is not a magic solution,'* Kazia had warned him. *'Sometimes it can stir up violent memories and, initially at least, make things worse.'*

Mullen wasn't sure if in his case things were worse or not. Getting the whole of the story out had been a relief, and yet it hadn't stopped the anxious thoughts spinning round inside his head. Nor had it stopped the feelings of guilt surfacing and resurfacing every time he tried to fall asleep. Sitting down in the kitchen to drink a cup of tea or pottering off for a walk with Rex were no longer relaxing activities. He couldn't suppress the thought that if he hadn't gone off to the pub and got drunk, then Ben might still be alive — or at least he probably wouldn't have killed himself that night.

One thing was clear: the therapy had failed to banish the lurid visual images of Ben: his body slumped under the lamp, his face brutally disfigured by the gunshot, the corner of his mouth smeared with lipstick and his body further disfigured by the bloodied dress.

Talking about it was not enough. Mullen came to that conclusion as he drank his second cup of strong tea. He was sitting on the sofa in front of the TV. He had been watching it to distract himself, but he had soon had enough of it. He would have liked to have talked to Becca. He had sent her a text but she hadn't responded. So he was sitting there with Rex as his sole companion, wondering what to do.

If in doubt, do something. If Mullen had a personal philosophy for dealing with problems, that was probably it. He ferreted through a drawer Professor Moody had assigned to him for his personal stuff until he found the newspaper cutting. He went back to the sofa and read it again.

Linda had had three children. Ben was dead, of course, but the others were presumably still alive. He vaguely remembered Sandra and Kevin. They had been at Ben's funeral. He hadn't spoken to them but he had noticed them. In particular he had noted Kevin's resemblance to Ben. Kevin had been how Ben must have looked when he was a gawky, spotty twelve-year-old. Except that Kevin at the funeral had seemed angrier than Ben had ever been. But perhaps he had had every reason to be so. How would he be feeling now that his mother had died, and how indeed would Sandra be feeling? One of them, possibly both of them, must have sent him the notice of Linda's death. But why? So that they could be sure that Mullen knew about their mother's death? It didn't quite make sense. What *did* make sense was the timing: he, she, they hadn't wanted him to turn up, unwanted and unannounced, at their mother's funeral, so they hadn't posted the notice to him until the day before the funeral. But why do it at all? To make him feel guilty for how he had failed Ben? Mullen couldn't come up with any other answer.

He made his decision as he stood outside in the garden watching Rex eat his supper. He needed to go and track down Sandra or Kevin and have it out with them. If necessary he would tell them the story of what had happened — though not the gory details or the fact that Ben had been wearing a dress and lipstick when he had died. On the other hand, maybe the homosexuality wouldn't be a surprise, and even if it was, it might help them to understand the bullying to which Ben had been subjected and that he, Mullen, hadn't been part of that. They might still blame him for failing Ben, but perhaps not hold it against him so savagely. *Perhaps.*

He took the decision quickly and acted on it immediately. He put Rex on his lead and walked round to Karen, his next door neighbour. Since her husband had died of pancreatic cancer, she had been only too glad to dog-sit Rex, but this time it was different.

When she opened the door, Mullen barely recognised her. Her grey bob had been replaced by something very different. His surprise must have been obvious because she ran a hand lightly through her hair. 'Like it, Doug? It's a spiky pixie cut.'

'Yes,' he said.

Her hair had also been professionally dyed, about three different shades, and she was wearing a bright red dress and red court shoes with (of course) matching lipstick. She looked, in short, anything but the grieving widow.

'I'm so sorry, Doug. I've got a date tonight.' She squealed like a young girl and Mullen felt a stab of jealousy at her happiness and at whoever it was who was taking her out. 'I would normally have Rex, as you know, but I'd like to keep my options open, if you know what I mean.' Another giggle. 'Another time, maybe.' And she shut the door carefully but firmly in Mullen's face.

Mullen looked down at Rex. The dog was looking up at him with a look of reproach on his face. It was his default when he wasn't trying to win favour with his 'aren't I cute?' expression.

'I guess we're stuck with each other,' Mullen said. 'Anyway, let's get the evening walk over and done with now.'

It was while they were still walking that Becca rang. No courtesies. No asking after him. No asking him how the therapy was going — though that was no surprise because he hadn't told her anything about it. Just straight in with the question. 'Any progress on the case, Doug?'

It had become a 'case', had it? No money had been agreed. Becca had indicated there wasn't a lot of money available and Marie hadn't asked him what his rates were or mentioned money at all. He ought to say something.

'Or have you got bigger fish to fry?' Becca pressed.

'Nothing specific to report,' he said. 'But I have been in touch with someone I know at Thames Valley Police, so I am waiting for her to get back to me.'

'Well, don't wait too long.'

'And how are you?' He tried to change the subject.

'Big. And getting bigger.' A pause and a laugh. 'Actually, I was wondering about a meal tomorrow night.'

'That would be nice.'

'At yours. You can dazzle me with more of your culinary skills.'

'I doubt it.' He knew she was flattering him for a purpose, but he was flattered nevertheless.

'I've got an antenatal in the afternoon, so I'll come round after that.'

'I'm out all day. Not sure when I'll be back.'

'Leave me a key. You can hide it somewhere, can't you?'

'Yes.' He caved in. 'Yes, I can.'

CHAPTER 6

Mullen and Rex travelled south the next morning — destination: Badgerhurst, on the edge of the New Forest. They set off at seven thirty and pretty soon hit traffic on the A34. Mullen wasn't worried. He had all day to play with. In fact, once he was past the Didcot junction, the traffic eased significantly and, insofar as his tired old car allowed it, he was soon rattling along at a very acceptable pace.

A brief stop for a loo break for both him and the dog plus a takeaway coffee was the only interruption and, rather to his surprise, they reached Badgerhurst shortly after ten a.m.

It wasn't a chocolate box village. A modern housing estate was being established on its northern approaches. Advertising hoardings advised that eighty percent of these *high-quality, desirable homes* had already been bought but, from what he could see, Mullen doubted that any of these new owners would be moving in before Christmas. Beyond them, a mixture of mid-twentieth century housing heralded the beginning of the inhabited village — detached and semi-detached brick-built homes lining both sides of the road. It was only when Mullen passed a service station that he found himself in what was clearly the original village. Much older, stone-built houses ushered him into the centre where a distinctly brown village green announced that he had arrived at the central point of Badgerhurst. He parked the car with a sense of *so far, so good*, got out, put Rex on his lead and looked around. He was puzzled. It was all very nice and English except for one thing: there wasn't a church.

Rex grunted. Mullen looked down. The dog was leaving what was, for a dog of his size, a pretty big deposit. Mullen bagged it up and then began to head across the green towards a bin. But it wasn't the bin that he focused on, rather the little gaggle of shops on that side of the green. Someone there might be able to help. There was a general store and newsagent, an undertaker (closed until one p.m according to a scribbled note stuck on the inside of the glass door), a florist and a café. The café was silent but appeared to be open. There were three sets of little tables outside, though none of them occupied. They were laid out with cutlery, cruet and tomato and brown sauce. There was an enticing smell of bacon being cooked.

It was three and a half hours since he had eaten two pieces of toast, so the promise of a full English breakfast — *'All local produce'*, according to the menu — was irresistible and within minutes he had ordered one for himself plus a coffee. Rex was welcome as long as he stayed outside (*'If that is all right with you?'*). With the sun shining from an azure sky, Mullen agreed that is was definitely all right with both of them.

'You on holiday?' The rather stout woman who delivered the full English to Mullen's table some ten minutes later asked the question without enthusiasm.

'No,' Mullen said.

'Not seen you round here before.' It sounded like a criticism, as if he had to be either a holidaymaker or a local. Perhaps this wasn't a place to which other people came.

'Actually, I'm on a mission.' Mullen smiled at her, hoping to enlist her help.

'Tom Cruise, are you?' Her voice and manner could not have been more deadpan. 'You don't seem short enough.'

Picking up on the cue, Mullen smiled. It wasn't a bad joke, after all. 'I was looking for the church. St Nicholas. I assumed it would be in the middle of the village.'

'Well, it's not. Built by some posh family back in the day.' She pointed. 'Down that road, second left. You can't miss it.'

He tried to make the most of the opportunity that had presented itself. 'Actually, I was hoping to speak to Sandra Wright, Linda Wright's daughter.'

'Were you, now?' The woman's guard was back up. 'And why might that be?'

'I knew her son, Ben.'

'Enjoy your meal.' Her tone suggested she rather hoped he choked on it. She disappeared back inside the café. Was the woman just being protective? She clearly knew who Linda was. But the drawbridge had gone up and the portcullis down with a mighty crash.

He looked down at his breakfast. It looked and smelled terrific. He put the woman out of his mind and set to. Rex whined at his feet and Mullen, whose thoughts had been drifting back to Becca Baines, did as she had done when he had cooked brunch for her in Oxford: he leaned down and slipped Rex a piece of sausage. He continued to think about Becca as he sipped his coffee. Had the father of her baby been a one-night stand and that was why she was so secretive about him? As for himself, did she actually fancy him? She seemed to like him, but liking and fancying were different things. Come to think of it, did he fancy her? The answer to that, he realised, was *yes*. But fancying someone was one thing. Taking her on when she was heavily pregnant with another man's child was very much another. Was he a fool to even consider it? He wished he knew. He also wished he knew what on earth he would cook her when he got home later. He'd have to shop en route.

His musings were interrupted by a sharp familiar tone. The woman was back with a piece of paper in her hand. 'That'll be nine pounds twenty-five.'

Mullen pulled a tenner out of his pocket. 'Thank you. Please keep the change.' Not a cheap breakfast, but a good one.

She said nothing. She thrust the piece of paper into his hand and removed his plate and mug. He studied the piece of paper. It was a printed bill and at the bottom there were four handwritten words: *Try the Nags Head.* He looked up to thank her again but she had retreated back inside.

* * *

The Nags Head looked a picture: stone walls, thatched roof, ye olde lamps in the car park. Mullen looked at his watch. Not so long ago, pubs didn't open until midday, but these were different times. Shouldn't a pub like this be offering coffee to passing punters? There were no cars in the car park, the front door was locked and there were no obvious signs of life.

But Mullen wasn't going to leave until he had checked it out fully. He walked round the building until he found a door at the back. His luck was in — the door was ajar. He pushed it open and slipped inside.

'Hello!' he called.

There was no reply, so he continued his progress, past the toilets (which smelled) and over grubby, patterned carpets (which looked as though they smelled) until he found himself in the bar area.

'We're shut,' said a voice out of the dark, female and gravelly.

'I just wanted some water for my dog.' Mullen picked Rex up and advanced a couple more steps. 'He's got a kidney condition,' he lied.

'Ain't we all.'

He could see the outline of the woman now, though not much else because the lights were turned off and the curtains were pulled across the windows. She was sitting on a barstool holding what looked like a wine glass in her hand.

'I'll say it again . . . We're shut. For a period of mourning. There's a pond down the road if your dog's thirsty.'

'Are you Sandra Wright?'

He'd clearly taken her by surprise. She didn't answer initially — unless taking another swig of wine could be called an answer. But she hadn't denied it, so Mullen pressed on.

'I was a friend of your brother, Ben. From the army.'

This time there was a noticeable change in her demeanour. She slipped down from the barstool and advanced through the shadows towards him. A flash of daylight from where one of the curtains had not been fully drawn gave him a brief glimpse of her face. Sandra could only have been in her mid-thirties but time hadn't been kind to her. She had dark bags under her eyes, sallow skin, greasy blonde hair and the down-turned mouth of a much older woman — one who had long ceased to enjoy life.

Soon she was standing in front of him, close enough for Mullen to know that this wasn't her first drink of the day. She stared at him through hooded eyes, trying to connect the face in front of her with the man of her memory. She was breathing heavily, as if the short walk across the room had been a serious act of exercise. 'You!' She spat the word out, exuding more alcohol fumes. She raised her glass high in the air as if she was about to propose a toast. 'Fuck you.' Mullen tensed, conscious that alcohol, anger and a glass could spell trouble with a capital T. And the dog, still in his arms, wasn't going to be much of a help. As if to underline that, Rex whimpered.

'Sandra . . .' He spoke softly, moving into sweet-talking mode, but he never got any further. The glass slipped from Sandra's hand, clipped the back of a chair and disintegrated as it hit the wooden floor. She gave a howl of anguish and disintegrated too.

* * *

'Why did Ben kill himself?' she said.

They were sitting either side of a small round table, still in the bar area but Sandra had let him turn the lights on.

The curtains, however, remained resolutely closed against the outside world. Instead of alcohol, they were armed with mugs of strong tea that Mullen had made. Sandra had stopped crying and Rex, either sensing that she was no longer a foe or — more likely— seduced by a treacherous greed, was sitting triumphantly on her lap and licking his lips after she had fed him a biscuit piece by delicate piece.

Why did Ben kill himself? Mullen had been expecting this question but, even so, he wasn't quite prepared for it. Over the last few days, he had asked it himself many times and he still hadn't come up with an answer that fully satisfied him.

'Ben was a fish out of water,' he began. 'I never quite understood what made him join up in the first place.'

She gave a hoarse laugh, as if he had just asked the most obvious question. 'To please his bastard of a father. Why else?'

The ferocity of her words took Mullen by surprise. Conversing with Ben's sister was like advancing through a minefield.

'He was gay,' she said. 'You knew that.'

He nodded.

'And you two were lovers?'

'No!' he said quickly. Too quickly perhaps, as if that would have been a thing of shame.

'Really? When he rang Mum, he was always talking about you.'

He shook his head. Whatever he said, he was in danger of stepping on an IED. 'We were mates. He did tell me that he was gay. But I'm not. I liked him. I tried to keep an eye out for him,' he insisted, plumping his size nine boot right down on top of a detonator. *Whoomp!* 'Tried?' This time her laugh was savage. 'Not very successfully!'

'No,' he admitted.

Sandra drank a slug of tea and stared at him. She looked just like her mother had at Ben's funeral — a furious clenched face, bulging eyes, down-turned red mouth. She was as hard as Ben had been soft. And she was waiting for Mullen to say more.

'The guys knew he was gay,' he said.

'And?'

'And he got bullied.'

'So you're saying he shot himself because he was bullied?'

He was being backed into a corner. 'I suppose I am.'

'Suppose?' Sandra spat the word out as if it was an uncooked gooseberry. 'How do you know someone else didn't shoot him and make it look like suicide?'

Mullen looked at her. She had taken him right off guard. He had never even considered the possibility that someone else could have killed Ben. Suicide seemed so obvious and logical. Bullied, gay, hating the army, afraid of jacking it in and going home to be confronted by his father — suicide was the obvious answer.

'Well?' She demanded.

But Mullen didn't have an answer, at least not the sort of answer that she clearly wanted. So he replied with his own question. 'Sandra . . . have you any reason to think it wasn't suicide?'

'He wouldn't have. He just wouldn't have.' She wiped her hand across her face.

How could she be so sure of that? This was a thought that he wasn't going to voice. *Don't push your luck. Discretion is the better part of valour and all that bullshit. Engage brain before opening mouth.* The clichés were hammering thick and fast inside his skull.

'Why?'

Mullen stared at her, uncomprehending.

She spoke one word at a time as if to a particularly stupid schoolchild. 'Why . . . have . . . you . . . come . . . here . . . today?'

'Ah!' The penny dropped with a resounding clang. He fished inside his jacket and pulled out the pink envelope. He passed it over and watched as she extracted the newspaper clipping and read it. And reread it. Eventually she handed it back, but without any comment.

'Someone posted it to me. It arrived on the same day as the funeral.'

Sandra straightened herself and looked Mullen full in the face. Her eyes were silver grey and deadly, like bullets waiting to be fired. 'So?'

'Was it you who sent it?'

'I don't even know where the hell you live.'

'Somebody does.' He held the envelope up in front of her. 'Do you recognise the handwriting?'

There was the briefest of delays. Was that a flicker of recognition in the killer eyes or had he imagined it? She shook her head. 'Nope.'

'Have you any idea who might have sent it?'

Another shake of the head but she continued to hold his gaze. If he wanted to play a game of chicken, she was up for it.

'Look . . . someone went to the trouble of finding out where I live in order to send me this. They wanted me to know that your mother had died. They wanted me to—'

But Sandra had had enough. She stood up without any warning, rocking the table and unseating Rex from her lap. He yelped in surprise.

'I want you to go. And I don't want to ever see or hear from you again. Not unless you can tell me what really happened to Ben.'

'It was a long time ago.' It was a feeble response and he knew it. Feeble and tactless.

'In that case, just fuck off out of here and don't come back. And take your yappy little dog with you.'

It wasn't hard to find St Nicholas church. He followed the instructions that the boot-faced woman from the café had given him and, sure enough, there it was just outside the village, above a field of sheep, up on the brow of a hill, flanked on either side by trees. He drove up the narrow lane that led to it, but stopped well short of the church itself. There was a parking place on the right, opposite the entrance to the churchyard. It could hardly have been more idyllic. A large open space, with graves (of course), but there was plenty of unoccupied space. Much of this had been left to grow wild — long grasses mixed with various wild flowers. Narrow paths had been mown through it and white and yellow butterflies careened and danced hither and thither in the sunlight. The church itself was higher up the slope but it wasn't the church that interested him. He headed for the graves.

It didn't take long to find the spot where Linda Wright had been buried. There was no headstone, but the mound of freshly dug soil was a giveaway, as were the three large wreaths that had been laid on top. Rex whimpered, as though in sympathy. Mullen ignored him, bending down to inspect the floral displays. He sat back on his haunches and looked around, checking to see if he was being observed. Then he pulled out his phone and photographed the three tags. He felt a pang of guilt. What the hell was he doing being so disrespectful? Except what was disrespectful about trying to do exactly what Sandra had challenged him to do? He just wanted to find the truth.

Rex whimpered again. Mullen glanced at the dog. He was staring into the long grass. Mullen followed his gaze and saw a deer, its head visible above the grass some ten metres away. For several seconds all three of them froze, and then the deer rose up onto its legs and skittered away up the slope and into the dark shadows cast by the trees.

Mullen turned back to the grave and realised that there were fresh flowers on the grave next to Linda's as well. That one had a headstone and he realised with a start whose it must be. He moved across and crouched in front of it so that he could read the inscription.

Benjamin Daniel Wright. Gone but not forgotten. Rest in Peace.

He was certainly not forgotten. But was he at peace? And was Linda now finally at peace? He hoped so, but he had his doubts because, back here on earth, Sandra certainly wasn't. And what about Kevin? Linda hadn't mentioned him. But then he hadn't asked her about her little brother. He really should have before she had gone ballistic.

Mullen wasn't a man who believed in God or life after death, but when you were face to face with the tombstone of the man whose memory haunted you, unexpected things could happen. He found himself saying things that came bubbling up out of his subconscious and were dangerously close to being what other people might have called prayers — not that he would have cared even if he had realised it. As the tears ran down his face, all he felt was an overwhelming tide of grief and guilt. But when that subsided, other things remained: an indefinable sense of anger and an intense desire to discover the truth. He needed redemption.

It was Rex who brought him back into the present. When whimpering failed to attract his master's attention, he tried licking his right arm, salty with sweat. And when that had no effect, he levered himself up as high as he could reach and licked his face. Only then did Mullen give the dog a hug and get up off his knees.

He checked his watch. He still had plenty of time to get home and cook the supper planned for Becca and himself. But first he needed a walk, and so did Rex, so he headed up along the grassy paths, past the church and out onto the lane beyond. A footpath sign stood conveniently on the other side, beckoning the pair of them to pastures new, and so Mullen walked on, letting Rex off the leash, and for an hour or more he tried to shut his mind to everything except what he could see all around him.

It was only when he returned to his car that he realised how time had marched on. He pulled out his mobile. Better just ring Becca and warn her that he might be running a bit late, but she didn't answer and it soon skipped to voicemail. As the robotic female voice gave its prescribed greeting, Mullen started to compose something short and conciliatory in his head along the lines of *'So sorry, I might be a tiny be late,'* but he never uttered even one word because the line went dead. He swore. Looking at the phone he could see that it wasn't the line that had gone dead — it was his phone. He swore again, though this time it wasn't so much the mobile phone he was swearing at as himself. It had been running through its battery faster and faster over the last few weeks and somehow he had never got round to buying a new one. As for the car charging cable, that had disappeared down some black hole weeks and weeks before. He liked to think Rex had been involved in that, taking it out into the garden and burying it so deep that it would only be found by archaeologists in some distant future. But when push came to shove, the bottom line was (he did love a bad cliché) that it was his own stupid fault.

Maybe God loved a good cliché too because the non-working phone was the first of three unforeseen problems to blight Mullen's return home. The second one became apparent as they drove down the hill into Badgerhurst: a red flashing light telling him that the car would like some more oil if it was to drive all the way back to Oxford. This was a minor problem in the overall scheme of things because, as he remembered, there was a service station in the village. So he sorted out the oil and took the opportunity to fill the tank with fuel because it seemed sensible to kill two birds with one stone. When he finally got on the road properly, another fifteen minutes had leaked away from his schedule.

'Belts on,' he told Rex, 'or we could both be in trouble.' Which was, Mullen knew, pretty unfair on Rex, but then dogs didn't talk back.

Problem number three was Lyndhurst, a pretty New Forest village, which, as any local would have told him, was a traffic bottleneck from hell. Heading north at this time of day shouldn't have been too bad, except that this was the summer and numerous caravan drivers had decided to head for home that evening rather than wait for the mad Saturday morning exodus. Throw in a burst water main and Mullen found himself moving slower than a cold war Soviet bread queue.

Eventually he got past the temporary lights, whereupon he and all the frustrated drivers in front of him began to drive much faster — though not actually that fast. He gripped the wheel as if he was negotiating the Monaco grand prix circuit and switched on the radio. Surely it would be plain sailing from now on? He had had his three problems. *Surely!*

But maybe it wasn't God who was taking an interest in Mullen that day. Maybe it was the devil and maybe he preferred the number four, because no sooner had he reached the sanctuary of the motorway and wound up his speed to a shuddering seventy-five miles per hour than he found himself kicking hard against his brakes. He swore. There was an accident ahead — not that he could see it, but what else could have caused everyone to grind to a standstill? He took two deep breaths and got cautiously out of the car. He looked forwards, focusing on a distant lorry. But however hard he tried to will it into movement, it stayed resolutely still. He opened the passenger door, grabbed the dog and his leash and headed for the grass verge. He might as well let the little guy have a sniff around.

* * *

Mullen eventually hit the outskirts of Oxford nearly two hours late. He wondered if Becca would be sleeping peacefully in one of the professor's armchairs — well, she *was* extremely pregnant. Or maybe — more likely — she would have stormed off home, leaving an extremely pointed note: *Where the hell have you been!* He tried to be philosophical about it but couldn't help feeling somewhat on edge. He had wanted to impress her with his cooking and his efficiency and (*Hah!*) his reliability.

The first hint of yet more trouble up ahead was a police car that roared past him as he headed up Cumnor Hill. But he didn't connect the blaring siren and flashing lights with himself. Why should he? That would be paranoia. Besides, his thoughts had now returned to Becca. It was only as he turned into his road and saw not just the police car, but a fire engine too outside the professor's house that panic bazookaed him. He pressed his accelerator and then a few moments later hit the brake pedal, screeching to a halt behind the emergency vehicles like a stunt driver.

He jumped out and rushed forward. Flames and smoke belched out of the house, not just from the front door, but from the upstairs windows too.

'Becca!' he screamed.

PART 3

AFTER THE FIRE

CHAPTER 7

Mullen kept seeing Becca Baines in his dreams — or rather his nightmares. Except that *'nightmares'* wasn't the right word either because when he did wake up, it was often in the daytime.

Oddly enough, she didn't seem to be burnt at all. It was as if she was suspended in mid-air. She would float towards him very gradually, growing bigger and bigger. Her face was pale and sad, a traumatised angel carrying the sins of the world on her shoulders. But it wasn't her face that he noticed most. It was her stomach, which was now flat and empty. He felt an overwhelming urge to cry but somehow didn't know how. All he knew was that Becca and her baby were gone and it was all his own stupid fault. If he had been there, or if he had rung her and told her to go home, or if he had bloody well gone and got himself a new phone, she would be alive and her child would be growing warm and safe inside her womb.

He didn't know how many times he dreamed this dream but it never varied and the ending never failed to devastate him.

* * *

He was semi-awake. The sun was low and spreading its orange light across his room. He had been allocated his own room. He wasn't sure why, but he wasn't in any sort of state to ask.

A nurse came in. Blue uniform, brown skin, no-nonsense face. 'How are you this evening, Doug?' Mullen hadn't a clue who she was. She didn't look familiar and he certainly didn't know her name. 'How's the pain? Would you like something to help it?'

'No,' he said, bluntly — rudely, probably. His face still hurt a lot but he had decided he needed to start fighting it. He wanted to stay awake rather than to take yet more painkillers and succumb to sleep and the horrors that came with it. 'Thank you,' he said.

She took hold of his wrist, assessing his pulse. She checked his temperature. She sniffed. 'Maybe we need to get you washed.'

He shut his eyes and listened to her rustling around the room. It was hugely comforting. Almost sexual. She straightened and smoothed his bedding. He sensed her close the blinds against the sunlight. He felt cared for, almost loved. 'Nurse . . .' He half opened his eyes. He didn't want her to go. He wondered if she would get him a cup of tea. Or was that below her pay grade?

'Yes, sweetie?'

Mullen screamed. *That voice!* He pushed himself up on one arm. There were two blue-clad nurses in the room now: the one with the brown skin and the don't-mess-with-me face and one who looked very like Becca. Another hallucination.

'How are you, Doug?' the ghost said. 'You look like shit.'

She came forward and leaned in, kissing him briefly on the top of his head. Her bulging stomach pressed against him. 'And you smell like it, too.'

She was definitely not a hallucination. She was one hundred percent real. He tried to speak but his words were more of a whimper. 'I thought you were dead . . . in the fire. I thought—'

'Well, I'm not.'

'They said you were dead. The firemen. The paramedics. They said you were dead in the house.' Mullen was on the edge of tears. All the emotion was welling up inside him.

Becca sat down in the chair by the bed and took his hand between both of hers. 'Not me, Doug. They think it is your Professor Moody.'

Her words didn't strike home. They didn't make any sense at all. How could it possibly be the professor?

'She came back from America. Turned up about seven thirty and found me in her house. She said it was a flying visit. Made a joke of it. Asked about the baby — whether it was yours. But she was tired and I was pretty pissed off with you, to be honest. I felt like a teenager who'd been stood up on a second date. You hadn't rung or texted. I had texted you, but you never replied, so I thought "Fuck it" and I left.'

Mullen shook his head, trying to take it in.

He felt her hand encircle his lower arm in an act of sympathy and support. Except that her grip grew tighter and tighter. It hurt. He tried to pull away from her, but she squeezed all the more, and her nails dug into his flesh.

'It could have been me, Doug. If Professor Moody hadn't appeared, it would have been me asleep in the house when it all went up in flames.'

CHAPTER 8

Mullen was feeling better, but getting bored. He had eaten his breakfast and had been helped to have a shower and now he was waiting for someone to say what was going to happen next. Another nurse, with green eyes, red hair and a brisk demeanour, had taken over and had indicated that they might let him go home. 'It's not up to me,' she had said. 'But the fact is that you're tying up a bed we could use for someone in greater need.' Sympathy didn't seem to be her strong suit, at least not from where he was half sitting and half lying in bed. He was tempted to point out that he didn't have a home to go to but he doubted it would cut much ice with her.

He was still pondering this quandary some minutes later when the door swished open and another visitor came in. He looked up to see a familiar, but not entirely welcome figure staring down at him.

'Do you feel OK to answer a few questions?' No polite enquiries after his wellbeing. Just straight down to business. It was DI Susan Holden. And at her shoulder stood another semi-familiar figure. It was the PC he had encountered and lied to (but only a little) in a previous life (or so it seemed). Except that she wasn't in uniform. 'You remember Detective Constable Benning?' Holden said.

'I do.'. He thought her first name was Lynn, not that they had been on first name terms but, ever the optimist, he had stored her name away just in case. People were always impressed if you remembered their name. 'Congratulations on the promotion.'

'Technically, it's a sideways move.' DC Benning smiled as she spoke. Holden did not.

'We're investigating the fire at the house you were looking after and the death of its owner, Professor Melissa Moody. We have spoken to Becca Baines because, as far as we know at the moment, she was last person to see Professor Moody alive. And we know she told you about her tragic death, but right now we need to ask you some questions.'

'Of course,' he said.

'We understand that you had invited Becca Baines over for a meal on the day on question?'

'Yes.'

'But you stood her up.'

'Not exactly. And even if I had, it's not a crime.'

'No, indeed.' Holden waited. Benning had disappeared and now she returned with two blue plastic chairs. Mullen watched as Holden took one (without a word of thanks) and put it close by the side of his bed. She sat down and adjusted herself. He could smell her perfume. It was unexpectedly delicate. 'So, Doug, why don't you give me your version of that day?'

'I spent the day on the edge of the New Forest. On a job.'

'What job was that?'

'A confidential one.' He was conscious that he wasn't being entirely helpful, but he felt he was being taken advantage of. Hell, he was in hospital and hadn't been given any warning. He breathed in and tried again. 'I took the dog. Rex. You remember him, I expect. Things took longer than I expected and my phone ran out of juice, and then there was a major delay on the A34, so I couldn't ring Becca to warn her. I got back to Oxford much later than I had planned and the house was on fire. I thought Becca was inside . . .' He stopped. The alarm that he had felt at the time was gripping him again.

'So you rushed in to save her, even though the fire services had arrived . . .'

'I had a key to the back door. God, she was pregnant. What the hell else was I meant to do? Stand and watch?'

'Is the baby yours, Doug?' The question was slipped in, slick as a stiletto.

'Mine? No!'

'Oh!' A pause. 'I thought it might have been.' Another longer pause. 'You haven't mentioned Professor Moody yet.'

'That's because I didn't know she had returned to Oxford. As far as I knew, she was still in the States.'

'It's her house and yet she flew back unannounced? Didn't she let you know? That seems odd.'

'Maybe she wanted to check me out. Make sure I was looking after her property and her dog. If so, I would say it was entirely understandable.' He didn't believe that — Moody used Skype to check things out. Whatever it was that had brought her to Oxford, it wasn't that. So why didn't he say so to Holden? He wasn't sure. But it just seemed the right thing to do in the circumstances.

'So, just to be clear . . . you're saying that the professor's return to Oxford was completely unexpected?'

Now it was his turn to pause. Perhaps he ought to give Holden something. 'Well, she had hinted that she might need to come back for a few days, but that was all. Nothing more. Nothing specific about when. Otherwise, I would have got in some extra food for her.'

'Did she hint at *why* she might have to come back to Oxford?'

'No, she didn't. Why should she have?'

'Why, indeed.' Holden stood up. 'Thank you for your time.' The interview was clearly over.

But Mullen had a question for her. The thought had only just occurred to him. 'Why are you here?' he said. 'I mean, why all these questions? The fire—'

'The fire was deliberate. Arson. Someone put petrol and a lighted rag through the letter box. So the question is . . . who did it? And who were they trying to kill?'

It was later that afternoon that Mullen was told he could go home. He was standing at the window watching the cars and people coming in and out when Becca appeared all smiles at the door. 'Come on, Doug. Get your clothes on. They want your bed.' She tossed a bag at him. 'I took them home and washed them all.'

'Oh.' His brain was still largely mush.

'You can stay with me until you get yourself sorted out. Unless, of course, you've had a better offer from one of your gaggle of girlfriends.'

He shook his head and emptied the clothes onto the bed.

'Don't mind me.' She pulled off his hospital gown and located his boxers. 'I've seen it all before.' He pulled the boxers up and looked at her. She was looking at him too, and not at his face. 'I've seen better, too.' She giggled.

But Mullen's mind was elsewhere. 'What about Rex?'

'Rex?'

'The dog. My dog now, I guess.'

'He's OK. He's staying with your neighbour. Karen.'

'Rex and me are partners.' He was conscious that he sounded like a cowboy in an old black and white TV Western. But he and the dog had been through a lot together. 'Can we go and pick him up? Please.'

She sighed. 'On one condition.'

'What's that?'

'You finish decorating the baby's bedroom.'

'What colour?'

'Two walls blue, two walls pink.'

He looked at her. Becca was a surprising person. That was one of the reasons he liked her. 'Hedging your bets?'

'I know what sex the baby is. It's all about being gender neutral. Not ramming pink down a girl's throat or blue down a boy's.'

'Well, I'm a boy and I like blue.'

'You're a walking cliché, Doug.' She smiled. 'Anyway, do we have a deal or don't we? Because if we don't, you'll have to beg bed space from the lovely Karen. And, by my reckoning, someone has already got in there before you.'

He pulled up his trousers and zipped up his flies. 'Yes, Becca, we have a deal.'

When Karen finally opened her front door, she wasn't in the best of moods. He had rung the bell twice and had been about to ring it a third time because he could hear Rex whining inside and Karen's car was parked outside. As was his: it was across the road in the place where he had abandoned it precipitately three days previously.

Karen's face was flushed and her hair askew. She was a tidy person normally: clean, neat, carefully made-up, as if she was always anticipating an unannounced royal visit. 'I wasn't expecting you today. You never rang,' she added, as if that was a serious failing on his part, as if she should have been at the top of his agenda. 'And the dog doesn't seem to get on with the food I'm giving him.' She was getting into her stride. 'He did his business all over the kitchen floor. Adrian nearly trod in it.'

'I *am* sorry.'

'I can't afford to lose a good lodger.'

'I didn't realise you had one.'

'The joys of Airbnb.' A distinctly smug smile spread across her face.

'Well I *am* grateful to you for looking after him.'

She grunted and nodded. And then her face changed. She had extracted the apologies that she wanted from him and now the contented smile was a look of genuine concern.

'I thought you were a goner the other night. I saw you darting round the back of the house. All the fire and smoke out of the front of the house. All the firemen shouting at you to stop. What on earth were you playing at?'

He shrugged.

'Anyway,' said Becca, butting in. She had clearly had enough. 'Doug is coming to stay with me for the time being.

And so is the dog. Which means, Karen, neither of them will be upsetting your lodger.'

'Good.' Karen's tone was curt. The tension between the women would have been obvious if only Mullen had been semi-alert. But his thoughts were elsewhere. Rex was at his feet, delighted to see him again, but Mullen's attention was torn between his loyal dog and his trusty (and rusty) car. He turned away from the women and made his way across the road. He put his hand on the driver's side window like a cowboy patting his long-suffering horse. He opened the door and Rex jumped in, ensconcing himself on the passenger seat. *His* passenger seat. Rex had definitely decided he was Mullen's partner, riding shotgun. Mullen was in a very silly mood. He grinned down at the dog. 'Let's hit the road, kid.' There was a tapping on the window. It was Karen. He wound it down. No electric windows for him.

'I almost forgot . . . I'm collecting the mail for the professor, God rest her soul. Passing it all on to the solicitor. But there was this one came for you.'

She handed it over to him. His heart somersaulted. The envelope was pink.

He didn't open it straightaway, though he was tempted to. That was largely because of Becca.

'I'm not waiting around,' she announced loudly as she stomped off towards her car. 'But you can you stay and chat if you like.'

He drove after her — and didn't she drive aggressively! He assumed she was low on blood sugar. The baby was probably hungry and demanding she do something about it. But when he got to her house and followed her into the kitchen-cum-living-room, it became clear even to him that her anger was something else, arguably even more elemental than hunger . . . *jealousy*.

'So, what's that pink letter all about? You and Karen got something going, have you? Because if so, you could have stayed with her. Not that I noticed her visiting you in hospital. Or taking your clothes home to be washed.' Becca grabbed a banana from a bowl and began to eat it. Three, four bites and it was gone. She dumped the skin on the table. Hunger *and* jealousy, Mullen decided.

'It's not from Karen.' He stared at the front of the envelope. 'It came in the post. She just passed it on.'

'For God's sake, Doug.' She moved three paces towards Mullen and snatched it from his hand. She sniffed it. 'No perfume.' Her lips twitched in a half-smile. 'Why don't *I* open it?'

He didn't answer.

'I'll take that as a "Yes."' She took a knife from a drawer and slit the envelope open with surprising dexterity. Had she watched surgeons cutting people open and unconsciously picked up their technique? She slipped a thumb and forefinger inside the envelope and pulled out a white card. As she studied it, her face morphed from curiosity to something close to horror. 'Oh my God!' She seemed to read it again, checking that she hadn't misinterpreted it. Finally, she passed it back to Mullen.

You are invited to the cremation of Douglas Mullen. Friday 13 July. No flowers. No donations.

Mullen read it but the words didn't sink in. Cremation? *His* cremation?

'That was the day of the fire,' Becca said.

He hadn't made that connection. His brain was working to rule. But of course it made sense, albeit a sick sort of sense.

'Which means that you were the target. Not me. Not the professor. You.'

He nodded.

'For crying out loud, Doug! Snap out of it. You need to ring the police. Suppose they try again. Suppose they come and set fire to my house.'

That shook him into life, but only just. 'I'll go and stay somewhere else. I don't want to put you at risk. Or the baby. I'll book into a cheap hotel.' He spoke as if he had a clear plan. But inside his skull his brain was on autopilot.

'No you bloody well won't. You'll ring your buddy at Thames Valley Police. Detective Inspector Holden.'

Holden was hardly his buddy. And she certainly hadn't been so stupid as to hand over her mobile number to him. But he wasn't going to point this out. So he rang the Thames Valley Police and reported what had happened.

The person on the other end of the line was polite and unrelenting. She asked a series of questions, at the end of which she told him to place the envelope and card in a plastic envelope and deliver it to the station the following morning. 'I'm sure DI Holden or one of her colleagues will be in touch but, as far I can see there is no immediate danger, especially as you are staying at the house of a friend.'

She made it sound so reasonable. And Mullen found himself agreeing with her. The arson had happened and he had survived it. Whoever had done it wouldn't know where he was now.

When the phone call was over, he tried to explain this to Becca. He was worried. She, so practical and bullish normally, seemed to be losing it. The baby factor, he guessed.

Or rather the food factor. Because in the time he had taken to report all the details to the police, she had cooked a giant pizza and was already more than halfway through it and as the food had disappeared, relative calm had descended.

'Do you want some?'

Mullen realised he was starving, and cut himself half of what was left.

'I don't suppose you're carrying a gun?' she said between mouthfuls.

'This is Oxfordshire, not the Wild West.'

'Even in rural Oxfordshire, bad guys carry guns.'

'If you prefer it, I'll stay downstairs. On guard in a chair.'

'Suppose the bad guy comes and you've fallen asleep.'

'Rex will bark. That's one of his characteristics. He's good at barking. And I'll wake up.'

'Let's hope so.' Her face indicated that she wasn't convinced. She stood up. 'I'm going for a long soak in the bath. Maybe you can clear up down here and then bring me a mug of tea.' And she stumped off up the stairs. Thud, thud, thud!

CHAPTER 9

Mullen couldn't sleep. He tossed and turned like the proverbial log, checking his phone every little while to see how late it was. Despite all the reassurances he had given to Becca, anxiety chewed away at him. Suppose the arsonist *did* know where he had gone? Suppose they had followed him? Suppose they had put a tracking device on his car? Not hard to do. Suppose they were out there in the dark waiting until they could be sure he was asleep?

He got up suddenly. He had made a decision. He felt his way across the room by the light of his mobile. He had noticed a rolling pin earlier, slotted into Becca's wine rack among half a dozen bottles. If you didn't have a weapon, find one. That was one of his handy hints for a tight spot, though he hadn't wanted to alarm Becca by telling her that. Nevertheless, once his fingers closed around the handle, he felt much reassured. He hefted it in his hand. It was a nice weight, easy to manipulate, long enough to thrust with and heavy enough to cause some damage if he ended up using it as a club.

He switched off the torch app on his mobile, opened the front door and listened. Rex wasn't going to wait. He went straight out and began to sniff around — and silently. Either there were no criminals lurking in the bushes or he had forgotten he was meant to be a guard dog. Mullen slipped out, too, and leaned against the house wall. The door clicked shut behind him, but the only other noise was from a snuffling Rex and an owl hunting somewhere across the fields. He peered around, allowing his eyes to get accustomed to the dark. No dark shapes loomed and there was no cracking of twigs underfoot. He slipped down onto his belly and then onto his back before edging himself under his car and switching on the torch on his mobile phone again. He played the beam around the underside of his vehicle, probing the shadows for a surveillance device. As far as private detectives went, he was something of a Luddite. Electronic tracking devices were something he treated with suspicion, not quite playing fair. Hence he had never fitted one to a car, but he had fiddled about underneath his Ford Focus a few times. So if there was something attached to his old crate, he reckoned he'd be able to spot it.

Eventually he rolled back out from under and raised himself onto his feet. Panic over. No sign of any tracking device. Back to bed — or at least the sofa. Rex whined. He stood at the front door with a plaintive look on his face. He'd had enough. Mullen took a final look around. As darkness went, it wasn't that dark. Nothing stirred. Mullen padded across to the front door — and swore. The door was shut. And, to be precise, it was also locked. He swore again. He didn't have his key on him.

* * *

There was a jackdaw tap-tapping on the surface of the coffee table. Mullen couldn't understand that because, a moment before, a giant chocolate cake had been there — his birthday cake, although it wasn't actually his birthday. And now the bird had eaten it all. How could that be? The jackdaw looked at Mullen. He had never been eyeballed by a jackdaw. He didn't like it. The jackdaw hammered its beak harder against the table and then uttered a strange mewing sound, more doglike than birdlike. The jackdaw stared at him again, opening its mouth so wide he could see its tonsils. 'Mullen!' it said.

Mullen jumped and opened his eyes and almost screamed. DC Benning stared in through the car windscreen, her knuckles poised to rap again. 'Are you all right?'

Rex whined as if to say no, he wasn't. Mullen levered himself out of the car. He was stiff. 'I got locked out the house,' he said.

'What the heck is going on?' This wasn't Benning. This was Becca, who had opened the front door and was looking at them as if she had caught them *in flagrante delicto*.

'I got locked out,' he repeated.

Back inside the house and huddled over a mug of hot tea at the table, Mullen was feeling rather sorry for himself. Benning had taken charge of the pink envelope and letter, but after that she and Becca had settled down to put the world — or rather Mullen's world — to rights. *They're like schoolgirls*, he told himself. He wouldn't live his stupidity down. Benning would tell it to her police colleagues and Becca would tell everyone in the hospital. He sipped again at his tea and realised that they had both stopped talking. Two pairs of eyes were focused on him — three in fact, because Rex was looking at him with reproach, as if he'd just decided that the man who was meant to be his master was a bit of an idiot. But it was Becca who spoke.

'DC Benning wants you to answer some questions, Doug,' she said, steadily and loudly, as if he was an old man with hearing and cognition issues. 'Then she needs to get back to the station before Holden loses her rag and busts her back to walking the beat on a Saturday night.'

'Sorry, I was thinking,' he lied.

'What I need to know,' Benning said, 'is this . . . Do you have any idea who might be trying to kill you?'

In reality there were a number of people who, if they had come across Mullen being beaten up on the other side of the roadside by robbers, would have walked on by without the slightest qualm: people he had tracked, people whose sordid secrets or affairs he had uncovered, a man whose ex-wife he had lied for. But walking by was one thing — setting fire to a house while expecting him to be inside was something else. Besides, if he had had any strong suspicions as to who it was, then of course he would have tackled the guy — or woman — himself. So he wasn't much help to Benning and he sensed her disappointment as she closed her notebook and headed for the door.

Becca headed for the door herself shortly after that, leaving Mullen to doze fitfully on the sofa. She had handed him a spare key, telling him pointedly to keep it in his pocket. 'I'm not cutting my shift short just because you get yourself locked out again.'

Mullen slept well, but when he woke up at just gone twelve thirty, his thoughts reverted to Benning's question and then he found himself asking another: did it have to be him whom the arsonist was trying to kill? The pink letter said he was definitely the target, but suppose the father of Becca's child had been tracking her and had got jealous when she saw her letting herself into his house, or suppose someone knew about Moody's arrival in England? If she had come back to England to deal with some problem or emergency, then it wasn't unreasonable to suppose that someone knew that she was returning and had decided to deal with her before she could spill any beans. But in that case, how was he to explain the second pink letter?

He was trying to weigh up whether he or Becca was the better bet as target when there was a knock on the door. He eased himself up from the sofa and hobbled across the room, his back stiff and aching. He opened the door. There was a woman standing there. Her face was familiar, but his fuddled brain still found it difficult to join all the dots. She smiled, but it was only when she said, ''Ello, Doug,' in a soft French accent that he made the connection.

'Marie!' he said, more loudly that he needed to. 'I wasn't expecting you.'

The smile faded and was replaced by a look of irritation. 'I do live next door.' Marie clearly didn't like to be forgotten. 'Besides, Becca asked if I would just check that you are all right.'

'I'm perfectly capable—' he started, before realising how churlish he must sound. 'Please, do come in. It's kind of you.'

She stepped over the threshold and surveyed the room. Mullen recognised the technique — he had employed it himself plenty of times, going into a house and looking for evidence: the blanket on the sofa, three-quarters of it splayed across the floor as if he had just thrown it off (as indeed he had), a dirty mug on its side on the carpet, margarine, bread and marmalade on the table next to a dirty plate. He saw it as she must be seeing it and felt embarrassed.

'Sorry, I was just catching up on my sleep. You must think I'm a scruff.'

She raised her eyebrows, too polite to actually agree. 'You have been through a traumatic time.'

'Yes.'

'Perhaps I should make us a coffee,' she said.

'Yes. No. I mean, I can do that. How do you like it?'

'Black, if that is not too much trouble.'

Mullen found himself going off Marie. Her soft accent was undeniably seductive, but it didn't hide the sharpness of her words. *'If that is not too much trouble.'* She made him feel like an archetypal man. He picked up the abandoned mug and tidied the blanket, dislodging Rex as he did. The dog had watched silently throughout but now he stretched his back and walked up to Marie, sniffing her sandaled feet.

'Oh!' She stepped back a pace. 'I do not like dogs.'

Mullen looked at her. Most people went all gooey at the sight of Rex. How could Marie not? 'He's harmless.'

'He is a dog.'

Mullen picked Rex up and put him on a small blanket that functioned (in theory) as his bed by the cooker. 'Sit.' Mullen lifted a warning finger. The dog said nothing.

Mullen turned his attention to making the coffee, while Marie peppered him with questions — about the fire, his time in the hospital, what were his plans, and so on.

'You must have lost all your clothes in the fire.'

He handed her a mug. 'Yes.' He glanced down, noticing what he was wearing. His clothes weren't exactly posh and they were pretty creased after sleeping much of the night in the car, but at least Becca had washed them while he had been stuck in hospital.

'I wish I had kept Robert's clothes. You could have had some of them. You must be the same size, I think, but I could not bear to see them hanging in the wardrobe, so I got rid of them all. The better ones I took to the charity shops in Headington. The rest went to the clothing bank outside the fire station. They will take anything if it is in a bag.'

'I'll be fine,' he said. 'Don't worry.'

'Do you mind if I ask you something?'

Something? The word was pregnant with meaning. And as far as Mullen could tell, she didn't seem to be a person who needed to get permission to speak. He braced himself. 'Go ahead.'

'Obviously your plate has been full with the arson and hospital, but I just wondered what you have learned about Robert's death?'

'To be honest, not as much as I would have liked.'

'To be honest? Are you not always honest?' This might have been a joke. Except that, coming out of her mouth, it sounded like anything but. She surveyed him through unblinking eyes. The question hung almost visibly in the air. The conversation had taken a very cool turn. Finally, she continued. 'You see . . . Becca may think you are the best thing since . . . how do you say it . . . sliced bread? But I do not. I listen to you say what you have been doing and you do not mention Robert once. So I conclude you have made no attempts to investigate his death.'

'I suppose that's what I meant.'

'What you meant, but not what you said. And now, I expect, you will be more interested in tracking down the arsonist who killed your professor. But who, Becca tells me, was trying to kill you.'

Mullen wasn't sure how to respond. Marie and Becca had clearly had a detailed discussion.

But Marie hadn't finished. 'Or, God forbid, the arsonist was trying to kill Becca.'

'I don't think so,' he said. 'After all, how would anyone have known Becca was in the house?'

'Maybe someone followed her? Tracked her to your house.'

'But why?'

'You call yourself a detective.' Her French accent, far from being sexy, was now dismissive. It was if she had weighed Mullen and found him wanting. 'It seems to me that the obvious culprit would surely be the father of Becca's child . . . whoever that might be.' She folded her arms and transfixed him with her hazel eyes: cool, unblinking, accusatory.

'Or maybe the culprit is someone who likes to start fires.'

Marie made a face as if that was the stupidest thing she had ever heard. She turned to go, but hadn't quite finished. 'Do you seriously believe that?'

He didn't, but he wasn't prepared to admit it. 'I'm not ruling anything out.'

She shrugged. 'Well, I will leave you to your not ruling out. But, before I go, let me make one thing very clear . . . You are not a proper detective. You are a person who claims to be a detective — a private investigator, but that is all. I cannot understand why Becca approached you to *detect* over my husband's death. Perhaps she had ulterior motives. Perhaps she wants to enlist your help for herself at a difficult time of her life. I would understand that. But she never asked me. I prefer to trust the British police. They have made a thorough enquiry and discovered nothing. This is because there is nothing to discover. My husband killed himself because he was a weak man. He abandoned me and he abandoned his child and that is something I will never forgive him for.'

'I understand your ang—'

'All you have to understand, Mr Mullen, is that I will not pay you a single penny. I do not want you to *detect* for me.'

She marched to the front door and wrenched it open. She turned and waved her arm in a broad arc. 'Look! You cannot even clear up your own mess.' Then she shut the door very firmly behind her.

It took Mullen nearly an hour to recover from the pasting to which Marie had subjected him. He took Rex for a long walk and tried to lose himself. He talked to Rex, he complained to Rex, he asked Rex what he thought and, eventually, when the circular walk brought them back to Becca's cottage, he had managed to unload some of his frustrations and to focus his thinking.

He had to forget Robert and his sharp-tongued widow and concentrate on Sandra. The pink envelopes and their contents pointed unequivocally to her or her brother, Kevin, who she had notably failed to talk about. Where the hell was he? Was it he who had sent him the letters, he who had torched the house? It seemed a reasonable guess — more than reasonable. It had to be him. Him or Sandra.

He scribbled a note for Becca, left it on the table, took a banana and got into his car. Rex flopped down on the passenger seat, more than happy to be driven wherever it was they were going. Mullen gunned the car into life and headed south. He drove down the A34 past Winchester, onto the M3 and then down the eastern side of the New Forest through Lyndhurst with its ever-present traffic queues, until he arrived again at Badgerhurst. It was nearly four o'clock when he pulled into the car park of the Nags Head.

The car park was as empty as it had been the last time he had come and the pub looked just as shut, too. He got out and let Rex have a pee. Then walked round to the door at the back. It wasn't ajar this time. He tried the handle and pushed. It was locked. He stepped backwards and stared up. There were two upstairs windows open. Curtains were billowing out, a bit of an invitation to any passing burglar with a ladder in their back pocket. He called up, 'Sandra!'. He paused for several seconds, then repeated the process, but louder. *'Sandra!'*.

'Yes!' the reply was equally loud and came from less than one metre behind him.

Mullen jumped and swung around. 'God!'

It wasn't God. It was Sandra. Unless it was God pretending to be Sandra, though what she said next seemed very unGodlike. 'What the fuck are you doing here? Didn't I make myself clear last time?'

'Someone tried to kill me. Arson.' He may have been taken unawares, but he had no intention of slinking off empty-handed. Fight fire with fire — as it were.

'What?' She seemed genuinely surprised. Mind you, for all he knew Sandra had gone through acting school and come out with a distinction. 'Are you serious?'

Five minutes later, they were sitting down with two mugs of tea. Sandra had made it this time. It was mud-brown and stronger than Mullen preferred, but he had more important things to discuss than tea. He gave her the bare essentials of what had happened: how he had driven home, how he had arrived late because of traffic problems, how the house was on fire, how he had been briefly hospitalised — he didn't want her to think he had just wrung his hands and watched — how he had received another letter, this one announcing his cremation.

When he finished, he waited for her to respond. Maybe he had subconsciously picked up operating tips from Kazia. Use silence to apply pressure. Wait until they cracked. Or maybe going silent was just easier than storming in mob-handed with questions. He sipped his tea. When Sandra looked up at him, he smiled bleakly — or so he hoped.

'So is that it?'

Is that it? By Mullen's reckoning, it was rather substantial. 'Someone died. I need to find out who did it.'

'And you think it was me?'

'The police have the letter and envelope. If they get forensics off it, it will be easy for them to rule you in or out.'

'It wasn't me. I went out. A guy took me to the Luna Caprese in Lymington. Italian. Very nice. Mind you, I was crap company. Went on and on endlessly about Ben and you. Still, he seemed to like it — me crying on his shoulder. Here . . .' She got out her phone. Her fingers flitted effortlessly over the screen. She showed Mullen a photo: her and a guy with broad shoulders and a shaved head grinning inanely into the camera. 'The waiter took it.'

'I'd like to speak to him.'

'Isn't this enough?' She waved the phone at Mullen.

'I like to double-check.'

'Rick is married.'

'I can be tactful.'

'You'd better be. He's a good friend.' She got up, found her handbag and dug out a business card. 'He's working up the road today. Pear Tree Cottage. On the left just before the garage. His wife has MS. Very advanced. He's very good to her, but sometimes . . .'

'I understand.' He had no interest in ruining people's lives. 'But what about your little brother?'

'Kevin? What about him?'

'Well, if you didn't send me the letters, I guess he must have.'

'And burnt your house down, you mean?'

Mullen nodded. 'And killed someone, too.'

'He's in prison. Has been for two and a half years. Will be for a while longer. He was brought to our mother's funeral and then taken straight back. In handcuffs. So, whoever it was, it wasn't him!'

'Which prison?'

'You're thinking of springing him?' She laughed. 'HMP Underhill.'

'Thanks.'

'Is that it?'

Mullen thought it was. He'd go and check out Rick, just because it would be so easy to, then head for home. It would be easy enough to check out Kevin, too, make sure he was where Sandra said he was, tucked away from the great British public at Her Majesty's Pleasure. He sighed. It had been a day of ruling people out rather than ruling people in — which was something, but far from everything.

'Thanks for your help.' He drained his tea and got up.

'I'm sorry about your friend.'

'So am I.'

'I'm also hoping you won't be coming back again. I need to get my life back on track.'

Mullen smiled. 'Fingers crossed.'

'You're serious about visiting Kevin?'

'Yes.'

'In that case, I can help.'

It wasn't hard to track down Sandra's Rick. A pretty cottage with a spectacular and well-fruited pear tree stood at the front. A small flat bed van was parked inside the short driveway. There was a pile of rubble in the back of it. Mullen pulled up in a parking area a hundred metres further on and got out. He attached Rex to the lead and went in search of his quarry.

'You Rick?'

The man from Sandra's photo straightened up and looked around. He had a trowel in one hand and several tattoos over the exposed parts of his body. Not a man to trifle with. 'Who's asking?'

'Doug Mullen. I'm a friend of Sandra.'

Curiosity in the man's face morphed into suspicion.

'Got some building work you want doing?' Rick waved the trowel in the air. 'Don't recall her ever mentioning your name.'

'I'm a private investigator.'

The trowel in Rick's right hand twitched.

'She tells me you took her out for dinner last Friday.'

Rick moved towards him until they were less than a metre apart. Mullen stood stock still, neither retreating nor advancing to meet him. They were of very similar height, but Mullen was under no illusions. Rick was solid. If he lost his temper, if he swung a fist and connected, then Mullen would be very lucky not to end up on his back. If he decided to use the trowel as a weapon . . . well, that didn't bear thinking about.

'She's told me about your situation.' Mullen tried to sound soothing. 'Believe me, I do understand. I'm not the sort of person who goes around telling tales.'

'I've nothing to say. So I suggest you leave.'

'I need to know.'

'Or what?'

'Or I remain very suspicious and I report my suspicions to the police.'

'Look, what the hell is this all about?'

'Hasn't Sandra told you? Didn't she ring you on your mobile and warn you?'

'It's on silent. In the car. I hate being interrupted. Like I hate you interrupting me now. I want to get on with pointing this wall before it rains.' He gestured to the sky, which was significantly darker than it had been all day.

'Someone deliberately burnt my house down last Friday evening. I just need to rule her out.'

'What?' For several seconds Mullen though Rick would explode. Push somebody hard enough and that was what could happen. But instead Rick burst into laughter. 'Is that what you think? Why on earth—'

'She blames me for her brother's death. I was his best friend in the army and she thinks I abandoned him. That's a motive.'

Rick's face hardened. 'Last Friday she was with me from about seven until eleven p.m. We went to the Luna Caprese. Well away from here and prying eyes. Luigi seated us at the back in a private corner.'

'What did you eat?'

He frowned. 'Veal escalopes. Some sort of white wine sauce. With chips. I'm not much of a pasta man.'

'What about a starter?'

'Hell . . . um, those little fish, deep fried. What are they called?'

'Whitebait?'

'That's it. Damn good they were too. And before you ask, I had ice cream for pudding — salted caramel. Followed by a large cappuccino.'

'OK.' Mullen nodded. He hadn't thought to ask Sandra what they ate, but the fact was that Rick sounded convincing. Just as the photo on Sandra's phone had seemed very convincing. It was hard not to believe they were both telling the truth.

'If my wife finds out about this, it'll really screw things up. Sandra and me . . . we know our priorities, but we also have needs.'

'I've no intention of ever speaking to your wife.' Mullen stretched out his hand and held it there until Rick shook it reluctantly.

'Come on, Rex!' Mullen and dog headed back towards their car. Mullen looked up. The sky was even darker and he felt the felt the first telltale signs of rain on his face.

When he got back to Becca's cottage, her red car was outside. He let himself inside quietly and discovered that she had parked herself in an armchair and was fast asleep. He gave a quiet 'Hi!', but she didn't stir. The only thing that stirred in Mullen was a feeling of protective love, the sort of thing male creatures throughout the animal kingdom experienced as they waited for their partners to bring new life into the world. He felt it and recognised it for what it was, even though the kid wasn't actually his. Soft. Soppy. Stupid. Whatever the most suitable word was, that was him.

'Doug . . .' Her eyes had opened and were taking him in. She smiled. 'I was just having forty winks.'

'You all right? Good day at the coalface?'

'Hardly the coalface. Computer admin, mostly. But yes. And you?'

'It's not Sandra and not Kevin.' He went on to explain.

'Just a minute, Doug . . .' She had levered herself up from the chair and now she made her way over to where he was standing. She kissed him. On the lips. Not exactly passionately, but she held it for longer than she might have. Then she rested her head against him. 'Call me stupid. But when I saw your note lying there, I got all tearful. I thought you'd done a runner. Then I read it and I began to think maybe you'd fallen for this Sandra.'

He didn't answer. He tightened his arm around her shoulder and let himself enjoy the moment. Whatever else happened, he wanted to remain Becca's friend for as long as she needed him.

'Tell me about Sandra,' she said. So he did. It was easier than talking about Marie. He had decided to bury that encounter. Fat chance.

CHAPTER 10

'I gather Marie called in yesterday.'

Mullen and Becca were having breakfast together and up to that point had been in virtual silence. Like a long-married couple. Mr and Mrs. Him and Her. Darby and Joan. Comfortable, undemanding, rather pleasant.

'Yes.'

'So how was that?'

'I don't think she rates me.'

'In what way?'

'In any way. I think she sees me a scruffy slob who can't even look after himself, let alone operate as a human being.'

'Well, projecting a professional approach to your work is hardly your strong suit.'

Mullen flinched. If he had been looking for sympathy, and he probably had, Becca wasn't dishing it out. 'Have you've been talking to her about me?'

'Mostly she was doing the talking and I was making excuses for you.'

'She said she won't pay me a penny.'

'Until probate comes through, money is going to be a problem for her.'

'I think it goes deeper than that. She despises me.'

'For God's sake, Doug, I can't stand people who play the "poor me!" card. If we're going to share the same house, we both need to be adults.'

Silence. He was at school again, being told off and not knowing how to get back in teacher's good books.

Becca pressed on. 'Also, because Robert's death is down as suicide, the life insurance won't pay out either.'

He was silent, but Becca's words seemed to kickstart his brain into some sort of life. For some reason, he had never considered that aspect of things. Never even thought about how much money Marie might or might not have. He was still smarting from some of the things she had said to him. It was easy to wallow in self-pity. Easy, but pointless — life had taught him that. But that didn't mean you could always stop it. He looked across at Becca, saw the firm set of her jaw and the irritation in her eyes. It was impossible to kick the feeling that she was on Marie's side rather than his.

Becca hadn't finished. 'Marie thinks I am a fool for attaching my hopes to you. Her husband gave up on her and her child. And she thinks you'll do the same to me.'

Would he? And had he already given that sort of commitment to Becca? She had offered him a place to stay. Washed his clothes. He was grateful. She had kissed him — on the forehead and on the lips. But he hadn't exactly gone down on one knee and pledged undying love — or even short-term love. He had promised to decorate the baby's room. That was just a way of thanking her. They didn't so much have a relationship as a working arrangement. That's what he had told himself. But Marie's assessment of him — that he would never stick with Becca when things got difficult — cut him to the quick. Was he that shallow? Sticks and stone may hurt your bones, but words can never hurt you? What idiot came up with that expression?

'Of course,' Becca continued, 'she's been damaged by her own experience. But I remain very optimistic about people. And that includes you.' She stretched her hand across the table and grabbed one of his, taking him by surprise. She gave it a squeeze.

Mullen waited for her to let go. 'I think I might go to Amanda's Café today.'

'Do some detecting, you mean.'

'Something like that.'

'Would you like some company?'

'No' would have been the honest answer. But truth and tact are often polar opposites. 'In theory. But I think it's best if I operate on my own.' He tried to sound casual. He didn't want to offend her.

'OK. You know best.' She got up. 'I think I'll make myself some more toast. Do you want some?'

'I'm fine.' he said.

He watched her as she stuck bread in the toaster and then waited for it to pop up, her back towards him. Something had changed. Was she disappointed in him? Could she see through him? Had she divined that he wasn't being a hundred percent open and honest?

'I'm taking this back to bed.' She held up her plate of toast and marmalade. 'I'm tired. See you much later.'

Much later. The words were like a knife being slipped in between the ribs. Why hadn't he just been straight with her? Told her that he wanted to see Kazia Ciesla while he was in Headington. But telling her that would require him to tell her a load of other stuff and he wasn't ready to do that yet. He liked Becca. A lot. But he really hadn't got the hang of living in her space.

'Leave the dog, if you want!' she called down the stairs, twisting the knife ever so carefully.

Mullen waited until he was halfway to Oxford before he rang Kazia. He pulled into the bikers' haunt just outside Berinsfield. Not that there were any bikers in sight. Sometimes when he drove past, it was awash with them, usually at the weekends, but today it resembled a sort of eerie deserted mid-Arizona fuelling station.

There was no chance of being overheard there. Not a single biker in sight. Not that there was much for anyone to overhear. Kazia's phone went straight to voicemail and Mullen told her he would like to meet up again when convenient.

By the time he had arrived in Headington and parked up in the Waitrose car park, Kazia still hadn't rung back. He told himself she must be busy working: holding a one-to-one session with someone in her garden office or maybe she spent some of her time in the Warneford Hospital or down at Littlemore. Or maybe it was her day off and the last thing she was going to do was return a call to a patient — especially one who hadn't paid her a penny. Because Professor Moody had been going to do that. Perhaps she hadn't got round to doing so? She certainly wasn't going to be doing so in the future. Perhaps he should offer to pay himself?

He felt a surge of guilt about Professor Moody. He had been so wrapped up in his own problems that he had barely thought about her at all. What was it that had caused her to fly back to the UK so unexpectedly? Maybe Kazia would know, or at least have some idea. Moody had known her well enough to entrust Mullen to her and pay for his sessions — unless, of course, Kazia had done it as some sort of favour. Had they known each other only through work or did they have some sort of personal relationship? Had they been lovers? He could imagine they might have been. Thoughts swirled round his brain like leaves in an autumn breeze but refused to settle into any sort of pattern.

He checked his watch. He was still old school enough to wear one. Mobile phones had rendered them unnecessary, but he only felt fully dressed with a watch on his wrist. It wasn't a flash-Harry one. It had survived several scrapes unscathed beyond the odd scratch and it hadn't cost him an arm and a leg. And right now it was telling him that it had just gone ten a.m. He'd give Kazia an opportunity to ring back — say until eleven. And if she didn't, he'd go and hunt her down at her house.

In the meantime, he was dying for a coffee and Amanda's Café was only a couple of minutes' walk away. That was where he would start.

He found himself a seat in the corner of the café and, almost immediately, Carly the waitress came over to take his order: a large Americano and a pecan and maple pastry. He didn't need the latter, except maybe psychologically, but since he had no idea when or if he would get lunch, it seemed like a reasonable precaution.

Amanda was barely visible. Once she appeared behind the counter, but when Mullen looked up again she had disappeared. Maybe there were things she had to help out with in the kitchen or there was admin to be done. The important thing was that she was around. Mullen pretended to read the paper while keeping an eye on what was going on. Carly came across and asked if everything was all right. Given that his pastry was long gone and his cup empty, he ordered another Americano. Anything to put off what had to be done.

He was halfway through his second drink when a vaguely familiar figure came in: tall, floppy fair hair, a slight paunch. Mullen had seen him somewhere but couldn't quite place him. The man ordered a takeaway latte and an almond croissant. Mullen felt a sudden pang of hunger. An almond croissant sounded really tempting. But then, as Carly turned away to make the coffee, Amanda appeared. The man ran his hand through his hair and that was when Mullen remembered where he had seen him before — in the hospital after Becca had had her fall. He had to be a doctor because he had said something about Becca and the baby being OK before he had swept out of the room.

He seemed to be a bit of a charmer. Amanda was smiling. Although they spoke quietly and probably inconsequentially, Mullen's guess was that they liked each other. As Carly handed him his coffee and croissant, he must have said something funny, because they both laughed. But the eyes that followed him as he left the café were Amanda's, and only when the door shut behind him did she withdraw to her hidden domain.

Mullen finished his coffee and stood up. He went to the counter and asked if he could pay. He did so with cash, left a generous tip on the counter and then asked if he might have a quick word with Amanda.

Carly looked at him suspiciously. Perhaps she had every reason to — he had spent a very long time in the café over two coffees and a pastry and, unlike the others, he hadn't been poring over a laptop pretending to work. 'Do you have an appointment?' she asked.

'No. I just wanted a quick chat.'

'She's busy.'

'Tell her it's about Robert Dench. Here's my card.' He handed it over. Not the fanciest one in the world, but the words *Private Investigator* were on it and that, he reckoned, would get her attention.

'Wait here.'

Mullen waited, and within thirty seconds she was back, accompanied by Amanda. 'Come with me,' Amanda said, and Mullen did just that, following her past a toilet into the kitchen, past the chef and out through the back door.

She lit up a cigarette and inhaled. 'What's this all about?'

'Robert Dench.'

'So you told Carly. But he committed suicide, didn't he.' It sounded like a statement rather than a question. 'It was all investigated. I went to the inquest.' She took another drag.

'Someone is unhappy with the verdict.'

'You mean his wife?'

'Obviously I cannot tell you who my client is.'

'I wouldn't trust her further than I could spit, if I was you.'

'When I work a case, I tend not to trust anyone.'

She laughed. A raucous, gravelly smoker's laugh. 'Well, I don't give a monkey's. All I know is that his wife gave him a hard time.'

'He told you that, did he?'

'Not in so many words. He was very loyal to her.'

'Were you and Robert having an affair?'

She didn't answer immediately, merely studied Mullen over her glasses, as if sizing him up or maybe buying herself some thinking time. She took a long drag on her cigarette before stubbing it out on the dispenser attached to the wall. 'What difference would it make if we were?'

'It would have given Marie a motive to kill him.'

'But she couldn't have, could she? Because she was at home taking a phone call from him when he shot himself. The inquest agreed that.'

'But suppose the inquest got it wrong and someone else shot Robert. What then? I guess if Robert had ended his affair with you, it would have given *you* a motive to kill him.' He tried to say this casually, as if this was a harmless and humorous piece of speculation — which it was, a shot in the dark fired from the hip.

But Amanda's face, which had so far been showing only signs of caustic amusement, hardened in horror and then exploded into fury. 'Don't you ever come to my café again, Mr Mullen. Because you sure as hell won't be welcome.' And she went back inside the kitchen. She banged the door shut behind her and he heard her slam the bolts into place.

Mullen wasn't sure how to react. He walked off, heading west down London Road. He needed to think. What had he done? Or rather, what did Amanda's behaviour mean? Had he been wildly off target or just the opposite? Had his question been too close to the truth? He paced on, down past the White Horse pub, past the girls' private school and then across the road into Gipsy Lane. If this had once been the home of gypsies, they were long gone. There were plenty of students though, because this was where Oxford Brookes University was based. Mullen barely gave the buildings a glance or indeed all the people going hither and thither all around him. He pressed on and it was only when he reached the crossroads and turned left into Old Road that his pace and agitation slackened a little.

He pulled out and checked his phone. Had he missed a call back from Kazia? Had his phone somehow gone on to silent mode? This was paranoia, he knew, but he checked anyway. Not on silent and no missed calls. There were no texts from Kazia either. Nothing. Should he ring again? But if she was deliberately ignoring him, then she would see it was him calling and just not answer. Mullen had a better idea: go and knock on her front door. He kept walking up the slope until he reached Lime Walk and turned left into it. Halfway along was a right turn and then a left past the church. Before he knew it, he was standing outside Kazia's house.

The side gate, which had been hooked open when he came for his two sessions, was shut. Not a good sign. No lights on inside the house, but then it was the middle of a very sunny day. Mullen hesitated. Suppose she was in: how would she feel about him turning up unannounced on her doorstep? He had already seriously pissed off Amanda and he didn't want to do the same to Kazia. But what harm could knocking on her door do? If she was in, then he could apologise and try to explain himself. And if she wasn't in, then no harm was done.

He walked up the short path to find there was no need to knock because there was a bell. He pressed the button and listened intently. It was working: a rather shrill tuneless sound. Then came the sound of someone approaching the door, leather soles clicking on a wooden floor. Mullen tensed himself, mentally rehearsing what he would say to head off her anger. There was the rattle of a security chain being released and the door swung open.

'Who are you?'

The man was taller than Mullen as well two steps higher and he looked down on him with barely concealed hostility. Mullen felt as if he was being judged and found guilty without any chance to argue his case. He also felt thrown off balance because he recognised the floppy-haired man from the café.

'Well?' the man said.

'Doug Mullen. Is Kazia in?'

'Do you have an appointment?'

'No. I was just passing and—'

'She doesn't do "just passing." Neither do I.'

'I tried ringing, but she didn't answer.'

'Doesn't the fact that she didn't answer tell you something?'

'I just needed to talk to her.'

'That doesn't make you any different to any other of her clients. So what I am going to do now is shut this door and what you are going to do is turn around and go back to wherever it is you came from and then you are going to wait until she returns your call.'

'Can you tell her I called?'

He smiled. 'I could . . . but I won't.' And with that he withdrew inside, shut the door with a bang and slid the security chain noisily into place.

Mullen made his way slowly towards London Road. When he got there, he stopped on the corner while he thought about a plan. He had come a full circle. Amanda's Café was diagonally across the road. He was hungry now but obviously couldn't return there for lunch. He started to walk along the nearside pavement. The fourth unit was a café. If there were two things Headington didn't lack, one was charity shops and the other was places to eat and drink. He went inside, ordered himself a toasted sandwich and yet another coffee and then carefully selected a table. It was set well within the café but nonetheless afforded a perfect view of the street and of Amanda's Café in particular. Not only could he keep an eye on the comings and goings from there, but he was pretty sure he would be invisible to Amanda even if she stood in her doorway and scanned the street for him.

He checked his watch. It was going to be a long wait. He could only guess when Carly knocked off work. Three, four, five o'clock. He would wait. Who said being a private investigator was glamorous and exciting work? Whoever it was, they knew nothing. But he was getting used to it and anyway, he'd had an interesting morning, which had given him lots to think about. First, there was Amanda: she was obviously antagonistic towards Marie, she had very possibly been having an affair with Robert and had possibly been very unhappy when he ended it. That was all hypothetical, he knew, but it made some sort of sense.

Then there was the tall man with blonde floppy hair, who Amanda had made a point of chatting to and, if he had read it right, was flirting with him. A doctor, because it was surely he who Mullen had encountered in the hospital when Becca had been admitted after her fall. And, extraordinarily, he had been the man who had answered the door at Kazia's house. It was one hell of a coincidence, and Mullen didn't believe in coincidences.

The toasted sandwich arrived, along with a flat white coffee and glass of water. Mullen nibbled the corner off the sandwich and wondered how long he could make it and the drink last. His mobile rang. He answered it.

'How's it going, sweetie?' It was Becca and without a hint of the discord that had surfaced like a U-boat that morning.

'Fine, thanks,' he whispered, but he was very pleased to have heard from her.

'What are you doing?' she hissed back. 'Stalking a suspect? Interrogating an unwilling witness? Discreetly handing brown envelopes stuffed with used fivers to dodgy informants?'

'I can't tell you. I'm in a café and besides, walls have ears.'

'Oh my God! I just had a thought. Your phone might be being tapped!' She was all mock surprise and horror. 'Someone might be listening to me and wondering what sort of code we are speaking!'

'It's all very dull,' he said, though he was well aware that listening in on people's phones was no joke. 'It's like watching paint dry, but less exciting.'

'Ah, speaking of paint drying, you won't forget my baby's bedroom, will you?'

'Blue and pink.'

'And when you've finished whatever it is you are doing, perhaps you can get me a few food items.'

'Sure.'

'I'll text you a list.' And with that she hung up.

Mullen took another bite out of his sandwich. Nibbling off tiny bits suddenly seemed ridiculous. Besides, he was hungry. Within five minutes it was all gone. He bought some time by sipping slowly at his coffee, but when he had got to the bottom of his cup, he went up to the counter and he bought himself another — would he ever sleep again? — and a large piece of carrot cake. There was no better cake, he told himself as he sank his teeth into it. *Fuck!* His mouth froze. Carly was leaving work. It was just gone one forty-five p.m. He had checked his watch before he went to the counter. What sort of time was that for her to finish her shift? He jumped to his feet and tried to get to the door past a woman in a mobility scooter — make that an immobility scooter. He tried to squeeze between her and the baby buggy at the next table but was losing the fight.

'Do you mind?' It was the mother of the toddler or maybe the woman in the scooter or maybe both. Mullen didn't much mind, but he blurted a quick 'Sorry!' nevertheless. He forced his way past them and reached the door despite their protests, before emerging into the bright light of London Road.

There! He thought he might have lost her, but he could see her disappearing down a side road. Mullen plunged across the road. A car hooted, a cyclist swore, but he carried on. On the other pavement he broke into a jog. He almost shouted after her but decided that this would alarm her. She glanced back, saw him and herself began to jog. It was a cul de sac, but at the end of it she turned right and disappeared from view. He accelerated, determined to catch up with her. He had never been this way before and he was amazed to find himself descending into what appeared to be a semi-subterranean corridor. There were stone walls on either side and up ahead he could see a short tunnel into which Carly was hurrying. 'Please stop!' he called, changing tactics. 'I need to talk to you!' Carly glanced back again and then tripped over.

He continued running. She was trying to get to her feet, but slipped down again. Maybe she had hurt herself. He slowed down as he drew near, held his hands out, palms down. He didn't want to alarm her. 'Please, there's nothing to worry about. I just need to talk to you. Are you OK? Are you hurt?'

'A little,' she said. She remained on the ground. She had capitulated.

He bent down. 'Here, let me help you.' He let her take his hand and braced himself as she pulled her to her feet. 'Carly, I am so sorry for alarming y—'

Suddenly both his eyes exploded. That was what it felt like, though as he later realised what had actually happened was that she had thrust her forefinger and second finger into his sockets. Mullen squealed and fell to the ground. *Open your eyes!* he told himself. But it was all darkness and exploding stars and sheer agony. Someone was shouting and swearing — himself. He waited for God knows what. The pain to ease, for a start. But he was already wondering if she had done him any permanent damage. He was also wondering if she was going to inflict more.

'I can explain . . .' he said. Nothing. He tried again to open his eyes. This time there was some daylight and significantly smaller explosions of pain. He could make out the shadowy rectangular shapes of the stones in the wall.

He saw another shape too: Carly. She was bending down. 'Are you OK, mate?'

Was it a trick? 'Been better,' he mumbled.

'Never done that before. Not for real. Only in the self-defence classes and then you don't actually do that to someone's eyes. Can you see?'

'A bit.'

'You really scared me. I thought you were going to mug me or rape me or . . .'

'Sorry. Stupid of me to chase after you and shout.'

'You're not going to report me, because if you are, I shall plead self-defence — which it was, and nobody's going to blame me for protecting myself.'

'I just need to know who the man was who came into the café this morning. Tall . . . floppy blonde hair. He was chatting with Amanda while you made him a coffee and got him a croissant.'

'Oh, is that all? He's Leo. Or, to give him his full name and title, Dr Leonard Francombe.'

'Works at the John Radcliffe Hospital, does he?'

'Maybe. I'm not sure which hospital, to be honest. Look, if you've got any more questions to ask, can you walk at the same time because I've only got half an hour's break.'

'Sure.' It suited him. This was the way to his car, and he suddenly realised that it must have been parked behind Waitrose for longer than the three hours he'd paid for.

'You go in front,' she said.

'Sure.' He walked slowly, still fighting the pain as he tried to formulate his questions. 'Tell me . . . are he and Amanda an item? They seemed friendly.'

She giggled. 'She'd like that to be the case. But he's a bit of a player by all accounts. And he likes his women to be younger models than Amanda. But he'll flirt with anyone with tits.'

'OK. Now I want to ask you about Robert Dench.'

'Yes?' Her tone was wary.

'Did he seem to you like he was a man who would take his own life?'

She didn't answer at first. He glanced back in case she had stopped, but she was right behind him. 'I don't rightly know. I've never known anyone else who's committed suicide. All I can say is that it came as a real shock to me.'

'So he didn't seem depressed?'

'Not depressed.' She paused, mouth slightly open, as if there was something that needed to be said.

'But?'

'Nothing,' she said. 'It's nothing.'

'Please.'

She shrugged. 'Look, Robert was OK. He was kind to me when I was learning the ropes here even though I didn't eat his food. "What's wrong with my cooking?" he'd say. There was nothing wrong with it. But I like to watch my figure and my weight.'

I can see that. Mullen didn't say so of course, but it was obvious enough. Anorexia was something he had never got his head around.

'It was like he needed approval. I felt he was quite a fragile person underneath. Tap him hard enough and he might shatter.'

They had reached the end of the passage and halted. They were no more than a hundred or so metres from the entrance to the car park behind Waitrose, but he sensed there were things that Carly wasn't saying. He tried a different line of attack. 'Just a couple more questions. Do you think it possible that Amanda and Robert were having an affair before he died?'

There was a long pause. She looked down at the ground as she considered the question. Finally she looked up. 'No. I don't think so. They often fell out over things. He wanted total control over the menu and the kitchen, but she wasn't willing to give him that.'

'Sometimes they had rows, then?'

'Don't all chefs?' She smiled. Her face was thin, the skin stretching taut over the bone structure. Why, Mullen wondered suddenly, did a woman with eating issues work in a café? To prove something to herself? Or was she bulimic, gorging herself on cake and then throwing up in the loo?

'But they always made up?'

'Made up? I wouldn't use those words. It was more like a thunderstorm. Lots of noise and lightning, and then half an hour later it would have all blown over. Look, Amanda has been kind to me, and so was Robert. But having an affair? I don't think so. Please don't go misinterpreting what I've said.'

'One final thing . . . Does a woman called Kazia Ciesla ever come into the café?'

'Look, people who come in for a coffee or a bite to eat don't start telling me their names.'

‘Reddish brown short hair . . . styled a bit like a close-fitting Greek helmet . . . favours dangling earrings . . . smart and strikingly dressed?’

She frowned. ‘I don’t think so. No.’

‘Maybe she has come into the café with Dr Francombe?’

‘Maybe. I’m not sure. Look, I only work at Amanda’s part-time. To earn a bit of money. That’s what students have to do.’

‘OK. Well, thanks for humouring me.’

‘Which way are you going?’

He pointed to the right. ‘I’m parked up there behind Waitrose.’

‘Good. Because I don’t want you following me.’ She folded her arms.

‘Thank you for your help.’ He crossed the road and headed for the car park. He walked fast, hoping he hadn’t got a parking ticket. As he got to the entrance, he glanced around. But Carly had gone.

* * *

‘Can I speak to Detective Inspector Holden?’ Mullen was in Cowley police station. He wasn’t feeling very comfortable about it. The only times he had been there previously were two occasions when he was being grilled by the police.

‘Got an appointment?’ The uniformed woman behind the tall desk and small glass window gave him a glacial stare.

‘I’ve got some information.’

‘Ah!’ she said, in a *they all say that* tone of voice. ‘What sort of information?’

‘For her ears only — that sort of information.’

She scowled at him. She clearly didn’t take kindly to smart alecs. ‘Got some ID?’

Mullen got out his driving licence and waited while she gave it intense scrutiny. She picked up the phone then returned the licence to Mullen. ‘Just wait over there for a minute while I ring through.’

A minute was an absurd understatement. Nearly fifteen had passed before a shadow suddenly fell across Mullen. He had almost nodded off. 'Mr Mullen?' He looked up. The amiable face of DC Benning was looking down at him. 'I'm afraid Detective Inspector Holden is not available. Was it about the letter in the pink envelope? Because I'm afraid forensics haven't come up with anything useful.'

'There was something else I wanted to run by her.'

'She's very busy. I'm afraid that really isn't going to be possible.'

Mullen tried not to let his sense of disappointment show. He had thought that he, Holden and Benning had some sort of understanding, yet here he was being kept at arm's length — and a very long arm's length at that. 'You can always ring our twenty-four-hour line if you have anything to report.' She said this as she ushered him towards the exit. 'Good day.'

Mullen pushed through the swing doors and turned left, heading down the slope towards the small row of shops outside which his car was parked. He got in and only then did he look at the piece of paper that Benning had slipped into his hand as she was wishing him 'Good day.' He unfolded the short note, handwritten in small capital letters: *LAY-BY JUST NORTH OF GOLDEN BALLS ROUNDABOUT, 7:00 P.M. LEAVE YOUR PHONE AT HOME.*

* * *

Mullen arrived at the lay-by at six fifty-five. He gave himself a pat on the back for being a sensible five minutes early. But as the minutes slipped by and Holden failed to show up, he became increasingly worried. By seven fifteen, he was conscious that his anxiety levels were tightening around his stomach. Handwritten notes, no phones, a rendezvous in a lay-by . . . it was almost as if someone was playing a joke on him — but from what he knew of Holden, she wasn't at all the joking type. At seven thirty a white van, unmarked and anonymous, pulled in. Mullen tensed. No phone, no gun, not even Rex as companion and guard dog. He had treacherously decided that staying with Becca was a much better bet. Mullen was about as unprepared for eventualities as anyone could be.

A man got out of the van, all bulging muscles, tattoos and beer belly, a laughable archetype if you were in the mood for humour. He glanced at Mullen but without much interest. If he was checking him out without appearing to do so, he was pretty good at his job. He went round the back of his van, stood in the shelter of its passenger side and urinated. Mullen pretended he was on the phone and made a point of avoiding eye contact as the man walked back around his vehicle. He didn't want to provoke the guy. He reckoned that hanging around lay-bys spying on men having a leak was a high-risk occupation. Even so, he watched surreptitiously as the guy got back into his van, started up the engine with unnecessary revving and then pulled out onto the road.

And there she was: a woman, or so he thought. It was hard to be sure. Jeans, trainers, black T-shirt, denim jacket and a baseball cap casting a shadow across her — or his — face. She walked steadily towards him. Mullen felt the sweat on the palms of his hands. Best to get out of the car — easier to react if this was a trap.

'Hi there,' the person said.

'Blimey!' It was DI Holden, looking nothing like herself. 'For a moment—'

'Let's drive.' She climbed into the passenger seat, strapped herself in and said nothing more.

Mullen started up and headed south. 'Isn't this all a bit cloak and dagger?'

'Straight on here,' she said. 'When you get to the Berinsfield roundabout, turn right.'

He drove and turned right as instructed.

'Don't exceed the thirty-mile limit' she said, in a distinctly teacherly manner as he headed steadily through the elongated village of Burcot until she waved him into another lay-by on the right hand side of the road. He switched off the engine.

'What happened to your eyes?' she said.

'I had a bit of a misunderstanding.'

'You know, if you were living in the United States, no health insurance company would touch you.' It might have been a joke, except that there wasn't a hint of humour in her voice. Maybe she only did deadpan. Mullen tried to imagine her on a boozy night out with the girls and failed.

'DC Benning told me there was no useful DNA on the letter or envelope,' he said.

'Correct.' Holden seemed very distracted. Was she afraid of something or someone? Everything about this meet-up, including her bizarre appearance, suggested she must be. She took a deep breath in and out. 'So Doug, have you got anywhere on the arsonist?'

'I've ruled one or two people out. But that's about it.'

'And were you the target — or was it Melissa Moody?'

'Me, I think.'

'And Robert Dench's death?'

'Work in progress.' He paused, but only to determine his approach. 'You were going to make some enquiries.'

'I was. And I did.' Another silence, longer this time. 'It didn't go down well.'

'Do you want to tell me about it?'

'Hell, Mullen. *"Do you want to tell me about it?"* Who on earth do you think you are? My therapist?'

He could have said that he knew a bit about therapy now, but he didn't. Instead he pressed her a little harder. 'Why didn't it go well?'

She pulled the baseball cap off her head and ran her hand through her hair. Even in these casual clothes, she gave off an unmistakable smartness. 'It was DI Greg Collins's last case. He's retired now and has no desire to have anyone digging around looking at it.'

'Any particular reason that you can see?'

'His pension and his reputation.'

'If he's worried about his pension, then surely that's because he's worried what a bit of digging might reveal.'

'Detective Superintendent McPherson has also told me in no uncertain terms not to spend any time looking at the case.'

'Because?'

'Because the case is closed. Because every investigation costs money. Because the Thames Valley Police has plenty more important things to investigate. Drugs . . . the grooming and abuse of young girls . . . ATM smash and grabs.' Holden's anger and frustration was a wild sea whipped up by a rising gale. 'Whatever gets into the headlines. Whatever the police commissioner and the media decide we should be prioritising. Sometimes, I despair . . .' She pressed her head back against the headrest and closed her eyes. Mullen had this sudden revelation that she was very close to the edge, close to some sort of breakdown. That would explain the rather strange way the evening had unfolded.

'Are you OK?' He would have liked to reassure her in some way, but putting a hand on a woman's shoulder was a high-risk activity nowadays. He knew the dangers and he also had no idea how Holden might react, so he did nothing.

'I can't do anything about Robert Dench's death,' she said with a firmness of tone suggesting she was now back in charge of her emotions. 'But you can. However, you will be on your own. You probably think I'm paranoid, but there's been a definite closing of ranks. Don't even try to contact me again. No phone calls, texts, emails. If you need help, you can trust DC Benning. These are her contact details.' She pulled a wallet from her pocket and extracted a business card. She scribbled an address on it, scratched a line through the mobile number and wrote another one in its place. 'Memorise the details then destroy the card. Don't come to the station. Don't ring her police mobile or try and contact her via the station. In all things, act with extreme discretion.'

'You know I'm staying with someone?'

'Becca Baines, you mean.' Holden smiled and he wondered how frequent an event a smile was in her life. 'DC

Benning told me all about it. Heavily pregnant, too, I understand. I suspect Benning may have been a little disappointed.'

'I'm not the father.'

'So you said in hospital.' Another smile, both teasing and probing. 'The gentleman doth protest too much, methinks!'

He tried to ignore her levity. 'I'm worried, really worried in case me staying in her house puts her at risk.'

Holden pursed her lips.

'It's a real risk,' he continued. 'God, if anything happened to her or the baby because of me . . . '

'In that case, you have to make sure you keep her safe.' Holden put her baseball cap back on her head, a sign that she had finished. 'Tell her what the risks are. It's important that she knows. But if you leave her on her own, she might be at greater risk. As far as they are concerned, you and she are linked.'

'Who do you mean by "they"?'

'Remember the arson, Mullen. Remember the closed ranks at Thames Valley Police. There's at least one person out there, maybe more, who wants you and maybe anyone closely connected with you dead.'

'Thank you,' he said. And he meant it. Either she was seriously paranoid or she was taking a real risk in contacting him. 'One more thing . . . Where does Greg Collins live?'

Holden's hand had moved to the door handle, but her head snapped round like a demented child's in a horror movie.

'I need to know,' he pressed. 'I'll find out one way or another, but it'll save me time and hassle.'

She considered this for some time. Eventually she shrugged. 'Abingdon.'

'Can you be more precise?'

'He'll be ex-directory, but he told me he's joined an Aunt Sally team and has bought himself an Oxford United season ticket. He likes to drink, but that's about it.'

'Thank you, Detective Inspector. It's nice to have you on my side.'

She gave him a look that might have sunk a thousand ships. 'Don't push your luck, not with me and definitely not with Collins.'

'Sure.'

'And take this.' She handed him a brown jiffy bag. 'It's a burner phone. Use it if you need to contact Benning. In the meantime, take a circuitous route home. Make sure you aren't being followed. And try not to do anything stupid.'

The circuitous route took thirty minutes or so and at no time did Mullen get any sense that he was being followed. An old Morris Minor managed to hang onto his coat tails for a couple of miles but, just as he was starting to wonder, it took a right turn and disappeared from view. Another car, a silver Audi, briefly took over the tailgating role but its female driver seized the first opportunity she had to overtake and her car was soon a speck in the distance.

The lights were off in the house when he got back. Not that it was that late. But there was no sign of Becca's car. Rex shot past him as soon as he opened the door and immediately peed on the grass verge. Inside there was a note: *At work! The dog will need his supper.* So would Mullen. He looked in the fridge and in the cupboards. The fridge was almost bare, but there was plenty of choice in the cupboards: puy lentils, couscous, coconut milk, tuna, mackerel fillets in tomato sauce, green pasta, wild rice. In the circumstances, and with Becca not being there to mock his choice, he decided on beans on toast.

He fed the dog first before eating in front of the TV while watching something purporting to be a comedy film about two slackers. He fell asleep without laughing once.

CHAPTER 11

Mullen woke at seven thirty the next morning. There was no sign of Becca's red mini, so he took the opportunity to have a leisurely shower. Downstairs, he fed Rex and then went for a walk up the road. Again there were no mysterious cars or indeed any cars parked in gateways or on the verges. Back at the house, he had just made himself a mug of tea and popped some bread in the toaster when Becca arrived. She looked tired and appeared to be in no mood to talk. He made extra tea and toast and they ate together in almost silence.

'How was work?' he said.

'Crap.' She killed the conversation stone dead. She made herself some more toast, smeared marmalade on it, ate it and headed off upstairs. 'See you later, alligator.'

As he washed and dried the dishes, he was aware of her stumping around (insulation between the ground and first floors in the cottage was virtually non-existent) but by the time he had tidied and wiped the work surfaces, he realised it had all gone quiet. Still working long shifts at that stage of pregnancy — she had to be exhausted.

He was thinking about this and his own feelings towards her when his phone rang. To his amazement, it was Kazia. He had pretty much given up on her ever returning his call.

'Hi Doug. You tried to contact me. I've been rather busy.'

'I just wanted to talk to you.'

'Lots of people want to talk to me.' She sounded testy, as if, as Mullen's mother used to say to him, she'd got out of the wrong side of the bed. 'You should have waited for me to return your call, not come and started banging on the door. That isn't how it works.'

'I'm sorry. I don't think your husband took kindly to me.'

'He's not my husband. Not that it is anything to do with you.'

'I really am sorry.' Mullen sensed he was in danger of losing all her goodwill. 'If I could just come and see you. For a few minutes.'

'I'm in London.'

London? Mullen's brain did a somersault, then pressed on. 'If you're not too late home, could I possibly call round tonight? Obviously, I'll fit in with you—'

'Let me spell it out, Doug . . . I live in London. I spend two days a week consulting in Oxford, sometimes more. When I do, I stay over in my friend's house, but otherwise I am based in London.'

Another somersault. 'In that case, I'll come to London.'

'Is it that urgent?'

'It's about Professor Moody.'

Kazia emitted a sound not unlike a drowning person trying desperately to suck in air and gulping only water. That was followed by silence. Then: 'Tomorrow, eleven o'clock. I live in Hackney.' She gave him her address. 'Try not to be late — and definitely not early.' She terminated the call.

Mullen sat there trying to assess this new development. The house was deep in silence. Even Rex had stopped snuffling. Mullen got up. That was tomorrow. But it needn't affect his plans for today. Today was to be devoted to Detective Inspector Greg Collins, the man who had investigated Robert Dench's death, the man who didn't like Holden asking questions about Robert Dench's death, a man, according to Holden, with protective friends. *'Try not to do anything stupid.'* That was what she had said, her final words to him. He was afraid he was about to ignore them.

If anyone asked Mullen how to go about tracking someone down, he would probably tell them to begin with research. The internet made it so easy. In the case of a detective in the Thames Valley Police, there were bound to be lots of news items concerning his cases, especially those in which he took a lead. You couldn't know too much about someone. Lots of it would be irrelevant, of course, but somewhere in all the dross would be the unexpected precious nugget — or semi-precious at any rate.

Mullen made himself another mug of tea and opened up his tablet. There were indeed a number of news items in which Collins featured, sometimes just a name, usually with a trite comment attributed to him, typically along the lines of *'It has been a very sad and difficult case, but I am delighted that we have seen justice done.'* Mullen turned up the cases of a seventeen-year-old stabbed in an Oxford park, the brutal — and ultimately fatal — assault on an eighty-two-year-old man in his Kennington bungalow, a paedophile arrested for offences against three young boys (*'My toughest and finest hour,'* Collins acknowledged to the press), a hit-and-run on a grandmother at a pedestrian crossing, a missing girl found locked in a room in a terraced house a year after her disappearance and, most recent of all, the death of Robert Dench.

That had been his last case. Indeed, he was already retired by the time the coroner had pronounced his verdict and it was Detective Superintendent McPherson who had spoken to the press afterwards and praised Collins for his work *'on this and many other cases.'* It sounded like PR flannel — aren't we coppers wonderful? Yet McPherson hadn't tried to take the credit from Collins. Maybe he and Collins were mates as well as colleagues. Or, to put it another way, maybe they were as thick as thieves.

But in terms of actually tracking down Collins, none of this helped. Holden had said he lived in Abingdon, but that was a pretty big pool — 36,000-odd people according to Google. He liked to drink, she had said, and he had taken up Aunt Sally. That would narrow it down a bit. But by no means every pub in Abingdon would be running an Aunt Sally team. Mullen had watched them play once in a pub in Oxford. He had stumbled into a match quite by chance and had been impressed by the skill of some of the guys and the seriousness with which the teams played as they battled to win their league. There would surely be a website where these leagues and the pubs involved were recorded.

It was a case of trial and error. An Oxford Aunt Sally website listed many leagues and pubs scattered round the county — a dispiriting amount to trawl through, especially as the pub locations were not always obvious. Mullen tried narrowing his search to Abingdon and Aunt Sally and to his delight he discovered Abingdon had its own leagues and website. Not all the teams were from Abingdon but Mullen reckoned this was a good place to start. His optimism was further boosted when he discovered the website contained not only the team scores for each fixture, but the individual player scores too. Within half an hour he had found what he had been looking for: a player named Gregory Collins. He had played four games for the Horse and Jockey B team and appeared to be a pretty recent recruit to a poor side. Collins himself had scored unspectacularly: two, three, and one, which, considering the maximum possible per match was eighteen (three rounds of six throws each), did not suggest he was likely to be promoted to the A team any time soon.

Wednesday night was Aunt Sally night. And today was Wednesday. Bingo.

The rest of the day was a day of domesticity. While Becca snored away upstairs, Mullen got on quietly with cleaning, filling the washing machine, walking the dog and then preparing a lasagne and salad for whenever it was that Becca woke and wanted a meal. In the meantime he made himself a sandwich and ate it sitting outside in the sunshine, surveying the scene around him and wondering whether pursuing

Collins was really as risky as Holden had made out. Holden, judging by her disguise and the cloak and dagger rendezvous, was verging on the paranoid. *There's nothing to worry about*, he told himself.

He whistled up Rex and they wandered towards the main road and then back the other way, past Marie's house. She was out — her car was nowhere to be seen — and Mullen was rather relieved. He didn't want another face-off with her. He was also relieved that there was no sign of anyone carrying out surveillance.

When he got back to the house, there was the smell of cooking. Becca was up. She had located the lasagne and had stuck it in the oven. She grinned at him. 'Well, here comes the secret chef! I do hope this lasagne was meant for me?'

'Both of us.'

She laughed. 'You should have made it bigger.' Loud and crude and jolly, just like her.

They sat outside afterwards and drank coffee in the sunshine. It was nearly seven p.m, but the breeze had disappeared and it felt warmer than it had been all day. They chatted like two old biddies, or rather Becca chatted and Mullen listened. Mostly it was gossip about the hospital and what a pain some of the consultants were, all very easygoing and trivial until Becca's tone changed.

During a pause, Rex for some reason decided that signified the moment when he should jump ship from Mullen and hop up onto her lap. She welcomed him, fondling his ears. And then, quite suddenly, she said: 'I was thinking today that I made a big mistake.'

A tractor pulling a giant empty trailer rattled past. 'What mistake?' Mullen said, when the noise had subsided.

'Not getting rid of the baby.'

* * *

Becca's words were still in Mullen's head as he drove to Abingdon an hour later. They bothered him because they seemed so out of character. If she was a person who was sometimes taken over by the black dog, she'd kept it damned well-hidden in the time he had known her. She was the last person he would have expected to say those words. Mullen thought about the little room that was earmarked to be the baby's and felt a stab of guilt. He had agreed to paint it — pink *and* blue — and yet he had done nothing. He promised himself that he'd start the next day depending on what time he got back from London. He'd show her that she wasn't on her own and that he'd be there for her for as long as she needed him.

Someone hooted, long and loud, snapping Mullen back to the present. He was sitting at the lights on Oxford Road and they had turned green. He bunny-hopped the car forward as if he had never driven one before and waved apologetically at the black BMW behind him. The driver hooted back, unmollified.

He parked in the car park next to Abbey Gardens. There were no restrictions or charges in the evening. The Horse and Jockey was down by the river Thames, only a few minutes' walk away — not that there was any great rush. The Aunt Sally would very likely carry on until nine thirty or later, he reckoned, so he meandered his way there, cutting through the gardens then down a narrow street that led to the old Abbey buildings. The western end had been converted internally to accommodate local amateur theatricals and a billboard advertised a play called *Jamaica Inn*. Mullen walked past it, down a path leading into a narrow pedestrian tunnel through the buildings. He had just entered it when he came to sudden halt. A man dressed in tricorn hat and frock coat emerged so unexpectedly from the building on the right that they almost collided. He touched his hat. 'Evening, squire' he said, with a distinctly west country accent, before disappearing through a door in the opposite wall. There was a gale of raucous laughter before the door closed and silenced it.

Mullen walked on out of the passage and turned right. Soon he was passing the old gaol, now converted into fancy and expensive flats. Mullen wondered what it was like living there. Did residents sometimes hear the rattle of chains and the moans of prisoners or had the designer kitchens, Farrow and Ball paintwork and beautiful furniture expunged all trace of the building's past?

The blue skies of earlier that day had been banished by a thick blanket of brooding cloud. As he made his way in the gloom down East St Helen's Street, Mullen found himself walking past more medieval buildings. He half expected to run into someone else from another time, a monk maybe or a distressed maid, but no such ghost or actor appeared and soon the noise of well-lubricated men shouting and guffawing brought him back into the present.

The noise came from the back of the Horse and Jockey. He pushed his way in through the front door and got himself a pint from the bar. Then he edged his way through a gaggle of drinkers watching the TV before exiting through the door marked: *To the garden*. The Aunt Sally session was in full swing and Mullen sat himself down on one of the few empty seats. *'Garden'* was a rather glamorous word for what was a wholly hardstanding area with three or four large tubs of flowerless greenery. Mullen checked his phone briefly before looking around.

The guy throwing his pieces of wood at the target — the doll — was good and he threw quickly. *Bang, bang, bang*. Three clean hits in three. Then a clang of metal as he fired too low, then two more perfect strikes. A roar of approval. He was the last of the visiting team from The Spread Eagle and their highest scorer. Mullen surveyed the board. There was only one Greg in the home team and he was second on the list. He sipped his beer. It wasn't long before Greg was throwing. He hit two out of six and wasn't very happy about it. Not that Mullen was interested in his score, only his identity. Unquestionably this was former Detective Inspector Gregory Collins. The receding forehead and the nose, which looked as if it had been broken and never straightened properly, matched the photos Mullen had gleaned from the internet.

The hair was unquestionably longer, hanging down rakishly over his collar and his gut was substantial, but otherwise he looked as Mullen had imagined.

Mullen continued to watch. The old man next to him gave him a running commentary on what was what, explaining that after three games, there would be a 'beer leg', the losers buying the winners of that leg a drink. He went on about this so much that Mullen took the hint and offered to buy him a drink. He went in and bought it plus a portion of chips for himself and returned in time to see Greg Collins hit a score of four in the beer leg.

'That's the one that counts,' the old man told Mullen before taking a pull on his new pint.

It was gone nine thirty before Collins drained his final drink and headed out of the pub into the semi-darkness. He walked with the exaggerated care of someone who is aware he has drunk too much and Mullen followed at a distance, padding quietly along, confident that he hadn't been rumbled.

He still wasn't quite certain how to deal with Collins. Holden had told him not to be stupid. What exactly did she mean by *'being stupid'*? Did following him home from the pub at night fall into that category? He suspected it might. Asking him questions about Robert Dench's death? Probably. Telling him he didn't believe his answers. Definitely. That was what Mullen suspected might well happen. But sometimes, stupid was the only way.

Collins made his way past the church of St Helens before forking right and heading for the town centre. Mullen increased his speed. Collins was, despite appearances, moving briskly. As he reached the far end, he veered slightly to the left, crossing the road and up into the colonnade under the county hall. Mullen broke into a fast jog as Collins disappeared. The last thing he wanted to do was lose his man, but when he got to the county hall and scanned the market square, Collins was nowhere to be seen. This structure had been designed in the seventeenth century to provide a space where traders could sell their goods protected from the weather. The base was three large steps higher than the surrounding area, and so it offered the twenty-first-century visitor an excellent view of the whole of the town square — though it was not so good on a dark cloudy night. Mullen swore. Collins had completely vanished.

Almost immediately, as if some higher power was having a laugh at Mullen's plight, it began to rain. Not just a light shower, but the sort of torrential downpour that comes at the end of a stinking hot, humid day. Hammer and tongs. Cats and dogs. There was no thunder and lightning, but there ought to have been. Mullen gave up on Collins and decided to leg it to his car — across the square, under the arch next to St Nicholas church and then through the Abbey Gardens. He slipped and almost fell in the gardens and was relieved when he reached the car, got in and slammed the door shut. He sat there, conscious of his heaving chest and soaking shirt and began to laugh. The evening could not have gone more wrong. A complete waste of time.

He started the engine. His car was an old friend, too old to have headlights that came on automatically in the dark, and so all he saw at first was a spectral shape appearing out of the gloom. A monk from the abbey, perhaps, condemned to walk the earth until his penance had been completed or, more likely surely, another am-dram performer from *Jamaica Inn* desperate to get to his car? Mullen smiled at the thought — but only for a moment or two. When he switched on his headlights, he realised immediately that he was wrong on both counts. It was Collins. And Collins was advancing towards him with unquestionable menace.

Mullen pressed his foot slightly on the accelerator, enough to make clear to the man that he was about to drive forward, but Collins didn't alter his pace or demeanour. The gap was closing fast. What to do? Drive forward anyway and call Collins's bluff? Swerve around him and leave sharpish? Or kill the engine and get out into the torrential rain and talk to him man to man?

Mullen did none of these. He sat there, engine ticking over, hands on the steering wheel, as if it was him caught in the beam of someone's headlights like a startled rabbit. *Do something*, his army training screamed at him. *Don't just sit there!* He killed the engine, removed the keys from the ignition and started to get out. Collins was close now, close enough to shout at him and to be heard despite the drumming of the rain on the car and sound of the wind ripping through the trees. But Collins said nothing. He merely dipped to his right, towards the passenger side of the car — a typical bully, keen to avoid a fight when someone challenged him.

'I think we need to talk!' Mullen called out, but Collins, who now glared at him across the bonnet of the car, said nothing. He raised his left hand. In it was a screwdriver.

'Do you reckon I'm brain dead? Did you really think I wouldn't fucking notice you? You might as well have hung a billboard round your neck saying *"I'm a private dick!"*'

He waved the screwdriver around, not directly at Mullen, more like a conductor trying to bring an unruly orchestra to order. Then, without warning, he ducked down below the level of the car. Mullen stepped back a couple of paces. He looked right and left and right again, anticipating a sudden assault from either the front or the back of the car.

Despite the noise of the rain and wind, he heard a noise that he couldn't quite place. A fizzing sound. Surely Collins hadn't squatted down to piss away his beer? Then Collins's head bobbed up again, just visible over the roof of the car. He grinned tauntingly and headed back the way he had come. Mullen made his way round to the other side of the car and only then did realisation dawn. His offside front tyre was as flat as pancake. It wasn't a screwdriver Collins had been carrying, or at least if it once had been, it had since been re-engineered into a sharper, more dangerous instrument. Mullen looked across the car park again but Collins was a barely visible shape, and moments later he had disappeared into the rain and the dark. There was nothing to be gained by giving chase. But at least, Mullen told himself as he set about changing his tyre in the pouring rain, Collins had only used the vicious tool to puncture his tyre, not him.

CHAPTER 12

Thank God for satnav. Mullen wouldn't have thought that a few years previously. He had been a dyed in the wool paper map man then. The sad fact was that reading a map had been one of the few useful things his father had ever taught him and he had clung to the skill long after it, or his father, was of any practical use. Because once you could pick up a 'brand new' satnav for a tenner at a car boot sale, who needed paper road atlases any more or even the wonderful *A to Z of London*? Actually, he did have an *A to Z*. It was on the passenger seat, being guarded by Rex, who seemed to be becoming more human than dog every day. He'd be demanding a seat belt next.

The only problem with a satnav purchased from a dodgy character on a grey Sunday morning was that it didn't necessarily have all the bells and whistles that it might otherwise have had. It had also been about ten years out of date when Mullen handed over his tenner so it didn't understand concepts like *fastest route* and it didn't have any awareness of the fact that its chosen route that morning was a road-repair hell. So despite leaving at six fifteen a.m. from Oxford, Mullen didn't get to Hackney until well after nine.

But if Madam Satnav was definitely being a bit of a bitch that morning, Lady Luck apparently was not. A large sign indicating *All day prarking* (sic) appeared magically on the side of the road as Rex's whining reached desperation levels. Mullen turned left down a narrow alley into the most eccentric car park he had ever encountered. Storage containers, kebab vans, a row of old telephone boxes, a giant giraffe and, in between all this paraphernalia, some real parked cars, rather better ones than Mullen's. That was a relief. If anyone fancied nicking a car from here, it wasn't going to be his wretched Ford Focus when there were smart-looking BMWs and Audis to be had.

Long before Rex had finished his extended leg-cocking on Mullen's driver's side front wheel, a guy in overalls materialised from somewhere and, like the car boot sale man, asked for a tenner. 'We lock up at seven sharp,' he warned. 'And don't leave your dog in the car. I had to rescue a chihuahua the other week. Had to smash the passenger window of a Merc.'

'We're inseparable,' Mullen promised, waving Rex's lead in the air to underline his point.

Inseparable was nice, except when you wanted a full English breakfast and your dog wasn't welcome to join you. 'Health and safety,' he heard from three different mouths on the Kingsland High Street. He was ready to give up and grab a sandwich from anywhere when an immaculately bearded guy beckoned him into his place. 'You keep the dog under the table, nice and quiet. OK?

It was a Turkish café, but Mullen wasn't complaining and when the breakfast came it seemed pretty English anyway. The coffee was damned good, too. The guy brought him a second cup, as well as a white bowl with water in it. He put this under the table together with something meaty and chewy that clearly met Rex's canine approval. So when Mullen got up to leave, he left a ridiculously large tip because it seemed only fair.

Kazia Ciesla lived in a block of flats some ten minutes' walk away. It was one of several such edifices off Amhurst Road, solid but unprepossessing brick relics of the 1930s.

They had been built as council flats, but Mullen assumed they were now partly owner-occupied thanks to Mrs Thatcher's vote-winning right to buy policy of the early 1980s. They weren't pretty, but who wanted pretty if it involved flammable cladding? Mullen had passed Grenfell Tower as he entered London along the A40 flyover, still standing and now covered in plastic, as if that would be sufficient to make people forget the horror of that appalling night.

Kazia lived in Flat Thirty-one. Standing outside the main entrance, Mullen keyed in the digits, pressed the *Call* button and waited. There was no reply. Maybe she was on the loo. He checked his phone. He was three minutes early. Give her time. He waited until his mobile phone registered eleven o'clock and then tried again. The same result. He was about to try again (third time lucky, maybe?) when he noticed there was a tradesmen's bell. He pressed it, something buzzed and he pushed on the outer door. It swung reluctantly open. So much for security. He picked up Rex and climbed the stairs. There was a lift, but he wasn't so decrepit as to need it.

Once he reached the third floor, he turned right along the external corridor and quickly found himself outside Number Thirty-one. The door was slightly ajar and there was movement inside.

'Hello?'

There was no reply.

Mullen tried again. 'Hello? Kazia? It's Doug Mullen.'

A woman appeared: tall, slim, dark-skinned. She looked him up and down but said nothing. She had a rolled rug in her arms.

'I have an appointment. With Kazia Ciesla?'

Still no response. Mullen wondered if he had come to the wrong block of flats. He tried again. 'At eleven o'clock?'

The woman opened her mouth. Her lips juddered, but no sound came out. Did she not understand? Could she not speak English?

'This is Kazia's flat, isn't it?'

She nodded. 'Kazia is dead.' She began to wail.

The woman's name was Florence and she had the flat immediately next door to Kazia's. It was there that she took Mullen. She made them each a cup of chamomile tea. He would have preferred builder's tea, but she insisted hers was better for calming the nerves.

'The police came round last night. Looking for her next of kin. But she lives alone. So of course, they tried my door and told me that she was dead.' She paused only enough to gather her breath and then plunged on like a swimmer doing her lengths, steady and relentless. 'An accident, they said. On the Underground. She fell in front of a train. God preserve her soul! Just as the train came in. One minute she was alive and the next she was dead. She was a non-believer, you know. I asked her to my church. Just up the road. Very friendly, we are. She came just once, when we had an Agape Meal, but never again. *"What has God ever done for me?"* she said. *"More than you will ever know,"* I said. She would have been most welcome. She was a lost sheep. We would have gladly gathered her into the fold.' Florence wiped away a tear and took a sip of tea.

Silence descended. Mullen had no tears running down his cheeks or even welling up in his eyes. It wasn't as if he had known Kazia in any meaningful sense. Two meetings and one phone call didn't add up to a relationship. But he nevertheless felt her loss. It was as if someone had just kicked away his crutch. He had come to Hackney ostensibly in the hope she might tell him things about Professor Moody. But what he had actually wanted to do was just talk to her. He had of course told her a lot about Ben and himself and his childhood and all the rest, but now that he had started, he knew deep down that there was a lot more ground to be covered. He needed not just to tell her about it but to understand his own thoughts and emotions. But now she was gone and it felt like a stiletto thrust into his heart.

Florence broke the silence. 'You don't think I was wrong to take the rug, do you?' Mullen looked up, remembering the rug, which she had obviously removed from Kazia's flat. 'I always admired it, and I just wanted something to remember her by. No one will miss it. Kazia won't mind. She will be touched.'

'Kazia was my therapist,' Mullen said. If Florence was coming clean, then he reckoned he should, too.

Florence nodded. 'Why don't we take your dog for a walk?'

* * *

'It's a big park,' Florence said, which was stating the obvious. 'Why don't you let him off?' Rex was pulling hard on the lead, anxious to explore a plethora of new smells.

'He's a small dog,' Mullen replied, which was also stating the obvious. 'That's why.' Mullen could see at least six dogs running free across the expanse of grass that was Hackney Downs and they were all a lot bigger than Rex. But it wasn't Rex he wanted to talk about. 'Was Kazia very depressed?'

'Depressed?' The question seemed to take her by surprise.

'If she jumped in front of a train, there has to be a reason.'

'Jumped?' Florence seemed alarmed by the very idea. 'Surely this was an accident? A lot of people. She was too near the edge. She stumbled.'

'Maybe.'

'She would not have jumped. Not my friend, Kazia. She was mentally very strong.'

Mullen considered her words. *Mentally very strong*. 'As I see it, there are three possibilities . . . suicide, an accident or it was murder.'

Mullen parted from Florence outside the flats. He had a plan. He had no desire to just cut and run back to Oxfordshire. Now he was in London, he might as well make the most of it.

Fifteen minutes later, he was on a bus. Half an hour after that, he was standing outside the London Underground station where Kazia had died, not that there was anything to mark her death, of course. Why would there have been? Merely people. People going in, people coming out, people rushing past with mobile phones in one hand and delicate little bags containing their lunches in the other. Mullen had picked Rex up and tucked him under his arm by this stage, fearful he might get trampled to death or, in trying to avoid that fate, hop in front of a hurtling Deliveroo bike. If you wanted a glimpse of dog hell, this was it.

Mullen braced himself. He didn't like the Underground. Give him buses or Shanks's pony any day — or even his battered Ford Focus. Rex pressed his nose into Mullen's neck and gave it a little lick. It was just what Mullen needed. Holding the dog tight, he plunged down into the subterranean world of Transport for London.

Of course, as so often was the case, the reality wasn't nearly as bad as the imagining. Two conversations later and he was shown into an office in which sat a young man who looked like he was barely out of school. But, given that he claimed to be the customer service manager for the station and had a badge attached to the pocket of his white shirt, which apparently proved it, Mullen decided Jack Jenner merely had one of those Peter Pan faces.

'I understand you have some information for me about an incident in my station?'

Mullen smiled. 'You ever played Chinese Whispers?'

Jenner's eyes narrowed.

'I whisper something to the girl next to me and she whispers to the girl next to her and she whispers to the boy next to her and by the time the message gets to the end of the line, it's all a load of gobbledygook.'

'So what you're telling me is that you don't have any information for me?' The schoolboy impersonating a manager wasn't daft, that was for sure.

'Actually, I'm hoping that it's the other way round.'

'Perhaps you should explain who you are and why you are here.' Jenner placed his hands together in front of him in a very precise manner, interlacing his fingers. Was this a technique he had learned on the *How to Deal with Difficult Customers* module of the Transport for London training school? Adopt a pose of polite conversation until you know exactly what sort of difficult customer you are dealing with.

'I am a friend of Kazia Ciesla's family,' Mullen said, stretching the truth. 'And as such I am trying to find out a bit more about the circumstances of her tragic death. The family needs to know what happened, otherwise it's hard to accept, but obviously I would like to protect them from the more unpleasant bits of the truth.'

'I see.' Jenner sat up even straighter than he already was. Apparently he was ready to speak. 'Ms Ciesla fell in front of a train. Right in front of it. There was no opportunity for the driver to stop. There were a lot of people on the platform, more than usual because of traffic and transport issues above ground. It is possible that she slipped or tripped or overbalanced. Alternatively, she may have thrown herself in front of the train deliberately.' It sounded like a pre-prepared speech, memorised from a training manual but with the travel problems above ground thrown in as extra defence. Jenner adjusted his red tie and folded his arms, a defensive move, which also indicated that his speech was over.

'Or with all the people thronging around, one of them could have pushed her,' Mullen said, staring right back at Jenner. 'Deliberately.'

Jenner lifted his head, as if to show off his Adam's apple, which pulsated fiercely. 'I cannot comment any further. In fact, I have already said too much. Ms Ciesla's unfortunate death will be examined by the coroner. I will not try to second-guess what he or she will decide.'

'Have you got it on CCTV?'

Jenner rose to his feet. 'I think our meeting has come to an end.'

Mullen stood up too. 'Is this your first death?' Mullen wanted to keep the conversation going a bit longer. He wasn't sure what he had hoped to get out of this spur-of-the-moment meeting but he knew that he hadn't got it yet. 'It must have been really difficult for you.' He turned on the sympathy. 'And I can't imagine what it must have been like for the driver or for the poor bastards who had to clear up afterwards.'

Jenner opened his mouth. Mullen half expected him call for help or hit some hidden panic bell, but instead he slithered back down into his chair as if his legs had suddenly turned to jelly. 'Jesus, I hope to God I never have another one.' He had turned so grey that Mullen was worried he was going to have a medical emergency on his hands.

He got up and moved round the man's desk. 'Loosen your tie. Get your head between the knees. Breathe, nice and steady. That's it.'

Two or three minutes passed before Jenner was sitting back upright on his chair, his face a slightly less sickly colour.

'Sorry,' he said, as if it was all his fault.

'Nothing to be sorry about. Look, I'm not an expert, but maybe you should have a few days off. Talk to someone about it.'

Jenner shook his head. *Classic denial*, Mullen thought. *Pretending it was nothing. Stiff upper lip bollocks.* 'It won't look good if I vacate my post at such a critical moment. I am the manager. It's my job to manage.'

Mullen nodded. He understood that. But then the man-boy in front of him said something that caught him right off guard. 'Actually, we were thinking it might be a hate crime.'

Mullen's brain did a somersault. 'Hate crime? I'm not with you.'

'Well, she was wearing a hijab.'

'A hijab?'

'Yes, a hijab. And we think we've identified her on the CCTV. So one line of thought is that someone with a hatred of Muslims gave her a push.'

'You mean, you've got someone pushing her on CCTV?'

Jenner held up his hands, realising he had said too much. 'No. Definitely not! Don't start saying that. What I mean is that her style of dress was pretty difficult to assess immediately after the accident. But we are pretty sure from matching CCTV footage and her remains that she was wearing a hijab. Maybe in due course we'll be able to tell more, but I hasten to underline that we have no clear footage of her death.'

'OK.'

'So please, this really is the end of our conversation. And please do not take this to higher management. I need this job.'

'Sure.' Mullen shook his hand. 'I will definitely not take this higher. You have been very helpful.'

Back at the flats, the tradesmen's bell was no longer offering Mullen a free pass. So he rang Florence's number.

'Who is that?' said a male voice.

'Doug, the man with the little dog. I wanted to speak to Florence.'

When Mullen reached the third floor, he found a short man waiting for him on the corridor just outside Flat Thirty-two. 'Cute dog, man,' he said with enthusiasm. 'You gay?'

'Is Florence around?'

'She's gone out.'

'Can I wait for her?'

'Whadda you want, man?'

Mullen surveyed him doubtfully. He would much rather have talked to Florence, but time was ticking on and if he didn't get to his car before they locked up for the night, he'd be well and truly stuck. 'Can you tell me something? Was Kazia a Muslim?'

The man laughed. 'I doubt it.'

'So she never wore a hijab?'

'You kidding me? Look, who the hell are you? Cos you sure aren't a friend of Kazia if you're asking these questions about her.'

'I've been to the station where she died. Spoken to the manager. He said she was wearing a hijab when she was hit by the train. So why would that be?'

'The manager must have got it wrong. She never wore hijabs or any of that sort of shit.'

'Yes, she did.' The voice came from behind the man. It was Florence, who now emerged from Flat Thirty-two.

'What are you talking about, woman?'

'What do you know about Kazia, man?' She spat the word out like it was a piece of lemon she had inadvertently tried to eat. 'You think Kazia is going to tell you stuff when all you want is to look down her cleavage?' She stepped forward, pushing her way past him. And he, to Mullen's surprise, withdrew without a word back inside her flat and shut the door firmly behind him.

'Does your dog want some water?'

For the second time (at least) that day — Mullen couldn't help but log the fact in his brain — Florence let herself into Kazia's flat. She got a cereal bowl out of a cupboard — she knew where Kazia kept her things — and filled it with water for Rex.

Mullen watched as the dog took a few delicate licks before abandoning the water and commencing a thorough investigation of the room.

Mullen tried not to be judgmental, but he couldn't help thinking that the flat was a bit of a mess. He had imagined Kazia in a modern flat, all clean lines and minimalist living. Instead he found himself looking around a flat that was anything but. *'Lived in,'* an estate agent might have said. Certainly Rex was finding it a haven of interesting smells. What was it? Drugs? Food debris? A cat's urine?

'Sorry about Joel,' Florence said. 'He's my brother and thinks he knows it all.'

'No problem.'

'How did you get on at the Underground station?' Florence said.

'Kazia was wearing a hijab when she died. Can you tell me . . . was that normal for her?'

'Of course I can. We were friends. She was forever knocking on my door wanting sugar or milk. Actually milk and sugar were usually an excuse. She just wanted to talk. She used to do so much listening to other people that I think she just wanted someone who would listen to her.'

Mullen tried to steer Florence back. 'What about the hijab?'

Florence frowned. 'A few months ago, Kazia had this idea of dressing up in traditional Islamic costume to see what it was like. She tried a burka, but the very first time she did, a guy with tattoos all over him threatened to cut her up with his knife. Kazia was a gutsy woman, but this scared her. In the end she decided to stick with a hijab. That was better. She went out a few times. Took some photos with her phone. Made notes of conversations she had. She was going to write a paper about it, I think. But that was a few months ago. She hadn't mentioned it recently. I assumed that she had finished — written whatever it was she wanted to write and moved on to something else that took her fancy. She was a bit of a butterfly.'

Perhaps Florence was a butterfly too, Mullen thought, because she flittered off out of the room just as she finished speaking. He turned his attention elsewhere. Photographs. Not a group of them in silver picture frames on a little bureau, but prints pinned up on a cork board. He moved closer. The photos formed a rough border, and in the middle were an assortment of business cards, flyers, emergency numbers, and a to-do list comprising only two items: *Renew mobile contract* and *Chase plumber*. The pictures seemed to be mostly of Kazia herself, starting with photos of a baby and then child. The self-conscious teenager and university student, apparently drunk or high, was more obviously Kazia. Then he noticed a formal one taken on graduation day complete with gown and mortar board, with an older woman standing next to her — her mother, he guessed. There was Kazia on a scooter, complete with red helmet and a wide grin, Kazia standing in front of a metal structure Mullen assumed was a piece of modern art and, yes, Kazia in a hijab.

'*There* you are!' Florence said, as if he might have got lost in Kazia's small flat. She had appeared from Kazia's kitchen and was holding a small white plate with a piece of indeterminate cake on it. 'Kazia loved her cake. You might as well have it.'

Mullen pointed to the photo of Kazia in a hijab.

'I took that one,' Florence said, with a hint of pride.

'Recently?'

'Maybe three or four months ago.'

'I'm surprised there aren't photos of family or friends.'

Florence shrugged. 'Father unknown. Mother died when she was small. Fostered here and there before she was finally adopted by the woman in the graduation photo. But she died of cancer three months later. Too many sad memories.'

'What about boyfriends?'

'No boyfriends. She was a lesbian.'

'Anyone special?'

'That was her business. She talked about them from time to time. But she didn't invite me round to tea to vet them.'

Mullen had a sense that Florence was holding something back. 'You live next door. Didn't you . . .?' Mullen let the question hung unfinished in the air.

Florence laughed. 'Did I did call round sometimes when she had a guest? Just to get a look? Is that what you're saying, man?'

Mullen flushed.

'No, I did not. She worked from home. She was a therapist, right? So people come and tell her their innermost secrets. We agreed that I would only come round if things got out of hand.'

'How would you know? If the noise level got too high?'

'She had me on speed dial. If she rang and didn't speak, that was my cue to go and knock on the door. It only happened a couple of times.

'Can you remember who they were? Give me any names?

'She never said who they were. *"It's a matter of confidentiality."* That was what she said. *"Even when they get violent?"* I said. *"Yes,"* she said.'

'Did she ever mention someone called Professor Moody? Melissa Moody.'

Florence's face lit up. 'You mean Mel?'

Mullen nodded. Personally he couldn't see what was wrong with the full name Melissa. It was rather nice. But people seemed to like shortening their names. He had himself only ever referred to her as 'Professor' and she had never objected.

'She and Mel were lovers for a while. But they seemed to have had a falling out. Mel got this job in the USA. It was only for a year, but Kazia was really upset at the time.'

'Mel flew into England the other day. Did Kazia mention that to you?'

'No. I can't say she did.' Florence's face and tone of voice was that of woman who felt rather miffed that she wasn't up to date with the latest gossip. 'Do you know Mel?'

'Not really.' Sometimes Mullen believed that truth had to be a little bit elastic. 'But I just wondered if maybe Mel flew back to the UK to see Kazia.'

'Maybe. Who knows? I thought maybe Kazia was over her.'

'Why do you say that?'

'Just an impression I got. Nothing concrete. I suspect maybe there was someone else in Oxford. Or maybe not. But I hope so. I don't approve of her way of life, but I don't condemn it either. God loves everybody.'

'I don't suppose I could have another cup of chamomile tea, could I? It's been quite a day.'

Mullen had already decided that chamomile tea was disgusting. Give him a proper cuppa any day. But he needed to look around the flat, and he would much rather Florence didn't witness his snooping. And it was his guess that she would have to return to her own flat to get him another tea bag of the stuff.

'I'll find something for the dog, too.' She gathered Rex in her arms. She seemed to like him. Or perhaps, Rex was to be her hostage, a way of ensuring he didn't do a runner with something he had nicked from the flat. Whatever the reason, she and the dog disappeared.

Mullen scoured the flat. Not that it took long. A living room, a small kitchen, a double bedroom and another room that was probably designed to be a single bedroom but appeared to be where Kazia had conducted her one-to-ones. It contained two modest armchairs, a small table with an orchid as a centrepiece and a filing cupboard in the far corner. Mullen pulled the top drawer, but it was locked. Private files on her clients, he guessed. He would have liked to rifle through it, even though his moral code was telling him not to. More significantly, he hadn't come equipped with a screwdriver to force it open.

Mullen returned to the bedroom where Kazia slept. The wardrobe was, as expected, full of clothes. He found the burka Florence had mentioned and a wide range of other clothes. It felt more like a theatrical wardrobe than anything else, as if to underline Kazia's apparent liking for dressing up. He opened the top drawer of the small bedside chest. This was Kazia's underwear store, but that wasn't what caused him to freeze for a moment or two. Lying on top was a photo of Professor Moody — he couldn't think of her as Mel. Not that she was looking too much like a professor. She was looking at the camera, head tilted to the side, a pouting smile and a loose red blouse only partially obscuring her breasts. *'Provocative'* was the word that jumped into Mullen's head. More interestingly, it was not on display even though it was in a very nice silver frame. Was that Kazia's doing, keeping it close to hand but out of sight, a precaution in case anyone else should join her in her bed? Or had that been the work of Florence, scouring round the flat and deciding, in her Christian wisdom, that it was too unsuitable for Kazia to have her lesbian lover on display?

He moved back to the main room and the kitchen, but before he could do much else a man appeared at the door of the flat. It was Florence's brother.

'Tea's ready. Florence has to go to work soon. So we need to lock the flat.' It was a heavy enough hint and Mullen took it.

Inside Florence's flat, he took the mug she offered him and had a reluctant sip.

'I couldn't see her laptop,' he said casually. 'Or maybe she had an iPad.'

'Don't ask me,' she said. 'I don't do technology.'

Mullen steeled himself to take another sip of chamomile. 'Delicious,' he lied. 'Maybe the police took it — when they looked round her flat.' *When* was a ruse. He didn't know if the police had been in the flat at all. But it was a simple way of finding out.

'They didn't go in.' Florence said. 'They asked about Kazia but they didn't go in.'

'Yes, they did.' Joel had materialised again, an unlit cigarette in his hand. Florence looked at him. He shrugged. 'When you were out early this morning, this woman in a smart suit came round. Said she was CID. Needed to check her flat.'

'Do you have a name for her?'

'Nah. She flashed her card. That looked genuine. Seen enough of them in my time.' He laughed. 'I let her in and locked up when she'd gone.'

'Describe her.'

'Well, what can I say? White . . . twenties . . . not that tall . . . reddish hair — dyed, I guess.' He laughed. 'Don't the girls all dye their hair these days?'

'Did she tell you her name? Or presumably she showed you her warrant card?'

Florence's man scratched at the stubble on his chin. 'To be honest man, the sight of a warrant card gets me on edge. Bad memories, you know?'

It took nearly four hours to get back to Oxford from Hackney. That included a break at the Beaconsfield services where, it seemed, every other wretch heading northwest along the M40 was also stopping to shit, piss and eat, probably in that order. Mullen got himself something from the Chinese bar and bought a sausage for Rex from somewhere else. Even when starving, Rex was quick to turn his nose up at anything as exotic as beef in black bean sauce. The dog, Mullen had concluded, was at heart a Little Englander who would, were he ever to meet them, get on fearfully well with Nigel Farage and his band of Brexiteers.

Mullen's stop, start, stop, start and stop again progress though London had been bad enough but things didn't improve much after his Beaconsfield pit stop as he found himself exposed to wind, horizontal rain and the spray from a thousand wheels speeding past his decrepit Ford Focus. By the time Mullen got home his brain had turned to mushy peas and not a single coherent thought had established itself. Kazia . . . Collins . . . Marie . . . Professor Moody . . . Amanda . . . Dr Francombe . . . the names circled around like butterflies caught up in a whirlwind. All he could manage was to make sure Rex cocked his leg in the garden before he collapsed onto the sofa and into a world of weird dreams.

CHAPTER 13

Rex woke Mullen at six forty-five the following morning. The dog needed to go rather desperately, so much so that he began to leak as Mullen struggled to open the door. Mullen pulled it open with a savage tug and let him out. He picked up the doormat and went and rinsed it under the outdoor tap. The sky was cloudless, so he draped the mat over an old tree stump to dry.

He looked around. The dog was happy, sniffing around. Pissing frequently was a sign of old age in humans. He guessed it was the same for dogs. How old was Rex? Not that old, surely. Five or six maybe? Mullen realised that he didn't know. He had to remember to ask the next time he went to the vet.

Another realisation was that Becca's car was nowhere to be seen. For a woman entering the last few weeks of her pregnancy, she was certainly being worked hard. Or maybe she was trying to earn extra money for the baby while she could. He felt a pang of conscience. He still hadn't done anything about painting the bedroom. But somehow other matters always seemed more pressing. Three deaths: Robert Dench, Professor Moody and now Kazia Ciesla — and three people with connections. It was impossible to say if Dench and

Kazia were murders or suicides or something else but, as far as Mullen was concerned, three such deaths in such a short space of time could hardly be coincidence.

The professor and Kazia had been friends and almost certainly lovers. Kazia knew Leo Francombe, who frequented Amanda's Café and so very likely knew Robert Dench. And then there was Marie, who seemed to have no doubts that her husband's death had been suicide. Why was that? Marie had spoken strongly about her husband's death being a cowardly betrayal of his family, but Mullen wasn't convinced. By his reckoning Marie had been jealous of Amanda and her 'buxom' charms, but did that mean Amanda and Robert had been having an affair? According to Carly, there had been fireworks in their relationship, but that had been over control of the kitchen and the menu. Also according to Carly, it was Leo who Amanda fancied, not Robert, but Leo hadn't reciprocated her feelings. *'Leo likes his women to be younger models than Amanda.'* Wasn't that what Carly had said?

Mullen would have liked to talk it over with Becca. After all, it was she who had asked him to investigate Robert's death. She knew them both. It was she who couldn't believe he had been suicidal because suicidal people did not plan secret holidays for their loved ones.

Robert Dench . . . planner of secret holidays . . . a man who had never been abroad (or so he had told Becca) . . . a chef with a temper. He was where it had all started and yet Mullen realised with a shock that he knew very little about him. He knew that Dench had urinated down his trousers just before he died. He knew also that Greg Collins most definitely didn't want anyone reopening the case. Which all begged the question: if it wasn't suicide, then what was it about Robert Dench that meant someone would kill him and other people would cover the tracks of that someone. In short, who the hell was Robert Dench?

An hour and a half later, Mullen had come to a startling conclusion: Robert Dench was not Robert Dench. He had searched for him on the internet, but had found out very little about him. There was a brief reference to Robert and Marie's marriage at the Oxford Register Office in Tidmarsh Lane. He had trawled through Facebook and other social websites but it appeared that Dench had not been the sort of person who put himself about on the internet. There was a Robert Dench who had played bowls for a team in Kidlington for a couple of years, but he seemed to have stopped after that — at about the time Robert and Marie had married. So it was a fair assumption that this was the same Robert Dench. He tried searching for *Robert Dench bowls* and then *Bob Dench bowls*. None of the results were any use to him unless he wanted to buy a set of bowls. He searched for Marie Dench, too, but there was no Facebook account for her either. He tried searching for her under her maiden name but again drew a blank.

He stood up and stretched. Still no sign of Becca. He needed to speak to people who had known Robert Dench. Why not try the bowls club in Kidlington? It was a lovely day. Perhaps he would find someone there.

Half an hour later, he struck lucky. There was no one playing bowls, but there was a groundsman there giving the green a very neat haircut. Mullen stood and watched, careful to keep Rex on a short lead and off the grass, until the man turned his machine off and walked over to him.

'Don't let him shit here.'

'He's very well-behaved and I have bags.'

'You're not a member.'

'I'm a friend of Robert Dench.'

This seemed to catch him off guard. He stroked his beard, which like the grass was neatly trimmed. 'He killed himself.'

'You remember him, then? He only played here for a couple of years, didn't he?'

'Is there a point to this conversation? Because I've got lots of things to do before tonight's match. It's a local derby. Everything needs to be just right.'

'Was Robert a good player?'

'If you're his friend, you'd know.'

'Never saw him play. We tended to chat in the pub, watch the football on the TV. He encouraged me to try bowls, but—'

'He was a bloody good player. Helped us win three bits of silverware. But then he became a dad and got married and stopped. I guess the wife laid down the law.'

'So he must have learned the game elsewhere?'

'Guess so. Yorkshire, to judge from his accent.'

'And—'

'Look, I really have to get on with things. And next time, if you want to try out bowls, leave the pooch with your missus.'

When Mullen got home, it was to find Becca's car stationed in its place and her stationed in a garden chair in the shade of the birch tree.

'Ah, the detective returns.'

'Long shift, was it?'

She laughed. 'Been a dirty stop-out, Mullen. Crashed at a friend's, so I'm just catching a few minutes' shut-eye. You could make me some tea if you like.'

'In a minute.' There was another chair under the tree, though not in the shade. He sat down. 'How long have you known Marie and Robert?'

'Eighteen months or so.'

'And you met through work?'

Becca's eyes narrowed, much as the groundsman's had. 'Why are you asking?'

He leaned forward, so that he could speak softly. Marie lived a couple of hundred metres up the road, too far to eavesdrop, but Mullen wasn't immune to a touch of paranoia. 'I've been trying to find out as much as I can about Robert. If he didn't kill himself, then there must be a reason why someone else would want him dead. I've scoured the internet and the odd thing is that there doesn't seem to be that much to find out.'

'Why is that odd? Not everyone lives their lives via Facebook.'

'Even so . . .'

'Lots of people have very dull lives that never get into the news.'

He considered this, then tried a different tack. 'What do you know about his life before he met Marie?'

She frowned. 'Nothing really. I've known them for less than two years. I'm more Marie's friend than his.'

'Did you never ask about his earlier life? Did he never talk about it?'

This time it was Becca who paused before replying. 'I did try asking once. He told me that his life began when he met Marie.'

'I understand he had a Yorkshire accent.'

'That isn't a crime.'

'I've also discovered that he played bowls for a couple of years for a Kidlington team, but stopped soon after he was married.'

'Nor is that.'

'The groundsman couldn't tell me much except that he was a damned good player.'

'Look, Doug, much as I would love to spend the rest of the afternoon chatting with you, I really do need to catch up on my sleep. I think I'll go upstairs.'

'I wonder if I shouldn't find somewhere else to live,' he said, and Becca, who was just easing herself up out of her chair, froze and then slumped back into the deckchair.

'What the hell are you talking about, Doug? What are you not telling me? And where would you go, anyway?'

'The puncture I had the other night. It wasn't an accident. A retired detective inspector did it. He followed me to my car and rammed a spike into my tyre. It was a warning.'

Becca said nothing, but Mullen could see anxiety creeping across her face. He pressed on. 'His name is Collins, and his last case before he retired was Robert's suicide. DI Holden at Thames Valley Police had warned me to be careful in my enquiries. It seems that Collins — and indeed, his superior officer — don't want me digging around. Which all goes to show that—'

'That there's something they want to hide. And that Robert didn't kill himself.'

'Exactly. So given that Robert Dench doesn't seem to have been keen to talk about his past and that he doesn't have much of an internet footprint, I'm thinking that maybe he changed his identity some time before he met Marie.'

'Wow!' Becca was suddenly alive, all thoughts of forty winks apparently banished. 'So how do we find out what he used to be called?'

'I'm not too sure.'

'You'll come up with something.' She smiled. 'As a special favour, I'll allow you to prioritise it over painting the baby's bedroom.' She stood up. 'Look, I really do need to lie down. Wake me at five, when my tea is ready.' She kissed him on the top of his head. 'You're a star, Mr Mullen. Please do stay.'

Mullen watched her walk rather slowly across the small patch of lawn and into the house. Well . . . more of a waddle than a walk. He suddenly realised how frighteningly vulnerable she looked. If Collins or one of his mates decided to pay a call and hurt her . . . God, it didn't bear thinking about.

All it took was two text messages, one sent by Mullen on his burner phone and the short reply he received some five minutes later. Then he set about making a spaghetti bolognese, feeding the dog, charging both of his phones and changing into dark clothes. At four fifty-five p.m he woke Becca, at five past five he fed her, and at five thirty watched her leave in her mini. He was relieved to see her go because she was surely much safer at work than stuck out here in deepest Oxfordshire. And he had to go out.

At five forty p.m, he and Rex set off. He had the burner phone with him, but his personal mobile was still plugged in. He left it there, switched on, in the kitchen. If 'they' really were tracking him using technology, then that ought to stymie them. He was aiming for Sutton Courtenay but he took a circuitous route via Stadhampton, Clifton Hampden, Long Wittenham, Little Wittenham and Appleford. If 'they' preferred to use tried and old school tailing techniques, then anyone remaining in his rear mirror view throughout his trip had to be following him. But no one did, and it was with a sense of relief that he parked near the George and Dragon in Sutton Courtenay and got out. He walked back down Church Street, turned right along Appleford Road past the fish restaurant — very nice fish at a very nice price, he noticed — then right along All Saints Lane, before turning right again until he reached a side gate into the churchyard.

There was a woman standing there checking her face in a circular compact mirror.

'Excuse me.'

She ignored him as she applied a fresh coat of alarmingly red lipstick. Only when she had finished did Mullen try again. 'I was wondering if you by any chance know where George Orwell's grave is?'

She made a final check of her face and slipped the compact and lipstick back into her handbag. 'I believe I do.' She spun around and stalked off across the graveyard in her absurdly high red heels. 'Here it is,' she said with an expansive wave of her hand. Her nails were also red, though her dress and thin raincoat were both pale grey.

For several seconds they stared in silent contemplation of the gravestone of Eric Arthur Blair, aka George Orwell. It had a rather tired rosebush growing out of it.

'Have you read any of his books?' she asked.

'Only *Animal Farm*. At school.'

'Doesn't everyone? You should try *Keep the Aspidistra Flying*. It is miserable. It will make your own life seem positively wonderful.'

He had never heard of the book, wasn't even sure he knew what an aspidistra was. But actually, he quite liked his life. And he didn't like being patronised. Anger flashed through him. 'Your outfit . . .' He waved his hand. 'It's not exactly merge-into-the-background, is it?'

'It's called hiding in plain sight, Mullen. Men will stop looking at their phones and study my profile and my legs. Women will glance at me with envy in their eyes. But no one who looks at me will think "undercover policewoman."'

'I have a theory that Robert Dench changed his name.'

'I see.'

'He was very good at bowls. He had a Yorkshire accent so presumably he was brought up there. But if you search for him on the internet, he doesn't seem to have existed before he popped up in Oxfordshire eight or nine years ago.'

'That doesn't seem to be a lot to go on.'

'I was hoping you could do some digging.'

'I'll check it out with She Who Must Be Obeyed.'

'There's a man coming.'

'How old?'

'Forties, well-dressed.'

'Attractive?'

'Not to me.'

'Piss off then, Mullen,' she whispered before turning round and stepping forward. 'Sir, are you by any chance local? I do hope so. I'm looking for Herbert Henry Asquith — Prime Minister during the First World War. Great-grandfather of that double-barrelled actress with the wild hair. I promised my father I'd take a photograph of his grave if I found it and—'

'Let me show you,' the man said.

Mullen was already making his exit with the dog tucked under his arm. He was tempted to look back, though not in anger. It was just that he doubted he'd ever see Detective Constable Benning dressed like that again.

He got home about an hour and a half later, having taken a different route back via Marsh Baldon, where he had walked Rex round the cricket ground and the adjoining green. After that he had treated himself to a pie and chips and pint of beer at the Seven Stars. So he was in a relaxed mood when he pulled up outside the house. He unlocked the door and went inside to check his phone in case Becca had tried to contact him. There was no particular reason why she should have texted or rung, but if she had . . . well, he wanted to respond.

He saw the mobile immediately, but it wasn't where he had left it. It was on the tiled floor and someone had clearly rammed their size twelve clodhoppers down on it with great gusto. He picked it up. Not a chance in hell of using it. He turned it over in his hands. The SIM card had been removed too. *Damn! Damn! Damn!*

He stood and listened, but the only sounds in the house were the snuffling of Rex and the unsteady hum of the fridge. Even so, he took Becca's rolling pin out of the wine rack and made his way up the stairs. But careful as he was, he couldn't stop the creak of a board every time his foot pressed down on the next step. He paused at the top, listening again. There was a sudden scampering at his feet, and Rex pushed his way past him and into Becca's room. Mullen followed the dog. He had never been in Becca's room: a double bed (unmade), a small bedside cabinet, a large white wardrobe, an Ali Baba basket full of dirty clothing, its lid lying abandoned on the floor, a small floral armchair with a deep pink nightie strewn across it. But there was no intruder, either in plain sight or in the wardrobe or under the bed. He checked the small unpainted baby's room and the bathroom. No intruder there either.

He headed back down the stairs and checked every door and window, but could find no sign of forced entry. Either the intruder was a real pro or he — or she — had a duplicate key, not so hard to achieve if you knew Becca or maybe had connections with the rental agency. *Or*, the thought suddenly struck him, *did Marie have a key? Or did Becca hide a spare one outside in case she lost hers? Under a flowerpot, for example?* Hardly original, but then he'd done precisely that himself at Moody's house. Didn't lots of people?

He tried to think. Should he ring Becca and tell her there had been a break-in? Since the arson, he had learned his lesson and written her mobile number down on the back of one of his own business cards. But would it help to tell her mid-shift? There was, as far as he could see, no sign of the intruder having run off with a bag of swag. His broken mobile told its own very clear story. If Collins and his police mates had been using Mullen's mobile as a means of tracking him down, the last thing they would have done was smash it to smithereens and nick the SIM card.

It was another warning: *Back off or else, Mr Mullen.* The big question was: or else what? First there was the screwdriver through the tyre and now there was this. If they were planning a further escalation, what the hell would that be? Maybe Holden wasn't being paranoid after all. Maybe it was he who was the fool for imagining he could ignore the threats and carry on investigating regardless.

What good would warning Becca now do? All he would achieve by ringing her mid-shift would be to alarm her. And then there was the risk that they were monitoring her phone and so would pick up the number of his burner phone — and then monitor it. Much better to tell her what had happened when she came home at the end of her shift and then try to persuade her to go and stay somewhere else, somewhere safer.

From outside there came a sudden drumming on the windows. Rain. And heavy rain at that. Something registered in his brain. He needed to do something and this seemed the opportunity. He attached a lead to Rex's collar, put on his anorak and headed outside.

Collins, and maybe others too, badly wanted him to stop his investigations into Robert Dench's death. But who exactly was Robert Dench? And why did Marie believe — or claim to believe — the coroner's conclusion that he had committed suicide? Mullen needed some answers and there was one obvious place to go.

By the time he got to Marie's house, he was soaked. He knocked on the door and picked up Rex. He was soaked too, and shivering. There had been two rolls of thunder as they trekked up the lane and of course two flashes of lightening. Not nice for a dog. Mullen waited. Marie's car was parked outside, so she was surely in. He knocked again, more loudly. She must have heard him. The downstairs light was on, so he doubted she had gone to bed.

There was a scrabbling at the door. It opened a little way and her face appeared behind a security chain.

'Sorry if this is inconvenient, but I need to speak to you.'

'No.' She shut the door.

'Please!'

'Go away.' Her words were muffled, but clear.

'It's about Becca!' he called. The rain was coming down harder, if anything, and Rex was whining. 'I said, it's—'

The door opened again. 'What about Becca?'

'Please, if we could just come in out of the rain.'

'I hate dogs.'

'He's frightened by the thunder and lightning. He's a bit of a wimp, I'm afraid.'

There was a long pause. *'Merde!'* She unhooked the chain and opened the door wide. 'What is wrong with Becca?'

'She's at work.'

'You said it was about Becca. As if—' Her face hardened. 'You were lying. It was a trick to get in my house and—'

'Yesterday someone damaged my car and this evening, while I was out, someone broke into Becca's house.'

'Did they steal things?'

'I don't think so.'

'Did they urinate on the floor or the furniture? I understand people do that sometimes.'

'They smashed my mobile phone.'

Marie frowned. 'Why? Don't burglars *steal* mobile phones?'

'Yes, they do. I think someone is trying to frighten me. I think they want me to stop investigating your husband's death.'

Mullen waited — while pretending not to. He was watching to see how she reacted. But Marie was playing it very cool. 'I do not understand. You say someone is trying to frighten you?'

'I thought maybe a friend of yours.'

'A friend of me?'

'Maybe someone who wants to protect you from the truth about your husband's death.'

'The truth is that he killed himself.'

'If he killed himself, if there is nothing new for me to discover, then why would anyone want to stop me investigating? It makes no sense.'

Marie looked at Mullen, but she made no reply. What could she say, after all? He pressed on. 'I think someone else killed him, but made it look like suicide.'

'I find this all very distressing. My son is upstairs, asleep. I am interested only in protecting him. Nothing else.'

'When did you meet Robert?'

'I would like you to go.'

'It's a simple enough question.'

She pursed her lips. 'Eight years ago.'

'How did you meet him?'

'On a blind date.'

'Really?' Mullen was momentarily taken aback.

'He was not my date. The guy I was meant to be meeting in a restaurant never turned up. I sat there waiting for nearly thirty minutes. I think I began to cry a little. It was so embarrassing. Robert was my waiter. He gave me a handkerchief and ordered me a taxi to get home. When it arrived, he escorted me outside and gave me one of the restaurant's cards. He had written his name and mobile number on it and he said to me, *"If you want to try again, I will be happy to be your blind date."*'

Mullen smiled. It was impossible not to.

'I thought at first he was just being polite, helping me out of a dreadful situation, but the next day I thought, why not ring him? It could not go any worse than that date. And six months later, we got married quietly at the registry office.'

'Do you have any photos of Robert?'

'Of course. She pointed towards a small round table in the corner of the room. Mullen went over to study the photos: bride and groom from the wedding, the two of them high on a mountain, four of their son James at different ages, a family group of the three of them — fairly recent, Mullen reckoned — and finally one of four adults and one fair-haired girl.

Mullen picked it up. 'Your family?'

She nodded. 'We go to France once a year. Those are my parents, my brother and his wife and their daughter.'

'What about Robert's family?'

'He had none. His parents were killed in a car accident. I never met them. He was an only child.'

A car crash? Both killed? Wouldn't that have made the news somewhere? He filed the fact away. Another thing to search the internet for. 'He was a chef, of course, and he was working as a waiter when you met him. What about before that?'

'He was a chef on board ships for several years. Merchant ships, going all around the world. This was after his parents died. I think he just wanted to get away from England. Eventually he came back and he had only been working as a waiter for a few weeks when he met me. Soon after that, he started to help in the kitchen. And soon after that, he was in charge.'

'Where did he grow up?'

'Yorkshire.'

'It's a big county.'

'Yes.'

'So where exactly in Yorkshire?'

'York, I think.'

'Did he ever take you there and show you the house he grew up in?'

'No. He never wanted to go back to Yorkshire. Too many bad memories. He preferred France. Better weather and much nicer food.'

Mullen nodded. He suspected she was right on both counts.

'Don't you have any photos of him when he was younger?'

She frowned, as if this was a difficult question. Then she got up and went upstairs. He heard her padding above him.

So she did have photos. In her bedroom? Where she could see them every morning and night? He got his mobile out and woke it up. There were more footsteps overhead, and then she was coming down the stairs.

'Ici.' The sudden reversion to French, albeit a common French word, caught him by surprise.

'Thank you.' There were two photos, neither in frames, both somewhat faded: an unsteady-looking toddler and a child in blazer, white shirt and tie. First day of school, maybe?

Mullen coughed and grabbed his throat. He coughed again.

'You are all right?'

'Water,' he gasped.

'Un moment.' She was on her feet and heading for the kitchen. Mullen only had seconds. Two quick photographs of the childhood snaps and then he slipped the mobile back into his pocket and grasped at his throat again.

'Ici!'

Mullen felt a fraud as he drank unsteadily at the water. But not so much that it was going to be giving him sleepless nights.

She gathered up the two photographs. 'He was a cute little boy, I think.'

Mullen nodded, prolonging the play-acting for just a bit longer. Then he plumbed his own extremely shallow well of French. *'Mais oui.'*

She stood up, and Mullen followed suit. He had pushed his luck far enough.

* * *

Back in Becca's cottage, he stripped off his soggy clothes and took a shower. Then he opened a can of beer and collapsed in front of the TV with his tablet on his lap. At least the intruder hadn't smashed that up. He thought he'd just check out his emails and watch a bit of trash before he crashed out. Ping — and there it was. An email from the prison. He could visit Kevin. It had all been so easy to arrange. Sandra had given Mullen all the relevant details, Kevin's prison number, date of birth, et cetera, and had given him the website for visiting prisoners. She must have spoken to Kevin as she had promised, so here was his invitation to visit. The first possible date was the very next day. Mullen's little whoop made Rex jump. He fired off an email to thank Sandra, then sat back to watch Mel Gibson playing a deranged cop in a film he had seen at least three times before.

When he woke much later, the TV was showing something featuring several stars he couldn't name. He switched it off, turfed Rex out for a final pee — it had stopped raining — and peered around. There was no sign of Becca's car. She had to be still be at work unless, of course, she was staying over *with* someone? *None of your business*, he told himself. But even so, he couldn't help it. Was that what happened with private detectives? Suspicion became part of your DNA? *Where is she?* he asked himself again. Even Becca wouldn't be clubbing in her condition. He went back inside, turned off the lights, stripped to his boxers and collapsed onto the sofa bed, dislodging a damp Rex in the process.

CHAPTER 14

When Mullen let Rex out the front door just after seven o'clock the next morning, he was surprised to see that the red mini was back in its normal place. Becca must have let herself in very quietly. He liked to think he was a light sleeper, but maybe he was conning himself. Maybe the dog was conning him too, failing to conduct his guard duties adequately. But maybe Rex was actually a great sentry, able to differentiate between friend and foe. Hell, he should give the dog the benefit of the doubt. He had saved his life once.

Mullen decided he was perfectly clean enough after his late-night shower, so he pulled on some clothes, fed Rex and settled down to his breakfast: toast and marmalade and a mug of strong tea. There was very little milk left and so he started a shopping list: milk, cheese, ham, eggs, salad stuff — he had soon got himself thirty or so items.

After that, he tidied his sleeping area, washed up, wiped the surfaces, and hand-washed his small pile of dirty clothing before hanging it out on the line. When she finally got up, he hoped Becca would notice how much he had done. *How pathetic you are, Mullen!* he told himself. He took the dog for a walk up the lane towards the main road, not especially for the exercise, but more to check out if there were any vehicles parked in any of the gateways to the fields. Paranoia had got its fingers hooked deep inside his brain. Then he checked his watch and decided it was time to get going. He left a note, apologising to Becca for leaving the dog, and hit the road before she could wake up and object.

If he hadn't spent a quarter of an hour negotiating his way through searches, scans and other security procedures, the room Mullen now entered might have been any anonymous community centre: cheap functional tables and chairs, pale green walls, garish lighting and a curious mix of sweat and disinfectant. Mullen was third in the queue and he paused to look around as the other visitors pushed past him.

He hadn't seen Kevin Wright for twenty years, when he had been a spotty distraught youth at Ben's funeral. So he was expecting identification to be a problem. But he knew him as soon as he saw him. He recognised the nose, the spitting image of his brother's, and the gestures: the sudden turn of the head and the lifting of his hand to his cheek, movements bringing memories of Ben flooding back into his brain. Kevin was staring back at him, eyes wide and unblinking as if he too could recognise Mullen now from his memory of Mullen then.

Mullen advanced towards him until he reached the table. 'I'm Doug Mullen.'

Kevin said nothing. He looked down and began to chew at his thumb nail, though his nails all seemed to be bitten down to the quick already.

'Is it OK if I sit down? I came to talk to you, Kevin.'

No reply again. Mullen sat down.

'Has your sister told you why I wanted to speak to you?'

Kevin looked up. His blue-grey eyes engaged momentarily with Mullen's before flicking evasively down.

Mullen slid an envelope across the table. 'I received this the morning of your mother's funeral.'

Kevin said nothing. He didn't move.

'Why don't you look inside?'

Kevin picked it up. He stared for several seconds at Mullen's name and address as if he had never seen it before and wanted to memorise it. Then, with a single movement of his right hand, he took the newspaper cutting out of the envelope and looked at it.

'Did you send it to me?'

'No.'

'I have a theory that you gave it to a visitor or a friend to post. Or did a deal with one of the guards.'

Kevin lifted his head, and this time their eyes locked. 'What if I did? It's not a crime.'

'Subverting a prison officer would be a disciplinary offence for him — or her.'

Kevin shrugged. 'It's a bloody clipping from a newspaper, telling you that your friend's mother died. Who's going to give a toss about it?' He leaned back in his chair and crossed his arms.

'Why didn't you get it in the post sooner?'

'Why the hell did you think? Because I didn't want you turning up.'

'How did you know my address?'

Kevin lifted his head and his mouth curled into a smile. 'You're not the only one who can find things out. You've been in the press with your do-gooder private detective shit. And I've had a lot of time to think in prison. About the crap deal life has handed out to me and my family. To think about how we suffered because you let Ben down. How my Mum was dying in agony from cancer while I was banged up in here. But not just physical agony. Emotional and mental too. She didn't believe in God. Didn't believe in heaven. Didn't believe she would meet up with Ben in some sort of cosy afterlife.'

'I am sorry.'

Kevin banged the flat of his left hand down on the table. 'Don't interrupt!'

Mullen froze, then looked across to the wall where a prison officer was looking like he was wired to spring into action. He lifted a finger of warning to his lips.

Mullen had no idea which way Kevin would jump — keep talking or walk out. So he waited in silence.

'I wanted you to know that our Mum was dead,' Kevin hissed. 'I wanted you to remember Ben and how you'd let him down all those years ago. I wanted you to feel as guilty as hell.'

'Did you want to kill me as well?'

Keven looked puzzled. Whatever he had been expecting, it wasn't that question. Mullen passed his second letter across the table. 'Someone torched my house. I ended up in hospital. Someone else died. And after I got out of hospital, my neighbour handed me this letter.'

There was no hesitation this time. Kevin picked the letter up immediately and pulled the letter out. He read it carefully. Mullen wondered if he had literacy problems.

'Are you saying I sent this? Cause I damn well didn't. It's not my writing.'

'Maybe you paid someone to write it for you.'

For a second time, Kevin's hand banged down onto the table. He rose to his feet and glared down at Mullen. He opened his mouth to say something, but two prison officers had raced across the room like speed skaters going for gold and grabbed him, one on each arm as if they did this sort of thing every day. They probably did.

Kevin twisted his head round as they frog-marched him towards the exit. 'Fucking well find the truth!' he yelled. 'I want justice!'

Mullen sat glued to his chair. He had blown it. He had well and truly blown it. And yet . . . and yet . . . He got up and made his way out, his brain whirling. *Two* letters. Sent by two different people.

* * *

'When are you going to paint the baby's room?' Becca was sitting in the armchair when Mullen walked in. Rex was sitting on her lap looking for all the world like he had finally weighed up the advantages of Becca versus Mullen and come down firmly on her side. *You're not the boss any more, Mullen. She is.*

He ignored her question — and Rex's insubordination. 'I've just been to prison.'

'And they let you out?'

'Hah!' He made a face. 'Don't worry, I will paint the room. You've got a few weeks to go, haven't you?'

'Maybe. Babies can come early.'

'I spoke to Kevin Wright. Ben's brother.'

'What's he behind bars for?'

Mullen ignored the question. 'He admitted that he sent the first letter, the funeral notice from the newspaper, but he denies sending the second one, the letter about my cremation.'

'Of course he would. Otherwise it would look like he was complicit in arson and so in murder.'

'I believe him.' Mullen pulled out a chair and sat down.

'Why?'

'Because he was genuinely surprised. And he got very genuinely angry.'

'I'm starving.' She pushed herself up out of the armchair, spilling Rex onto the floor. She went over to the cooker, opened the oven and took out a cottage pie. It was, to Mullen's surprise, homemade.

'It smells terrific.'

'I was going to give you until seven thirty, and then I was going to eat it on my own. All of it, most likely. I don't want baby to starve.'

Not much likelihood of that, a caustic voice said inside Mullen's head. But out loud he said, 'Of course you don't.'

'So,' Becca began, her mouth full of potato, 'who did you tell about the first letter? Apart from me, of course.'

He had just put a forkful of food into his mouth, but she wasn't waiting for him to answer.

'Because whoever sent the second letter must have known about the first one. He or she has been trying to muddy the waters, making you think they were from the same person to get you to focus on Sandra and Kevin.'

He was impressed. He had heard people, men mostly, talk about how pregnant women's brains turned to mush towards the end as the hormones took hold, but Becca's seemed as sharp as a scalpel.

He took a sip of beer. 'I told Kazia Ciesla.' He spoke the words reluctantly. They sounded like an accusation, and yet he felt only gratitude towards Kazia. The idea that she might have betrayed him was intolerable. He couldn't, *wouldn't* believe it.

'Is she one of your girlfriends?'

Sudden anger arced through him. How could she joke over such a serious matter? Three people dead and she was making cheap cracks at his non-existent love life. He stared at her, hoping she would notice his disapproval.

'Well, who is she?' Becca snapped, before thrusting more cottage pie into her mouth.

'My therapist.'

The two words stopped Becca mid-chew. She swallowed, half choked, drank a slug of water and waved her fork at him. 'You have a therapist?'

'Not anymore.'

'You mean you've finished therapy. But what on earth made you see a shrink?'

Mullen shook his head. He had been holding his fork in the air, as if it were a conductor's baton and he was about to strike up the orchestra. But now he laid it down on the side of his plate.

'Aren't you going to tell me? Are you saying you can't trust me?' There wasn't a trace of humour now. She also laid down her fork. 'Don't clam up on me, Doug.'

'Kazia is dead.'

'What?'

He wished she would stop asking questions but then if he had a fairy godmother, she clearly had better things to do with her time than waiting around to grant him his wishes. Becca pushed on, remorseless. 'How did she die, Doug?'

He blew out his cheeks and tried to focus. 'She was a friend of Professor Moody. I think they were lovers. And now they're both dead. Kazia fell in front of an Underground train in London a couple of days ago. Possibly an accident. Possibly suicide. Though I tend to think she was pushed. Deliberately.'

'Murder? Why do you think that? Do you have a witness that she was pushed? CCTV coverage?'

'I spoke to the station manager. He told me that she was dressed in a hijab when she died. She wasn't a Muslim, but she was interested in the psychology of being a Muslim in Britain. The manager did say they were open to the possibility that it was a racist attack.'

'You mean they have got it on CCTV?'

'To be honest, the manager was cagey. In fact, he clammed up. I think because of the hijab, they're looking into the possibility that it could be a racist attack.'

'So you don't actually have any evidence to support your theory that Kazia was murdered? Nothing to say she didn't slip? Or why couldn't she have committed suicide? She wouldn't be the first.'

He felt his exasperation growing. He had thought Becca would be on his side, but here she was picking holes in his thinking. He looked down at his plate and piled more food onto his fork, only just managing to get it into his mouth before it fell off.

'Doug, I'm not saying you're wrong. I just want you to convince me that you're right.' She was less provocative now, firm but calm, like a mother responding to a truculent teenager or his teacher when he got into trouble at secondary school. His thoughts flashed back to Mrs Pink: grey hair, half-spectacles, beige clothes. He sighed and looked across at Becca.

She looked back, her face stern and unyielding. 'Well?'

'Firstly, I don't believe in coincidences. Three people, all connected, die — in suspicious circumstances.'

'Actually,' she said, 'as far as I can see, only two are connected. Kazia and the professor. Good friends or even lovers. But there's no saying either of them knew Robert.'

'And there's no saying they didn't.' He'd had enough. 'Kazia Ciesla lived in Hackney, but for two or three days a week she practised in Oxford. In Headington. Less than half a mile from where Robert worked at Amanda's Café. She stayed at a house belonging to a hospital doctor, name of Leo Francombe. I think you know him, don't you, Becca?' He was in full flow and had no intention of stopping. 'When you were in hospital after your fall at the hospital, I met him in your room. He even told Marie and me that you and the baby were going to be all right.'

'You get doctors in hospital, Doug.'

'So you know him, do you?'

'Through my work. The odd coffee in the canteen. OK?'

But he hadn't finished. 'And another thing . . . A woman claiming to be a police detective visited Kazia's flat after her death. Maybe she was a detective or maybe she wasn't, but if Kazia's death was just an accident, why would anyone have done that?'

He stopped talking then. He was shaking all over, trembling uncontrollably. All the tension and anger and frustration and fear rippling through his body. He pushed his fork into his meat and potato, but his hand refused to be behave. As he lifted it towards his mouth, a glob of food fell into his lap. He slapped his fork back down on the table, and began to sob.

'Doug! What is it?' Mullen could hear her speaking, but he couldn't look up. Couldn't bear to see the expression on her face. He heard her scrape back her chair, felt the thud of her feet as she moved around the table, felt her hand grip his upper arm, pulling him to his feet. Then he felt both of her arms encircling him, holding him tight. He could smell her too, sweat overlaid by perfume. He didn't know how long they stood like that. Maybe a minute, maybe ten. It didn't matter. But eventually he was calm and had stopped shuddering and the tears had dried on his cheeks. Only then did she release him. She stepped back half a pace and they stood motionless, staring into each other's faces.

'I believe you, Doug,' she said. 'You've convinced me. But the question is, what are we going to do now?'

CHAPTER 15

By eight the next morning, Mullen was on the road again, this time heading north. On the passenger seat, rather to his surprise, sat Becca, with Rex ensconced on her lap. She was asleep and Rex was a picture of contentment. 'You look like the cat that got the cream,' Mullen quipped. But the dog ignored the disrespectful joke. Becca grunted something unintelligible. Mullen wondered if she was about to wake up, but she merely adjusted herself in the seat and resumed her gentle snoring.

When she had asked the previous evening, *'What are we going to do now?'* he had assumed that she was really saying *'What are* you *going to do?'* but he had underestimated her. After he had recovered from his own little crisis, she had made them each a mug of tea and then they had settled down and done some research. In fact, she had very quickly taken over his tablet. It was much faster than hers and her keyboard skills were hugely more impressive than his. She'd taken charge of it when he'd gone to the loo and then refused to relinquish it when he returned.

They had been following up on two things. First was five-year-old Robert's school uniform. The photo was faded but the colour was sufficient: grey shirt and trousers, blue blazer and tie (royal blue, probably). There was a badge on the blazer, but badges on pre-digital colour snaps that had been photographed with a mobile phone before being printed end up blurry. This hadn't stopped Becca. Determination personified, she scoured the internet for the primary schools of York and its surrounding area and checked out their uniforms.

'There's no saying the school will still exist' Mullen had said. 'And, if it does, they may well have changed their uniform since Robert was a child.'

'Maybe, but how often do schools change their colours? Stop being such a misery guts and go and make me a mug of tea. Two sugars — if you want me to stay awake.'

Later they had switched their attention to bowls clubs.

'He might have moved since childhood,' he'd said. 'There's no saying that he stayed in York or played bowls there.' But Becca had merely pointed at her empty mug and carried on regardless.

So now the three of them were heading north up the M1. Becca had not only printed off lists of possible schools to investigate and bowls clubs in and around York, she had also booked them into a dog-friendly hotel. 'I've booked a twin room. Much cheaper than two singles,' she'd told him. 'But I have priority over the bathroom.'

Her reasoning behind having 'priority over the bathroom' became very obvious on the trip north. Three times they stopped at services so that she could visit the ladies. Mullen was wise enough not to comment on this. He focused instead on trying out a different takeaway coffee at each stop.

The fourth and final stop was just a few miles south of York, where they ate a fast food lunch. 'I'm starving,' Becca said. 'I could eat a horse.'

'Not sure they have them on the menu.'

She didn't laugh. 'I've been thinking, Doug . . . Why don't I do the snooping around the bowls clubs while you look after Rex, because it strikes me that the little chap isn't going to be terribly welcome. The last thing they will want is him doing his business on their lovely green turf. And you can't leave him in the car in this heat.'

* * *

They started in York itself, and Mullen let Becca have her way while he walked around the nearby roads with Rex. He had this extremely optimistic hope that he would stumble across Robert Dench's primary school. The photograph taken of him on his first day of school appeared to have been taken outside the school building, but the background was fuzzy. He had been standing in front of a black wrought iron fence, but what was the chance of them still being there more than thirty years later? How easy was it anyway to tell one set of school railings from another?

Two hours later, they had made no progress. Rex had done his business twice and Mullen had dutifully cleared up after him, but he was feeling rather low. Wasn't this all a bit of a longshot: recognising a school from one old indistinct photograph — and an even longer shot tracking him down via the local bowling clubs?

He was waiting outside the fourth one on Becca's list when he heard her voice, loud and excited. 'Doug!' She was waving from the doorway. 'Doug! Come here!'

Rex was lying sullen and resentful on the path. Mullen scooped him up and marched towards the club where Becca was waiting. He assumed that the urgency in her voice meant that she had discovered something. He expected her to have a smug grin on her face, but it was the opposite. Her features were as unyielding as granite. She gestured at him to follow her and turned back inside. She led him along a long corridor that seemed to bisect the clubhouse. She stopped and turned left. 'What do you see, Doug?'

What he saw were photos. They were lined all along the corridor, photos of men with fixed grins proudly holding a bowl. Had Becca found Robert Dench? That was the obvious conclusion, but hard though he tried he couldn't see anyone who looked like Robert Dench in any of the photos. He turned to Becca for help.

She was grinning now. *Smug or what?* thought Mullen.

'Well?' He was irritated with her, but also with himself.

'What do you *not* see, Doug?'

Mullen looked again, at the faces, at the background — always the same, at the names and dates and — finally, the penny dropped. 'There are two years missing.'

'Exactly!'

Mullen looked at her, waiting for her to explain.

'These were the two years that Fred Rossiter won the pairs cup with his mate Alan Jackson. He was shit hot at bowls, apparently. They had their photos up there, of course, as is the custom, until the day that Alan Jackson came in and smashed both photos to smithereens with his own bowling ball.'

'Why?'

'Fred Rossiter had been accused of abusing Alan's son, Joe. It went to court, but the case was thrown out. Rossiter walked out of the court a free man. Alan Jackson went down to the pub, got rolling drunk, then staggered up here to the club and blitzed the photos. No one ever dared replace them.'

Mullen glanced at Becca. Over her shoulder he saw a short man in a green waistcoat scurrying along the corridor towards them. He was executing a fast walk, arms swinging. Running was probably forbidden. 'We don't allow dogs in here.'

Mullen nearly said something, but Becca cut in. 'Doug, this is John. He has been marvellously helpful.' She turned fully towards the man and greeted him as if he was a long-lost friend. The man simpered back at her, clutching his left hand with his right. Mullen marvelled that she had managed to turn this petty functionary into a pathetic devotee. 'John, please don't worry. Despite appearances, my friend is very aware of dog hygiene issues. I can promise you he won't let the dog out of his arms, and we'll be gone in less than a minute. But perhaps you could look at a photograph and tell us if it is the man you once knew as Fred Rossiter. It would be so, so helpful.'

Becca held out her hand, while Mullen ferreted in his pocket — not so easy to do without putting Rex down. They had printed off a photograph of Robert Dench, the same image that had been used in the press at the time of his death. She took it from him, opened it up, refolded it to hide the press report, and held it in front of John.

'Here you are, John.' He stared at it, and tried to take it off her, but she held on, merely moving closer to him. Little and Large. Mullen imagined her pressing him against the wall, crushing him until he squealed.

'Take your time, John,' Becca said. 'It is so important that you're certain. Don't say it's him just to get rid of me.'

He gave a little yelp. 'Oh yes, I would say that is definitely him. Of course, he looks older, but that definitely looks like Fred to me.'

She gave him a little squeeze with her left arm. 'You've been an absolute star, John.'

'We aim to please, madam.'

Mullen turned to go. He'd had enough. But Becca looped her arm through his. 'There we are, darling. One just needs to be nice to people and they will be nice back. You should try it sometime.'

They walked steadily down the corridor and out into the fresh air. 'It's all an act, darling,' she whispered. 'I can see you didn't like it, but needs must.'

'Despite appearances? You said *"despite appearances"*. Was that really necessary?'

'Well, you do look a bit of a scruff, Doug. And you haven't brushed your hair today.'

When they reached the car, her arm was still hooked through his. He tried to detach but she held on. 'Let's do this properly, Doug. A quick kiss. John is watching us.' Mullen glanced toward the clubhouse. John was indeed watching them. He leaned down and kissed her. He was aiming for her cheek, but she turned her head so he couldn't avoid her lips.

He felt a frisson run through him: irritation at being trifled with, but also something more primal. After a few seconds, longer than he had intended, he pulled away. She smiled, lifted her hand and ran it down the side of his face. 'Thank you, darling. That was very nice. But, for the record, you haven't shaved either.'

* * *

There now seemed no point in staying the night in York. They had got what they'd wanted from the trip. Becca cancelled the room, pleading that her mother had been rushed into hospital. She persuaded the person on the end of the phone to make a refund. Mullen listened silently as he headed south, leaving York in his rear mirror. He had lied in the past. It was sometimes necessary in his line of work, but he was impressed by the ease with which Becca did it. He was also somewhat disturbed. Was this something she might do to him? There was part of him, the insecure boy, that wondered if she wasn't playing him now, playing him for a fool. He had found himself thinking about her more and more now, craving her approval like a lovesick teenager, wishing he was the father of her baby and wanting her to come clean about her past and what it was that she wanted in her future.

'Penny for your thoughts?'

He shrugged and kept his eyes focused forward.

'Come on. Spill the beans, Doug.'

He felt his hands tighten on the steering wheel, his blood run fast and furious. 'If you must know,' he said, 'I was wondering if you have feelings for me.' He regretted his words immediately. *That sounded so bloody silly.*

'Hell, Doug. Feelings for you?' The car was rattling and groaning along as it always did, but all he could hear was the silence as she considered her answer. Rex lifted his head as if he could sense the significance of the moment. 'Well, Doug, darling, that really is a biggie.'

It was when they stopped for a second comfort break on the M1 that he made the phone call. He'd been mulling over the options as Becca slept and had finally reached a decision. 'I'll give the dog a little walk,' he said. 'Perhaps you can grab me an espresso after you've been to the loo.'

She muttered something he assumed to be the equivalent of *yes* and stumped off towards the main building. He led Rex to a wide grass verge and got out his burner mobile. To his surprise, Benning answered almost immediately.

'Doug, how lovely to hear from you.'

'I need to see DI Holden. Tomorrow. ASAP.'

'You need to practice your small talk, Doug. Especially when you ring a girl up late on a Sunday evening.'

'Can you contact her?'

'Of course I can, Doug.'

'Or give me her contact details, so I can ring her myself?'

'Not a good idea, Doug.'

'I know where she lives. I could call round later and—'

'*Very* bad idea, Doug.' The flippancy had disappeared from her voice. 'That would be very bad indeed. I'm the intermediary. I'll contact her. And then I'll contact you. Goodbye.' Benning terminated the call.

* * *

Benning scrolled through the four contact names she had on her mobile and found Holden's burner phone. Holden picked up on the fourth ring.

'Mullen wants to meet you. Urgently. Like tomorrow, soonest.'

'I see.' A delay followed. Benning wondered if she had interrupted something. Holden's private life was a closely guarded secret. Benning wasn't even sure which way she swung. Maybe both. It was all too easy to imagine Holden bawling out anyone she hooked up with and as a woman whose relationships fell apart when they had barely begun. Oh, to be a fly on her bedroom wall!

'Radley. St James the Great Church. Seven a.m.' Holden rang off.

Benning found Mullen's number, rang him and told him the details. It was less traceable to speak rather than text, less dangerous if either of their mobiles fell into the wrong hands. You couldn't be too careful.

She picked up her glass, drained the wine and looked across the room at the man on her sofa.

'Very fortuitous that he should ring at this time,' he said. 'Save you the trouble of ringing me.'

Benning nodded.

'I'll be off, then.' He got up off the sofa. 'Thanks for the drink.'

Benning was silent.

'Cat got your tongue?' He chuckled. 'You're doing a good job. And soon it'll all be back to normal.'

'Bye.' Benning saw him out and watched him walk down the street and get into his car, a high-end silver BMW. Not exactly two a penny, but there were plenty of them around Oxford. She shut the door, slipped the security chain across it and went to refill her glass. He'd insisted on starting a bottle of wine. She might as well finish it. But the real question was: when would this all finish? And how? And, most importantly, was she making a serious mistake?

CHAPTER 16

Mullen got up quietly, threw on his clothes and then stood at the doorway while Rex went out for a quick pee. He didn't want the dog to go AWOL, but Rex had no apparent desire to do so. As soon as Mullen called him in, he nipped past his ankles and straight up the stairs. Mullen waited for a squeal of fury from Becca, but none came. Perhaps the dog had located a nice bit of discarded clothing to lie on or maybe he had jumped up on her bed and she'd welcomed him under her duvet. Bad for discipline or what?

But it was six twenty-five a.m. and Mullen had more pressing matters than the fickle affections of a small dog. He needed to get to Radley. It wasn't far away, but he wanted to get there early, check out the lie of the land and make sure they were unobserved.

The church of St James the Great was old, a lot older than the civil war damage visible in the walls. He had learned that via his tablet. There was a car park a hundred metres or so down the road and he parked there, tucked in the corner behind the hedge, the only occupant. He would have been amazed — and suspicious — if there had been anyone else at this time of the day.

Benning had said the church, so he walked casually up the road until he reached the church gate. There was no immediate sign of Holden. The rain began to fall hard enough to encourage him to get under cover. There was a wooden porch at the entrance to the church and it seemed like a good place to wait. It was unobtrusive but afforded clear views. And unless there was a malevolent vicar hiding inside the locked doors of the church, there was no chance of anyone surprising him from behind.

Holden arrived five minutes later. Mullen didn't see her car. One moment he was checking his burner phone for any possible texts, the next he looked up to see her hurrying up the path. She wore a light summer mackintosh over what he assumed were her work clothes. No attempt to disguise herself this time. He took that as a good sign.

She shook the rain from her hair and sat down on the internal bench opposite him. 'Well?'

'Becca Baines and I drove to York and back yesterday. We've discovered who Robert Dench was before he changed his name.'

'Yes.'

'Fred Rossiter. He lived in the area.'

'What else?' Holden was irritable, impatient and possibly paranoid. She kept glancing around the churchyard as if she was expecting Genghis Khan and his hordes to come galloping in.

'He was accused of abusing his best friend's son. Taken to court, but the case collapsed.'

'Names?'

'The best friend was a chap called Alan Jackson and the boy was Joe. Alan and Fred played bowls together. Won tournaments. But never after that, it seems.'

'Why did the case collapse?'

'I don't know. I thought it best not to do any searching on the internet in case someone was monitoring me.'

'Very wise.' Holden sat there in silence. Deep in thought, he presumed — hoped so, anyway.

'Were you followed?'

'No.'

'You sure?'

'Absolutely.'

'Neither was I.'

He nodded. He wasn't sure where this was going.

Holden pulled out a packet from her pocket and lit a cigarette. She took a deep pull on it then blew out the smoke. He hadn't thought of her as a smoker. 'I'm pretty sure someone arrived before us,' she said.

'What?'

'I imagine they were waiting for us to arrive. When I say "us," maybe it was for you or maybe it was for me? Not that it matters. What matters is there's a leak. Or there's a bug. Or someone with a big mouth.'

He said nothing, but didn't like the implicit criticism.

Holden pressed on. 'How much do you trust Becca Baines?'

He gulped. Of all the questions she could have asked, of all the things she could have said . . .

'Well?' Holden snapped. 'Could it be her? After all, she was with you all of yesterday. Maybe she rang someone and tipped them off.'

'Dammit, I'd trust her with my life.' He felt anger bubbling up inside him. What right had Holden to be making such groundless accusations?

'Well, let's hope you're correct. Because your life might be in her hands.'

'She hired me in the first place. Why on earth would she—'

'Calm down, Mullen, for God's sake. This is no time for you to be throwing all your toys out of the pram.'

'What about Benning?'

'What?'

'What about Detective Constable Benning? Do you trust her?'

'Why ever shouldn't I?'

'Her hair is red, right?'

'Well, it is at the moment. It changes from time to time.'

'The evening after Kazia Ciesla died, a woman claiming to be a police detective came to her flat to check around it. She had red hair according to one of her neighbours who let her in.'

'Plenty of people fit that description.'

'In her twenties, medium height, even flashed something that looked like a warrant card.'

'It looked like a warrant card?' Holden raised her eyes.

'My informant has clearly had run-ins with the police in the past. He'd know a warrant card when he sees one.'

'But he didn't check it carefully enough to get a name from it.'

'I guess, with his background, recording her name wasn't at the top of his agenda.'

Holden grunted.

'Anyway, my point is that if you're looking for leaks, you should maybe look closer to home.'

Holden stood up and tightened the belt of her mackintosh. It was already pretty tight, he reckoned. She lit another cigarette, took a single drag and then stamped it out on the stone flags under her feet. She was obviously very stressed. Even so, when she spoke again, she did so with apparent calm. 'On the other side of the road, twenty metres to the left of the church gate, is the entrance to a close containing three houses. There are several cars parked there, but one of them has a man — or possibly a woman — sitting in it. Go and find out who it is.'

Mullen didn't move. He didn't much care to be ordered about by her. It wasn't as if he was in the police. He trusted her, admittedly, but he hadn't warmed to her.

'For crying out loud, Mullen! Pretend you've lost your little dog. Rex, isn't it? Stupid name for a black Westiepoodle but that's Professor Moody's fault, not yours. Just go and bloody look for him.'

Mullen paused, but only for a moment, just enough time for him to process the realisation that the detective inspector had remembered all the details of his dog — and presumably knew and had stored away in her memory banks plenty of other trivia about him, too. He wasn't sure whether to be touched or alarmed. He got up from the bench and began to make his way down the path to the road. 'Rex!' he bellowed, as if the dog had just run in front of a rogue tractor taking a trailer load of wheat to a grain silo. He paused, ostensibly looking around for the non-existent pooch, then he cut across the road into the close where, just as Holden had said, there stood a silver BMW — with a figure in a cap hunched behind the steering wheel. Mullen stared wildly around the close, calling Rex's name and whistling, as well as taking in the fact that although there were lights on in the upstairs of the far house, there wasn't another living soul around outside. He wasn't sure if that was a good thing or a very bad thing.

He turned towards the BMW as if he had only just noticed it, holding his hand out in alarm and supplication. 'Have you seen my dog?' he shouted. 'A little black terrier!' But the driver was revving the car's engine and pulling his cap down even further over his forehead. As Mullen drew closer, the vehicle lurched forward with a spin of its tyres towards him. He hurled himself sideways, sliding and rolling across the gravel as it swished past. He twisted round and pushed himself up on one arm, just in time to see the car swing left out of the close. He registered the first four characters of the number plate, but no more. OU18, he thought — or maybe OU13. Hell, he wasn't sure. How bloody amateurish was that?

He hobbled across the lane and back to where his own car was parked. He eased himself into the driver's seat and slammed the door shut. His left leg was throbbing and so was his head. Had the guy been trying to scare him or kill him? Or had he just panicked? Not that it mattered which. What mattered was that he was alive.

There was a noise. Mullen jumped. The passenger door opened and Holden slipped in. 'Are you all right?' she said.

'I thought you'd scarpered.'

'Scarpered?' She clearly disliked his choice of words.

'With all this secrecy stuff, I thought you'd want to keep your head down.'

'What sort of woman do you take me for?'

'Well . . .'

'You think I'm the sort of person who scarpers when things get scary?' She had turned into a venom-spitting cobra. 'Bottle it?'

'No, no!' He held his left hand out as if to deflect her anger. 'Definitely not. It was just that I assumed — stupidly — that you'd gone.' He realised he wasn't being honest. 'Actually, I suppose I thought that you were using me as a decoy.'

'A decoy?'/

'Well, weren't you?' He wasn't going to be bullied.

She pursed her lips as if she was sucking on a very sour boiled sweet. 'Maybe I was.' Then a quick change of tone — to brisk and businesslike. 'Anyway, are you OK?'

He grunted.

'Look at me!' she snapped.

He turned, and to his surprise she took hold of his head, one hand on each temple, and looked into his eyes. 'Hmmm! A bit of a mess, but you seem OK. No concussion as far as I can see.' She removed her hands and looked him up and down. 'Ruined your jeans, though.'

'Only a fiver from Oxfam.'

'Anyway, ripped jeans are very trendy.' The hint of a smile. 'Did you recognise the driver?'

'He — or she — was wearing a cap, pulled down over the forehead. 'Maybe it was Greg Collins.'

'Maybe? Either you recognised him or you didn't.'

'More of a hunch, I guess. He slashed my car tyre the other evening.' *Slashed* was a slight deviation from the truth, but what the heck? He wasn't in court swearing on the Bible. 'He didn't much like me watching him play Aunt Sally.'

'You do seem to have a knack for winding people up, Mullen. What is it about you?'

'I guess I ask awkward questions and I keep on asking them until I'm satisfied with the answers.'

'You're not so different from me, then.' There was another half-smile then a dense silence. The conversation had side-stepped from the solid ground of strictly professional cooperation into the uncertain shallows of the personal.

'So, did you get the registration number?'

'OU something.' He felt a complete fool admitting it. 'I guess when someone tries to run you down...'

'Not to worry.' She held up her mobile, like it was a trophy of war. 'Amazing cameras these things have nowadays.'

'Yes.' He felt wrong-footed. Holden had been messing about, asking him about the registration.

'I've got him trying to run you over.'

She handed her mobile to Mullen and he studied the short video. He didn't reckon Holden would win any prizes for her video skills — far too shaky for that — but he was alarmed to see quite how close the driver had come to hitting him. *Driver*, not *Collins*, he told himself, because he doubted that the video was going to prove who was driving the car. The registration number was almost readable, and no doubt some whiz-kid at Thames Valley Police would be able to make it clear enough, but would it prove to be genuine? As for the driver — head down, cap pulled low, early morning sun reflecting off the windscreen — it would be hard to prove anything.

'So what are you going to do?' he said. 'Arrest him?'

'You're in one piece, aren't you? I'm not going to waste my time on cautioning Collins for bad driving — assuming it *is* him behind the wheel. The fact is they *know*, Doug. They know that we know about Robert Dench's previous life. They knew we were meeting here today. They know that we don't believe Dench killed himself. In short, they know that we're onto them.'

'They being Collins, you mean? And who else?'

She ignored his question. 'It's one thing to suspect or even know something. It's another to be able to prove it.'

'But it's not just Robert Dench. What about Professor Moody? What about Kazia Ciesla?'

'Unless we can get them to confess or we can find some compelling evidence, then none of these deaths will matter. A suicide in the woods, an arson attack directed at you by a disgruntled person, an unfortunate accident on the London Underground. That's all they are unless we can prove otherwise.'

'And do you want to prove otherwise? Or is it only me?'

Mullen was close to seriously losing his temper, but if anything this seemed to make Holden even calmer. 'Let's talk about it over breakfast. There's a nice café on the Thames in Abingdon.'

'What? Isn't that a bit public? I thought you wanted to keep things under cover?'

'Our cover is blown, Doug. So let's make the most of it, stop pretending and see what happens. Besides, I'm starving.'

'I've got a better idea.'

'Oh, yes?'

'Amanda's Café in Headington.'

Holden grunted.

'Where Robert Dench worked.'

'I have read the file.' She was testy, as if he'd just doubted her professionalism.

'Of course you have. Unfortunately, I made rather a bad impression on Amanda and her sidekick Carly when I paid a visit.'

Holden grinned. 'It sounds perfect. As long as they don't spit in our food.'

It didn't take long for Mullen to be spotted. He and Holden had hardly sat down at one of the window tables before Amanda was striding towards them. 'It's you again!' She stood over Mullen with arms akimbo. 'Didn't you get the message last time? You're not welcome. Not when you come in here making wild accusations.'

'My companion and I just want breakfast.'

'Why don't you try the one across the road?'

'You were recommended by a friend.' Holden's voice was sweet as honey. 'Are you Amanda, by any chance?'

'I'm not serving him.'

'Yes, you will.' Holden pulled out her ID. 'It really won't be in your interests to upset me.'

Amanda froze. There was a flash of alarm in her eyes. Few people felt comfortable with the police, but Mullen couldn't help wondering if there wasn't a particular reason. 'I'll get Nabil to come and take your order.' And then she was gone, heading across the room and already gesturing at a man standing upright and still by the counter.

'Please, what do you want?' Nabil bowed slightly as he reached the table, his attention fully on Holden.

'Eggs Benedict on brown toast. And an Americano. No milk.'

Nabil seemed uncertain. 'Eggs . . . '

'Eggs Benedict.' Holden held the menu up and pointed it out.

'Ah, yes. Very nice.' He scribbled something on his pad. 'And Americano.'

'Full English for me.' Mullen decided it was easiest to keep things simple. 'And a cup of tea.'

'Are you from Syria?' Holden's interest seemed aroused.

He nodded. 'Yes. Syria. But very pleased to be here in Oxford. Very nice place.' He backed away. 'I get your food very soon.'

Mullen looked across at Holden. What was that all about? Of course, she was a copper and she was on duty, but he didn't like the idea of being involved if she was going to start arresting illegal immigrants. 'It's not a crime, is it? Being Syrian?'

'No. But exploiting them is.'

Mullen decided not to pursue this anymore. Holden was checking her mobile for something . . . emails . . . texts . . . the weather forecast . . . immigrant statistics . . . he tried not to care. He leaned across to the next table and picked up a crumpled copy of the *Metro*. He'd barely read the first paragraph of the main front-page article before a woman's voice interrupted.

'You're getting Nabil alarmed.' It was Amanda, but she was speaking to Holden, not him. 'I told him to be nice to you.

I told him you were police. And next thing you're asking him if he's Syrian and he assumes that you're going to arrest him.'

'Is he illegal then?'

'He's applied for asylum. He has a wife, a small child and a baby on the way.'

'So what's the deal with you?'

'He gets thirty quid a week to survive on. He can't take a job. So he volunteers here. Three days a week. No money changes hands. But I feed him during his shift. His wife and child come in at the end of the day when it's quiet and I feed them, too. If there's food going out of date, they take some of that home. Share it around. I'm not exploiting them. There's nothing for me to be ashamed of.'

Holden held up her hand. 'I'm pleased to hear it. Please reassure him that all I am interested in is my coffee and my breakfast.'

Amanda made a face. 'I do hope so.'

Mullen watched Amanda as she retreated. But Holden was watching him. 'What are you thinking, Doug? I can almost see the little cogs whirring around inside your brain.'

'I'd like to have a chat with Nabil . . . maybe show him a few photos.'

She nodded. 'OK, but let's eat first.'

It was a good breakfast, though not a peaceful one. Holden ignored two phone calls and then kept checking her mobile as texts came beeping in. 'I'll have to go. You settle up.' She pushed a twenty-pound note across the table. 'You may have more luck with Nabil if I'm out of the way.'

It was with Amanda that Mullen had to settle up. 'Sorry about the other day,' he said. 'I may have overstepped the mark.'

She didn't respond, merely pointed at the card reader.

He tapped his debit card and waited for the receipt. 'I think I may be able to help out Nabil,' he said. She looked at him. 'From time to time in my line of work, I need an extra pair of eyes. Who notices or would suspect a migrant?' It was a load of guff, mostly. It was only as he had finished drinking his coffee that he had come up with it as a line. But the more he had thought about it, the more convincing it had seemed.

'He doesn't need to be doing anything illegal,' Amanda said. 'Not in his position.'

'Of course not. But if I could just chat to him for five minutes outside, I would really appreciate it.' He smiled and pushed a business card across the counter. 'In any case, here is my card for you. You never know when you might want someone like me on your side.'

'I really can't imagine such a situation,' she said. But she picked it up and pushed it into her apron pocket nevertheless.

Mullen had been waiting outside for several minutes before Nabil appeared from out of the side door, and in that time it had started to rain. They stood close up against the wall, protected from the worst of the weather. 'Five minutes only,' Nabil said. 'Or Amanda get angry.'

Mullen got his mobile out and found the only photo he had of Kazia. It was the one that had appeared on a couple of websites, those that had bothered to cover her death. He didn't know who had provided it but it looked pretty recent.

Nabil studied it intently. 'Good-looking woman.'

'Has she been into the café? Have you seen her here? She stays in Oxford sometimes.'

'I do not want to get into trouble.'

'I am not the police. You will not get into trouble. But I need your help. This woman is missing. She is in trouble. Big trouble. I want to help her.' *If you were going to lie, make it good.* Kazia Ciesla was beyond all help, but she deserved it nevertheless. If she had been pushed in front of a train by someone, then Mullen was determined to bring her killer to justice. It was the least he could do for her.

'She come in sometimes.'

'Recently?'

Nabil frowned. Mullen wondered if he was struggling with understanding the word *recently*. 'I think maybe two weeks ago. Maybe more. I not sure. Green dress. Long earrings. Hair shorter than in the photo. She like pecan Danish. She buy two.'

Mullen tried to process this. Nabil's description was pretty damned good. The green dress, earrings, hair — Nabil could have been remembering her from the day of his own first session with her. It was a short walk from Francombe's house, easy enough for her to have developed a pattern of popping in here for a coffee and a sticky bun. Yet Carly had claimed not to know her. She had been insistent that Kazia had never been in there. Why the hell was that?

Mullen found another photo on his phone and showed this one to Nabil, too. 'What about him?'

Nabil nodded. 'Him a doctor. Leo. Very nice man. Talks to me.'

'Does he talk to Amanda?'

Nabil shrugged. 'A little. But *pouf!*' He made a strange noise, and threw his hands in the air. A volcano exploding, Mullen guessed. 'I think doctor prefer Carly to Amanda. She is more young. And thin. Not like Amanda. I see them in street the other day. In a doorway. The shop was closed. They were talking. Her hand on his arm. Very friendly. I think maybe they . . .' He laughed. 'You know what I mean?'

'Yes.'

'Look, I need to go back in or Amanda get cross.'

'Wait.' Mullen pulled his wallet out and extracted a business card. 'Here . . . if you need help, if you are in trouble, ring me.'

Nabil studied the card as if it was something rare and precious.

'And here.' He held out the twenty-pound note Holden had given him.

'I not take tips,' he said with sudden alarm. 'Amanda tell me. She take all money.'

'Not a tip. A gift. For your wife. *Not* for Amanda.'

There was another moment of hesitation, then he removed it carefully from Mullen's fingers. 'Thank you. You are a good man.' And with that, Nabil slipped the note into his pocket and scurried back into the shop.

Mullen frowned. Amanda *"take all money."* What did he mean? That she handled all financial dealings with the clients? That was maybe fair enough. That she kept all tips the customers left? She had said she gave him food, nothing about tips. Was that to keep the guy safe from allegations of illegal work or was Amanda not quite the saintly person that she claimed to be?

* * *

'There you are, guv. I was beginning to wonder if you were all right?' Holden had barely hung up her dripping coat and sat down at her desk before Benning had been at her side. 'The boss wants to see you. He's in a bit of a mood.'

Holden grunted acknowledgement, stood up, and made her way to the loo to check on her appearance. Only then did she take the stairs up to the realms of higher management and human resources, both of them areas that she would prefer never to enter.

McPherson pretended not to notice her as she entered the open door and stood there, legs slightly apart, arms hanging tense on either side of her body, ready for battle.

'You wanted to see me, sir.'

After a meaningful delay — *I'm the boss, you can damn well wait until I'm ready* — he glanced at her. 'Only just got in? What time do you call this?'

Holden was tempted to check her watch and answer the question literally, but even in her current frame of mind — what Benning would doubtless call 'being in a mood' — she was wary of saying anything quite so incendiary.

'Been meeting a contact.'

'Would you like to expand on that?'

'There's nothing particularly to expand on.'

'Does he have a name?'

‘Everyone has a name.’ She was echoing Mullen’s quip — and pushing her luck. ‘And many contacts have identities they would not want me sharing with anyone.’

‘Detective Inspector, may I remind you that I am not *anyone*. I am your senior officer. Who was this man you were meeting?’

‘What makes you think it was a man?’

McPherson didn’t answer. He shifted his lanky frame in the chair, as if he had suddenly realised that there was something sharp sticking into his back. ‘You’re meant to be running Operation Windrush, not chasing around like some maverick DC trying to make a name for herself.’

‘Robert Dench was murdered,’ she said.

‘I told you to stay away from that case. I warned you. The coroner determined that it was suicide.’ McPherson’s hands were clenching and unclenching on his desk as if part of a curious exercise routine.

‘I think the coroner may have got it wrong.’

‘It’s a closed case. End of discussion.’

‘What about the death of Professor Moody? That’s not closed, is it?’

McPherson cleared his throat, but Holden pressed on.

‘Then there’s the death of Kazia Ciesla, a psychotherapist who knew both Moody and Dench. She was pushed in front of a London Underground train.’

‘London? The Underground? That’s not our area of responsibility, as you well know. As for being pushed or stumbling or jumping — I’d have thought it was very hard to prove the difference.’

‘The three deaths are connected. I know it.’

‘You know it? As in you’ve got a gut feeling, you mean?’ The sarcasm in his voice was palpable.

‘It’s more than a gut feeling.’ There was silence. A stand-off. Two gunslingers waiting to see if the other backed down. ‘Please, sir.’ Holden rarely pleaded. But here she was, virtually bending her knee. If she had been a dog, she would have been lying on her back, legs held limply in the air, belly exposed in an attitude of surrender.

'You're off Operation Windrush, with immediate effect.' He stood up, indicating the end of the meeting. 'And you're also on leave for two weeks with immediate effect. And . . .' McPherson paused as he considered his words. 'And, unless you can magic up some cast iron evidence, I don't want to hear you utter the names Robert Dench, Professor Moody or Kazia whatshername ever again. And certainly not Greg Collins, either. Otherwise, I'll put you in charge of car theft and see how you like that.'

'Thank you, sir.' She moved towards the door, fighting back the urge to smirk. *Mission accomplished.* 'Thank you, sir. I really do appreciate it.'

'Now bugger off out of the station before I change my mind.'

* * *

McPherson took a deep breath as Holden disappeared from view. He picked up his mug, took a sip of his coffee and swore. It was lukewarm. Not that lukewarm coffee was the worst of his problems. He walked over to the window. It offered a rubbish view, unless you could find something aesthetically pleasing about a car park. He stared out nevertheless, looking at but barely registering a couple of uniforms having a quick fag.

His mobile rang. He pulled it out of his pocket and studied the flashing screen until it stopped ringing. He went into his settings and put a block on that number. Then he deleted all the texts he had received from it. Almost immediately another text came in informing him he had a new voice message. He rang 121, listened to part of the message — a mixture of wheedling and anger — before deleting it. *You're on your own, mate.*

He looked up from his phone, out of the window, and saw Holden approaching her car. For a moment she turned and looked up and their eyes met. Then she got in, slammed her door shut and drove away. *You're on your own too, Inspector.*

He returned to his desk and slumped into his chair. He ran a hand through his thinning hair. *We all are.*

* * *

Becca Baines woke up at much the same time as Mullen and Holden were tucking into their food in Amanda's Café. She could hear rain pattering against the windows as she rolled over and swung her legs out of bed. There was a yelp. It was the dog. She leaned down and ruffled his hairy coat. 'Sorry, Rex.' He looked back at her with dark button eyes. He was a cute little chap. In her advanced state of pregnancy, Becca had found herself finding lots of things cute. Like the pink matinee jackets that one of her fellow nurses, Marina, had been knitting with alarming rapidity. 'So cute,' she had said, and meant it, as she was handed a pile of five, each of a slightly different design, but each of the same startling shade of pink. 'So cute,' she had said to Jamina when she had brought her own beautifully brown but slightly snub-nosed twins into the hospital café to show them off. Sometimes she even found Mullen cute in his own peculiar way.

And now here she was admiring a dog who had clearly been sleeping on her clothes. She knew she had abandoned them rather carelessly on the floor last night — well, it had been very late when they got back — but the fact was they could easily have been worn for another day. But not now.

The dog licked her feet. They were probably salty. She watched him for several seconds before pushing him gently away. It was time for a shower and some food. She yawned. Maybe another snooze later. Thank God it was her day off.

Half an hour later, she was washed and dressed and enjoying a leisurely breakfast. First a bowl of muesli and then granary toast with marmalade. She got up and put two more pieces of bread in the toaster. That would be enough, surely, even though she was eating for two. The baby inside her seemed insatiable.

She was just switching on the kettle to make a second mug of tea when there was a knock on the door. She sighed. Maybe it was Marie checking up on her. She wasn't sure she was in the mood for any more of her interrogations about how long Mullen was going to stay and whether he was going to marry her and if he wasn't the father, then who was, because whoever it was should jolly well help support her financially.

She opened the door. Momentarily, she was all at sea. Then she said, 'Oh, it's you!'

'I need to talk to you.'

'Me?'

'I'm in trouble. I need help.'

Becca paused. All she wanted was to finish her breakfast and then go back to bed. Rex whined at her feet.

'Oh, she's a cutie!' Her visitor bent down and held out a hand. 'What's her name?'

'Rex,' Becca said. 'She's a he.'

* * *

Mullen needed a walk to clear his head. It had been one hell of a morning and his brain was a maelstrom of questions and paranoia: What if . . .? Who could he trust? What should he do next? He didn't think about where he was going, he just walked — away from Headington's small shopping centre down Windmill Road. There had been no sign of any Windmill, old or not. He went as far as the Nuffield Orthopaedic hospital, then right along Old Road and then right up Lime Walk.

What should he do next? It was as if he had known the answer to the question all along, but he needed his legs to lead him to the answer. When he got as far as All Saints Church, he turned right and then left. He was in New High Street, which he thought of as Shark Street thanks to one particular house with a twenty-five-foot fish protruding from its roof. But he wasn't heading for that particular house. Instead he stopped and stood again in front of Dr Leo Francombe's and tried to calm himself. Perhaps he wouldn't be in? He half hoped that would be the case, but he caught a flash of movement through the downstairs window. He took a deep breath, advanced to the front door and rang the bell before he could change his mind.

The door was opened by a young woman: dark curly hair, round face, grey T-shirt, denim shorts, sandals and a rucksack hanging casually from one shoulder.

'Hi there,' she said. She barely looked at him as she slipped past him and then headed left towards London Road. A student, a lodger, a daughter, a lover?

Mullen stepped onto the doormat and called out. 'Hello? Dr Francombe?'

There was the sound of footsteps coming down stairs. It was Francombe. 'What the—'

'I just want a quick word about Kazia Ciesla.'

He frowned and stared, 'You're one of her clients.'

'Yes.'

'You were here the other day.' There was more than a hint of irritation in his voice — and of nervousness in his face.

'I was.'

'You were trying to get hold of her, weren't you?'

'It's all right. I know she's dead.'

'You do?' He seemed relieved. 'It was a terrible thing.'

Mullen edged forward. 'Can I come in? I need to talk.'

Francombe hesitated before nodding. He led the way past the stairs into a kitchen diner with grey bifold glass doors offering a view of the garden and the little outbuilding in which Mullen had unloaded himself to Kazia. He felt a sudden lurch of emotion and when Francombe sat down at the table, he followed suit with alacrity.

'If you want to talk about what happened,' Francombe said, 'I'm not your man. I'm not a therapist, but I could probably put you in touch with one.'

'That's not why I came. I've been house-sitting for a Professor Melissa Moody in Botley while she was teaching in the States. But the house was burnt down a week or two ago by an arsonist, the day that the professor flew back. She died in the fire.'

'I read about it, on the BBC website.' Francombe had gone pale.

'Did you ever meet her?'

'I don't think so.' *Don't think so? Liar.*

'Even though she was a close friend of Kazia?'

'Was she? You seem to know more than I do.'

'Kazia lived in your house for part of the week. Didn't she talk about the professor sometimes? Or Mel, as she called her?'

'Kazia and I weren't best buddies. It was a financial arrangement. It suited both of us. But I didn't actually see that much of her. She worked hard during the day and at night she often went out. Typically we would cross paths over breakfast, but we didn't go in for long intensive chats.' Francombe looked at his watch. 'That's your five minutes. Now I really have got someone coming shortly.'

'It's not Carly, by any chance?' It was a wild throw of the dice. He really didn't think it would be Carly, but that wasn't the point. It was how Francombe reacted that mattered. For a moment his face froze, caught in indecision or surprise.

'Carly? I don't know what you're talking about. Carly who?'

'Carly who works at Amanda's Café. I understand you're quite a regular there. Rumour is that you and she are . . .' Francombe stood up so abruptly his chair cartwheeled behind him with a crash. 'Get out of my house.' His voice was controlled, but ice-cold. 'You get out, and you don't come back again. Who the hell do you think you are, anyway? I've tried to be polite and—'

'This isn't a game, Leo. I'm investigating three deaths. And someone I've talked to thinks you're having an affair with Carly.'

For a moment, Mullen thought he had pushed his luck too far, but to his surprise Francombe burst out laughing.

'We flirted a bit in the café. Why not? No harm done. She even let me cook her dinner one evening. There's no law against it. We're both consenting adults. Not that we ever got that far. That was one of Kazia's nights in the house, so I asked her to join us. It seemed . . .' He paused, his eyes and thoughts far away. Then he focused back on Mullen. 'It wasn't me she was interested in. I was a means to an end, an old fool. I'm a man. She preferred her own sex, and above all, she liked Kazia.'

'I see.'

'Do you? I don't care whether you *see* or not. Now I really must insist that you go.'

'Thank you.' Mullen stood up. 'I'm sorry if I overstepped the mark . . .'

'You're sorry? I doubt it very much.'

Mullen withdrew along the corridor and out onto the street. The door banged shut behind him, but he barely noticed. Thoughts and questions were whirling around in his head. Had Carly really been having an affair with Kazia or was Francombe covering his own tracks? These days, older men hitting on younger women ran the risk of being viewed as predatory rather than consensual. But if he was telling the truth, why had Carly pretended to Mullen that she didn't know Kazia by name and that she only understood who he was talking about when he described her? Mullen sighed. The only thing that was certain was that one of them was a liar.

But then there was Francombe's reaction to his questions about Professor Moody. He claimed never to have met her. He denied knowing that Kazia had had a relationship with her. That was hard to believe. But perhaps even more curious was his extraordinary lack of interest in her death. How many people faced with the man who had been living in the house when it burnt down, for crying out loud, would not have asked questions (*What exactly happened?*) or offered sympathetic concern (*God, how awful!*)? What sort of man was Francombe?

Mullen walked on towards London Road, barely noticing the shark that Bill Heine had famously installed in his roof. He paused at the main road and checked the time. His parking ticket would be running out soon. Time to get the car and head for what currently served as his home. He checked the traffic both ways — *look right, look left, look right again* — his mother's influence lived on. He was about to step into the road when he froze. On the far pavement was a woman. In profile, she was elegant and impressively slim, the sort of woman who could wear a fine summer dress, white with blue flowers in this case, and make you immediately want to purchase one for your loved one. She was walking smoothly and serenely through the pedestrian traffic as if she was in one world and everyone else in another. For a moment he was tempted to call across at her and wave, but she was looking determinedly in front and didn't deviate until she reached Amanda's Café. Then she swung right and in through the open door.

It was Marie. Mullen stepped out to cross the road. A woman in a red convertible hooted at him but he barely noticed her, merely waving his hand in apology as he reached the far side. He turned left. He was still full from breakfast, but he could certainly handle another coffee.

* * *

Mullen didn't believe in coincidences. Absolute coincidences rarely happened in his experience. Marie's husband had worked there for several years after all, and no doubt Marie had called in plenty of times for a coffee and snack and a brief chat with him. Just because he was dead, it didn't mean that the pattern of her going there when she wanted a drink or food or just somewhere to take her weight off her legs should change. Anyway, this was his opportunity to 'bump into her' and quiz her, wait until she was settled with a fresh cappuccino and a pastry and then move in. Talking to her in a public place might yield different results.

He stopped on the pavement and took out his phone. He needed to send Becca a text. He felt guilty. 'Sorry. Got delayed. Leave Rex in the house if you need to go out.' He hoped it would cover the bases. Becca was getting harder and harder to predict. He wanted to blame it on her advanced state of pregnancy, but he hadn't dared share that theory with her, or indeed with anyone else. Maybe if Kazia had still been around, he would have discussed it with her. He'd only had two sessions with her but her death had left a hole in his life. Absence made the heart grow fonder. And her absence was permanent. *Get a grip!* he told himself. Oddly enough, he could imagine Becca saying exactly that. But not Kazia. He *got* a grip and homed in on the café. To his surprise, Marie came out.

'Hello,' he blurted.

She checked. 'Mr Mullen!' Her face was blank with surprise. '*Bonjour.* Sorry, but I am in a hurry.' She breezed past him, back up the pavement from where she had come only a very short time before.

He was tempted to call after her, but memories of the last time he chased a woman — Carly — in this area were still fresh. So he went inside and up to the counter. Amanda looked up and observed him coolly.

'Can I have a flat white? To take away.'

'You're a bit like the bad penny, aren't you? Always turning up.'

'Your coffee's very good.'

'And your flattery's very bad. It doesn't cut any ice with me.'

'I just want a flat white.'

There were a couple of seconds of silent stand-off until Nabil appeared from the kitchen area. 'Mr Mullen! Back again! Very nice to see you.'

'Flat white to go for Mr Mullen, Nabil.'

Mullen handed over a fiver. 'That was Marie Dench, wasn't it? Went out just as I was about to come in.'

She gave Mullen his change. 'You're full of questions, aren't you?'

'What did she want?' Would Amanda be stupid enough to lie?

'Most people come here for a coffee or a snack or whatever.'

'I'm not asking about most people.'

She ran her hand over her hair as if she was in front of a mirror and had found something slightly out of place, but had mislaid her brush and comb.

'She asked if Carly was here.'

'Oh!' Mullen waited, eyes trained on Amanda.

'She should have been, but she texted me to say she was ill. Thank God I was able to get Nabil to come. This isn't his usual day.'

'Are Carly and Marie friends, then?'

'She babysits Marie's son sometimes. Or she did do when Robert was alive. I guess she'll still need her now — perhaps even more so, if she is to have any life. So maybe that means they are friends — of a sort.'

* * *

Holden was stuck in a queue on the ring road when the call came. She pressed the green phone button on the steering column and snapped a 'Hello.'

'Hi, guv.' It was Benning's voice.

'Yes?' Holden wasn't bothered about pleasantries. Certainly not today with Benning. If Benning decided she was in a mood, then so much the better.

'The number on the car is cloned. Belongs to a Skoda in Hartlepool. Owned by an Oxford United fan.'

No surprise there. She would have been amazed if it hadn't been cloned. As for Oxford fans living in Hartlepool, nothing about football fans' obsessive support for their childhood team would surprise her. The traffic started moving again.

'Anything else, guv?' Benning sounded off-key. A little too keen to help, maybe? Anxious to keep Holden's trust? Was she leaking information to Collins or McPherson? Holden reckoned it was odds on she was. But even if she wasn't, she was pretty damned sure that the rumour mill would already be churning away at the station. *Do you know about Susan? Have you heard about her bust-up with the super?*

'Whose side are you on, Constable?'

There was a marked silence before she replied. 'I don't understand, guv.'

'It's not a good idea to fall out with me, Constable. Certainly not a good idea to leak information to Greg Collins.'

'I really don't know what you are talking about, guv.'

'I think you do.' She paused, letting her warning sink in. 'However, despite all that, I do have a job for you. Robert Dench wasn't always Robert Dench. Before that he was Fred Rossiter — accused of abusing boys in York. He went to trial, but was found not guilty. Not everyone was happy with the decision. The father of the boy involved killed himself. I want you to find out everything you can and then let me know. Pronto. Just me. Not McPherson or Collins or anyone else. Do I make myself clear?'

'Yes, guv. Thank you, guv.'

'Good.' Holden terminated the call. She wasn't sure which way Benning would jump. Had Collins got something on her? As for McPherson . . . well, he still had clout. Were they in it together? Divide and conquer, as some old guy said a long time ago. Or, as she preferred to think, stir the pot and see what shit bubbles to the surface.

* * *

Mullen arrived back at Becca's house with his stomach comfortably full of breakfast and his head full of confused thoughts. Becca's car was parked outside in its usual place and Rex was waiting to zip out past him as soon as he opened the door. He watched him do his business before calling him back inside. He made a cup of tea and cleared away Becca's unwashed breakfast things. That was going to be a bone of contention if he stayed with her for too much longer. Of course, she had an excuse now, but when she gave birth she would have an even more convincing one for leaving a trail of debris behind her. The more he thought about it, *it* being him and her living together long-term, the more improbable it seemed. Chalk and cheese. He took his tea outside, sat down on one of the two seats and fell asleep.

* * *

Holden sat in her car, eyes shut and trying hard not to sleep. The sun had banished the rain and was casting its soporific spell over her. Too many early mornings and late nights. Too much work and not enough fun. She needed some holiday. Here she was on enforced leave, courtesy of Detective Superintendent McPherson, trying to prove herself and Mullen right when what she needed was to be checking in to a flight from Heathrow to somewhere totally, wonderfully, blissfully relaxing. Instead she was slumped in the Tesco car park off the ring road sipping at a black Americano and waiting for God only knew what.

Her phone rang, pulling her back into the present. It was Benning.

'What have you got for me?' No niceties, no *'Thanks for ringing so promptly,'* just the blunt question.

'The father of the boy who was allegedly abused by Fred Rossiter was a friend of his, Alan Jackson. They were bowls partners.'

'I know that!' Holden snapped. She was being unreasonable, she knew, but she really didn't care. 'What about the boy, Joe? How old is he now? Where is he?'

'Joe is dead. He had childhood leukaemia. That's when the allegations of abuse came out. Some nurse was concerned about something he said in hospital. Fred was charged, but the prosecution collapsed when it got to court.'

'What about Alan?'

'Alan killed himself shortly afterwards.'

'What about Joe's mother?'

'Lorraine. Has severe mental health problems. Lives with her sister when she's not in hospital.'

'Any other children?'

'Just one. A girl.'

'How old?'

'Twenty. She's a student.' Benning paused. It felt to Holden like a theatrical pause, making sure she had got her fullest attention.

'Is that it?' Holden was pushing her intolerance to new levels.

'No. Her name is Charlotte and she's studying psychology at Oxford Brookes University.'

'Fuck!' Another pause, though this time it was of Holden's making.

'Is everything OK, guv?'

'I need her photo and her address.'

'I'll contact the university.'

'And one more thing . . . How did Alan Jackson kill himself?'

'He shot himself. In the head.' Another silence. 'With an old army revolver.'

* * *

Mullen was dreaming of Ben again. He couldn't actually see him, but he knew he was there somewhere and he knew he was in danger because he could hear the sound of shots being fired in the distance. *Ping, ping, ping!* He woke up. It was his phone. The pings were the sound of texts and they were all from Holden.

Alan Jackson shot himself.

His wife Lorraine has severe mental health problems.

His daughter Charlotte is studying at Oxford Brookes Uni.

This is her photo.

The final text was a photograph, and a single word: *Charlotte*.

Charlotte? No it wasn't. Mullen swore and fired a text back: *Charlotte is Carly. She's a waiter at Amanda's Café.*

Moments later Holden rang. 'Where are you?'

'At home.'

'Where the hell is home, currently?'

He told her.

'Well, make sure you stay there. I told you before not to do anything stupid. So I'll tell you again. Don't. Do. Anything. Stupid. Do you hear me?'

'I hear you.'

'I'm handling the case from now.'

'Yes,' Mullen said. He terminated the call.

* * *

Holden stood outside a modern townhouse in the Vineyard area of Abingdon and pressed the bell three times. She could hear its fake *ding-dong* tones and waited impatiently for the sound of footfalls. Collins's car was parked outside the house in its allocated space. Except for the number plate, it was unquestionably the self-same car that had done its best to run Mullen down. There was a slight scrape on the rear nearside of the car, which looked a good match for the one on the video. She pressed the bell again. If he didn't answer, she'd ring his mobile. If he didn't answer his mobile then she'd begin to seriously worry.

There was the sound of a security chain being released and then the door opened. Greg Collins stared out at her. 'What the fuck do you want?'

'I think you know, Greg. So perhaps I can come in and we can discuss it.' She paused. 'In private.'

He led her inside and into a small sitting room, modern and tidy — surprisingly so. She'd reckoned him to be a bit of a slob at home. Maybe there was a woman's influence at work.

'You nearly ran over Doug Mullen this morning.'

'I've no idea what you're talking about.'

'I have a video that suggests otherwise.'

Collins shifted in his seat, but said nothing.

'Don't worry. That's not why I'm here. I'm here because I have reason to believe that Robert Dench was murdered and that you were involved.'

Collins grunted. '"Reason to believe?" No actual evidence of murder, then?'

'How thorough were your investigations, Greg?'

'Thorough enough.'

'Tell me about them.'

'Marie told us Robert rang up. He was very distressed and he told her he was sorry.'

'Sorry for what?'

'Sorry for what he was about to do. He said goodbye and the next thing was, he blew his own brains out. Of course, I didn't just take her word for it. The forensics matched her account. His prints were on the gun handle. The residue of gunshot and the cranial damage all pointed to him holding a gun to his own head and pulling the trigger.'

'What about phone records, Greg?'

'I checked those. I'm not an imbecile. Robert made a phone call to Marie's landline at the time she said. It lasted long enough for the conversation she described. It added up to suicide, just as she'd described.'

'But he wasn't the suicidal type.'

'How can anyone know that? How does anyone know precisely what was going on inside his head that evening?' Collins's eyes were glaring, his face tightening, hands balling into fists. Holden tensed. He might be past retirement age but if he turned to violence, she had no doubt he would still be a dangerous adversary.

'He urinated down his trousers just before he died. Oddly enough, that detail isn't in your report. He was scared. Only a week or two before this, he had asked advice from a friend on a good place to go abroad — a surprise present for his wife and child. Not the act of someone planning to take their own life. And no one I've spoken to has described him as being notably depressive or suicidal.'

'People hide that sort of thing. Did you ask Marie? She thought he was very low.'

'Marie is hardly a reliable witness.'

'Why not?'

'Because she had a reason to want her husband dead.'

Collins didn't respond. Didn't say, *"What reason?"* Didn't say, *"What are you talking about?"* Instead he began to show signs of panic. His normally red face paled and his eyes showed the alarm of a man who knew his hunter was drawing close.

'Robert Dench's real name was Fred Rossiter. He changed it after he was accused of abusing a boy, the son of his best friend, Alan Jackson. He was acquitted, but the police received a lot of flack for errors they'd made. Dench was in serious danger himself as a consequence, not least from Jackson. So he disappears, changes his name and reinvents himself here in Oxford. Then he meets Marie. They have a baby. The boy grows to be the same age as Alan Jackson's boy had been and Alan Jackson's daughter comes to study at Oxford Brookes. She takes a part-time waitressing job at Amanda's Café where Dench works as a chef, and of course she recognises him, whereas he doesn't recognise her because she looks nothing like the chubby ten-year-old girl he might have remembered Charlotte Jackson as. And besides, she's now calling herself Carly.'

Holden paused, waiting for a response. There was none.

'I was checking through your record. I was struck by what you described to the press as your "finest hour" — arresting a man who was found guilty of abusing three boys.'

'What the hell is wrong with that? I was proud of it. Still am. Bastards who abuse kids deserve everything they get.'

'So what happened? You found out about Robert Dench's past and then decided to kill him.'

'I did not! I was the investigating officer. It wasn't a secret. The case — and I — were all over the local press. But I just did my job. I started to assemble and sift the evidence. I checked the telephone records. I interviewed Marie. And then I got a note pushed through my door.'

'From Carly?'

'From someone signing themselves *"A friend."* Telling me about Dench's true identity and his past. So of course, I trawled the internet and I realised it was all true. I'd already met Marie. And her son, James. I knew that if Rossiter had carried on living, he'd have turned his paedophilia towards the boy. So I turned a blind eye to one or two things — cut a few corners in my investigation. I didn't know who'd done it. Probably Marie or some close friend or lover. It didn't matter. What mattered was saving that lad.'

'Was Detective Constable Benning helping you?'

He chuckled. 'Keeping me in the loop, yes. That was McPherson's suggestion. He didn't like the idea of you and that bloody Mullen working a closed case that no one in their right mind would have wanted reopening. What do you think it will be like for Marie Dench and little James when this is all splashed across the internet? Another family ruined. And all because of some private eye who wanted to rake up some dirt — and because of you, Detective Inspector.'

'I'll want you to come to the station and make a full statement of everything you've told me.'

'I'll come to the station and see McPherson. Anything else I'll do with my lawyer present.'

* * *

Mullen had been tempted to tell Holden that she wasn't his boss and she couldn't tell him what to do, but killing the call had seemed a better option. He hadn't wanted to argue the toss with her. He wanted to think. It had to be Carly. She had the opportunity and the motive. She must have seen Robert every day she worked there. Developed a friendship with him — maybe even more than friendship. Lulled him into a false sense of security and then lured him out and killed him. Made him ring Marie, tell her he was going to kill himself and then, as he had urinated down his trousers, she had blown his brains out.

He stood there for a bit longer. The dog was whining at his feet, as if conscious of his master's internal voices but unsure how to respond to them. Mullen looked down. 'I need to pee, Rex, if you don't mind.' He went inside and tramped up the stairs to the bathroom.

When he had finished, he hovered on the landing. He didn't want to alarm Becca but, in the circumstances, he really ought to warn her. She was, after all, a friend of Marie. Her door was ajar. He pushed it open and walked in. The curtains were drawn, so it took him a moment or two to register that she wasn't there. Her bed was unmade — no surprise there — but she was definitely nowhere to be seen.

He went downstairs and looked outside again. He hadn't imagined it. Her car was parked out there in its usual place and she was definitely not crashed out in it sleeping off a hangover. So where was she? Gone for a walk? Becca wasn't the walking kind, at least not in her current state. Perhaps she had gone to see Marie. Why not? That seemed the obvious answer and, as if to prove it, his mobile received a call from Becca.

'Where are you? At Marie's?' he said quickly. 'I was worried. Your car's here, but you're not.'

'Ten out of ten for observation, Doug.'

Mullen's heart jumped into mouth. 'Who is that?' But he already knew who it was. He recognised her voice all too well.

'Now listen very carefully, Doug. Becca is a guest of mine. And she will remain a guest of mine until you come and take her place. I will text you directions to an address. I insist that you come alone. Absolutely alone. You will not inform the police. No one will tail you. No drones will fly over the area. If even a one-legged country yokel stumps up the lane after you, the deal will be off. And if I am forced to call the deal off, then you and you alone will be responsible for what happens to Becca and her baby. Do you understand?'

'Yes.' Of course he bloody did.

'You have twenty minutes.'

'None of this has anything to do with Becca!' He blurted the words out, knowing they would achieve nothing. But standing mute was not something he could bear to do.

Carly didn't reply. The line was silent. Moments later a text came through. The game was on.

* * *

Becca had been so easily fooled. She hadn't been able to place the woman at first. It was only when they had got in the car that she had suddenly realised who she was — not by her name, but where she had seen her before: the girl from Amanda's Café. *Girl* because, although she was clearly of university age, she was alarmingly thin and distinctly childish-looking. In retrospect, it was easy to see that her eyes gave a hint of the demons beneath the surface. But at the time she had been seduced and fooled by the little girl lost look.

She had pulled a gun out of her handbag in much the same way as most women might pull out a pack of paper tissues and had pointed it casually at Becca's baby bump. 'I won't hesitate to shoot,' she had said. 'Believe me, I've nothing left to lose.'

The woman had handcuffed her and made her lie down on the back seat of her car, pulling down sun blinds over both rear windows.

Then she had driven her here, to this old windmill, which had clearly seen better days. The mill machinery had long been stripped out and the building had now become a storage area for agricultural kit that the owner couldn't quite bring himself to throw out: wooden trays (which she reckoned had something to do with potatoes), hand tools, rolls of plastic, a small stack of straw bales (last year's to judge from the discolouration and dust on their outside) and an alarming clump of fuel cans. The woman had tied her loosely to a central post with a rope. 'Just to reiterate,' she said, 'if you make any noise or shout out or try to escape, then I *will* shoot you. Or rather, I'll shoot your baby and then I'll leave you half dead and set fire to all these lovely bales. And then you'll wish you were dead.'

* * *

There was no time to waste, not least because the last thing Mullen wanted was Holden turning up and interfering. He ran to the car and swore. Rex was sitting on the grass by the driver's door. He thought he had shut him inside the house. The last thing he needed was a midget-sized dog under his feet. 'Here!' he said firmly. *'Here!'* He moved back towards the house but Rex showed no sign of obeying orders. He knew what the keys in Mullen's hands meant and he had no intention of missing out.

Mullen moved back to the car and unlocked it. Rex was inside before the door was fully open, ensconced on the passenger seat, sitting upright and alert. He gave Mullen the full stare treatment. *In case you've forgotten, I go where you go. Comprendez?*

Of course he comprendezed! He understood Rex's dog language only too well. 'On your head be it, chum.'

Partner, not chum! He felt Rex's reply.

At least the satnav was working, third rate though it was. Mullen's brain was half attuned to not taking a wrong turn and half to coming up with a plan. The only problem was that he had drawn a complete blank on that front. A few ideas had presented themselves but none of them had convinced him even momentarily.

Walk up to Carly and charm her with his most innocent smile . . . *Yeah, right, that'll work. Not!*

Disarm her . . . She knew how to use a gun — think Robert Dench's death. Chances were she'd be carrying at least one — how else could she have got Becca to cooperate? So just grab it off her while Becca causes a distraction . . . *Not such a bad idea, if only Becca was party to it.*

Fall to his knees and plead for Becca's life . . . *Romantic, but futile.* If he seriously thought she would be willing to let Becca go if only he blew his own brains out, then he really was crazy.

Summon Holden and an armed response unit . . . *Too little time and too risky.* Carly was ready to die as long as she took him and Becca with her.

Talk her down . . . *Don't make me laugh!* She'd already killed three people. She had a real taste for it now.

They were less than two miles from their destination according to satnav. It was time to look out for the landmarks Carly had described.

First was an old pub, which had long since ceased to be a pub and was now a crumbling ruin engulfed by brambles, sycamores and ivy and presided over by a rookery. A few hundred metres further on, Mullen slowed down, peering right until he saw what he was looking for: a rough-hewn farm track and an unfriendly notice. *Keep out. Trespassers will be prosecuted.*

'Better than "Trespassers will be shot."' He was keeping Rex fully up to date with things.

He drove slowly, not that there was any other option given the state of the track. Twice his wheels spun briefly in slaked mud and pools of water from that morning's downpour. A cock pheasant flew low across the front of him. A grey squirrel minding its own business on the central grassy hump of the track looked at Mullen's slow advance and decided to get out of the way up the trunk of a huge oak. A couple of crows or rooks — Mullen was an ornithological dunce — called from somewhere to his left. As the road curved round to the right, the shape of a long-neglected windmill hove into view: no sails, no smart new coat of white paint, just a husk.

He stopped the car a hundred metres short of the windmill. 'We'll play it by ear, then.'

Rex responded by hopping across onto his lap. He was shivering.

Mullen hesitated. What use could the dog be? Carly would probably shoot him for sport.

He got out of the car, leaving the keys in the ignition. All set for a fast getaway — hah! He stuffed his burner phone under his seat. He had decided not to risk ringing Holden with it, but maybe at some point she or Benning would have the wit to track it and trace his last movements. In the meantime, this was his battle.

'All set, partner?'

Rex had stopped shivering, so Mullen reckoned that must mean *Yes*.

He walked towards the windmill. The sun was now out in all its glory, various small birds were chattering away in the bushes and bees were humming. How could anything bad be about to happen?

Up front, a slight figure appeared from the doorway of the windmill — Carly. He kept walking. She stood still, hands hanging loosely by her thighs, baseball cap on her head and sunglasses over her eyes — a modern-day gunslinger, except there was no sign of a gun. Not yet.

Mullen didn't pause for a moment or vary his pace. He'd keep walking slowly until she told him not to. *Get inside . . . Find Becca . . . Check out the lie of the land. Then do something heroic, preferably without ending up dead.*

Apart from the sounds of nature, it was strikingly quiet. No noise from any distant ring road or the dreaded A34. No planes flew overhead. No combine harvesters or farm tractors plied their trade. The calm before the storm. Except that Mullen felt anything but calm. Every sinew in his body was screaming *Action!* The adrenalin was kicking in. *Fight or flight,* it was screaming. But he kept walking, step by steady step.

Into the valley of death rode the six hundred. The words emerged suddenly from the hidden recesses of his brain. Not from school, because Mullen had prided himself on not concentrating on things like poetry there, but from his stay in the army, where someone who *had* paid attention at school insisted that they all learn it. 'The Charge of the Light Brigade' . . . A highly appropriate poem, Mullen reckoned, if you overlooked the missing 599 and the speed of his own advance. But they were in a valley of sorts, rising land to the left, a mixture of grass and woodland and a much steeper and more rugged ground to the right.

He was some thirty metres from Carly when she ordered him to stop. He froze.

She kept advancing and he realised that she *did* have a gun. It was in her other hand. *Mental note . . . she's left-handed.*

'Hands in the air!'

He complied, lifting Rex as he did.

'Hell! What on earth have you brought a dog for? If you can call it a dog.'

Never insult a man's dog. 'He jumped in the car before I could stop him.'

'Inseparable, are you? You and your toy dog. Anyway, now you're going to have to dump him on the ground and lean against that tree — arms straight, legs apart.'

'Man's best friend.'

'Full of shit and clichés, that's what you are. Now move.'

He put Rex down a few metres from the tree. *'Sit!'* He hoped against hope Rex would comply.

'He even thinks about biting me and I'll blow his little brains out.' Mullen set himself against the tree as she moved closer. 'I have a very twitchy trigger finger. So strip off very slowly.'

He gradually removed his shoes, socks, jeans, T-shirt and started finally on his Y-fronts.

'OK, leave the pants. I've no desire to see your dick.' Mullen pulled them back up, ever so slowly. 'Now into the windmill and take your wretched toy dog with you.'

Mullen picked up Rex, who hadn't moved from his spot. Maybe he understood the seriousness of the situation, the danger implicit in a deranged girl-woman with a gun. Or maybe, finally, he had learned the importance of following orders. Mullen walked on towards the windmill, promising to himself that if Carly had hurt Becca then he would kill her or die trying.

'Doug!' Becca's wobbly voice came from somewhere in the shadows cast by the blazing sun.

'Are you OK?' *Stupid question.*

'You shouldn't have come. She'll kill us both now.'

As his eyes adjusted to the light within, he glimpsed her now in deep shadow. Her hands were tied or handcuffed together — hard to tell which — and she was roped to one of several thick wooden posts that supported a circular wood floor running right around the inside of the building like a miniature running track above his head. He scanned the interior, desperately looking for something he could use as a weapon. Anything at all.

'I couldn't bring the cavalry.' He tried to sound light-hearted. 'So I've brought Rex instead.'

'Cavalry?' Carly snapped. As words go, Mullen's hadn't been well-chosen. 'If anyone comes along that lane, it's fucking curtains for both of you.'

'No one's coming. I told you. But you did promise you would let Becca go.'

'And you believed me?' She laughed. 'What a fool you are, Doug. And what a plonker you picked, Becca. Muggins. That's what you should call him. Doug Muggins . . . the plonker.'

'It's me you need to punish — if punishment's what you're after.'

'Becca hired you, didn't she? She asked you to investigate Robert Dench's death. Against Marie's wishes. Against everyone's wishes.'

'So Marie was involved, was she?' Mullen saw an opportunity and went for it. 'Where is she now, then? Has she scarpered and left you to carry the can?'

Carly let out a shrill laugh. 'You think I'd have trusted her? I chummed up to her. I picked her brains. I told her who she was married to — a child abuser.'

'It was never proved.'

'Only because the police screwed things up. Fred Rossiter was as guilty as hell. When I discovered him masquerading under the name of Robert Dench and that he had a young son, I knew I had to take things into my own hands. But the last thing I was going to do was let Marie in on my plans. No way. She talked about leaving him and returning to France, but I wanted revenge. Don't you see?'

'Of course.' Mullen could feel the situation slipping away from him, but he refused to give up. 'I understand. I really do. But please, why involve Becca? She has a baby inside her. For God's sake, let her go and kill me.'

'She hired you. So it's her stupid fault and besides . . . she knows everything. So I can't do that.'

'You seriously think that if you kill her and me you'll be able to drive off into the sunset and live happily ever after?'

She didn't reply. It was impossible for Mullen to estimate how she was reacting. She stood in a patch of sunlight entering through one of the small square windows high above, but her eyes and her face were cloaked in darkness under the visor of her cap.

'Killing someone thought to have abused young children is one thing, but murdering an eight-months pregnant woman and the child inside her — now that really is beyond the pale. No one is going to cover for you, no one is going to turn a blind eye. Not even Greg Collins.'

'Shut up!' Carly hissed. 'Shut up or else!'

'Or else what? Scratch my eyes out like you tried last time? Ooh, I'm scared.' When you riled someone, you did your best to distract them, to throw them off balance. It was all about timing: when to continue pressing, when to risk all.

Or, sometimes, when to toss the dog into the fray. If Mullen had had time to think about it, he would have patted Rex on the head and thanked him for being the best partner ever and said sorry for what he was about to do. But of course he didn't. Instead he lobbed Rex high into the air above Carly and almost simultaneously hurled himself forward at her. There was the explosive crack of a bullet, an agonised yelp from and a warlike scream from Becca, sitting helpless but not voiceless on the sidelines. There was also a very satisfying thump as Mullen's shoulder hit the lightweight Carly and sent her spinning backwards into the straw.

But Charlotte Jackson hadn't been taking self-defence lessons just for the hell of it. She cannoned off a bale and, like a children's toy, bounced up back onto her feet.

'Good try, Muggins, but not good enough.' She giggled.

Mullen was also back on his feet, swaying slightly and crouching low. He advanced two steps forward and tried to grab her, but she slipped away out of reach.

Another giggle. 'Try again.'

He was confident that if he could just get a firm grip then he would be able to overpower her, but sometimes confidence was misplaced. The next thing he knew, she had jabbed him hard in the left eye. He should have expected it, should have been ready to counter the sudden two-fingered jab, but he plummeted to the floor. He tried to rise, hoping somehow that with his one working eye he could even the odds, but as he tried to focus on Carly, something solid smashed into the side of his temple. He sank down again.

It's not going to end well. His mother used to say that from time to time and had usually been right. Mullen ignored the words of wisdom circulating in his brain and pushed himself up onto his knees. Carly had withdrawn two or three metres away. She was standing next to a pile of straw bales and was pouring petrol out of the can with which she had just cracked Mullen around the head. She stared at him, demons in her eyes.

'God, your house was a sight when it went up in flames. Shame it was your professor in there and not you, Doug.'

Mullen screamed, a final cry again the dying of the light, and forced himself to his feet. He ran at her or at least he tried to, but she sidestepped him and sent him sprawling into the petrol-sodden straw.

She laughed. 'Now, where are my matches?' she asked theatrically. 'They must be here somewhere.'

But theatricality is one thing — a loaded gun is another. Carly's gun had spun into the air when Mullen and the dog had come hurtling towards her, but she hadn't recovered it. Hadn't needed to, because she clearly felt she was more than a match for Mullen. More than a match for any man who tried to lay a finger on her. But she had reckoned without Mullen's best friend. It was the dog who recovered the gun. It was the dog who saw Becca stretching at the end of her rope to grab it. It was the dog who remembered all the bits of sausage she had disobediently dropped on the floor for him and the warmth of her body when he had snuck into bed with her. It was the dog who used his snout to push the gun inch by inch into her reach.

But it was Becca who picked it up in her cuffed hands and pointed it in Carly's direction. As Mullen went down for the third time, Becca fired it into Carly's central body mass — or at least, that was where she aimed, but she had never fired anything more powerful than an air gun in her life, so she wasn't ready for the kick. The barrel jumped alarmingly in her hands. She bellowed in frustration. She cursed herself for her stupidity and tensed her whole body, ready to try again. But Carly, to Becca's amazement sank to her knees, a puppet in slow motion, mouth gaping, eyes rolling in their sockets. She stared blankly at Becca, apparently unaware of the blood pouring out of the neat hole in her neck. Becca stared back at her, ready to shoot again if needed. She didn't notice, not until it was too late, that Carly's twitching fingers were desperately scrabbling to light a match. There was a flash of ignition and then, as Carly fell forward onto her face, a wild explosion of flame as the petrol fumes ignited all around her.

Becca had only a hazy idea of how they got out. She tried shooting through the thick rope tying her to the post, but this turned out to be harder than she thought. The fumes and smoke were already swirling around her, causing her to choke and cough, and her eyes to sting. In desperation, she fired another shot and then Mullen materialised at her side, taking the gun from her and, like a good boy scout, producing a rusty old bit of metal with which he began to saw furiously at the rope. One by one, the strands began to ping apart.

'Quick!' she croaked (as if he wasn't doing his damnedest to hurry), and then wonderfully the rope split asunder and Mullen was pulling her, gasping and spluttering, through the smoke until they emerged into the bright, clean air outside.

CHAPTER 17

It wasn't hard to track down Sergeant Major Bates. After a career of bullying young men into the brutal realities of being a squaddie in the British army, he had earned himself enough of a reputation to be given a retirement send-off in the local media and then invited by the local second division club to be their guest of honour at their Forces day. Neither was the sort of gig to live long in the public memory, but for Bates they clearly mattered. Mullen could tell that from the photographs the internet had helpfully provided. Despite the passage of time, Bates was still recognisably Bates, albeit significantly older than the image imprinted in Mullen's memory. His hair, insofar as it was visible under his army cap, was a mix of grey and white. His eyes stared out at the viewer with a wild intensity that made Mullen shiver with apprehension.

There was a third, more recent event in Sergeant Major Bates's life that had briefly caught the attention of the press. Nine months previously he had been involved in a brawl at the back of a pub called the White Hart. Bates had tried to beat the shit out of a seventeen-year-old who had mocked him. But this got only the most short-lived of coverage because Bates had had the wisdom, or maybe luck, to teach his tormentor a lesson beyond the intrusive of reach of any

CCTV cameras. He did get taken to court, but, according to the local press, received only a suspended sentence and a verbal warning from the magistrate.

It was a miserable damp day when Mullen drove up the main street of the miserable grey town Bates now called home. There were empty shop units, bookmakers, fast food outlets, sale signs and even a charity shop with a sign saying *Closing Down*. The consequences of several years of austerity were much sharper here than back in Oxford.

The pub was on a street corner just beyond the main run of shops. He turned left up the side road and parked his car. The White Hart was red brick and rundown, boasting cheap food and drink deals and endless sports coverage. Mullen gathered Rex into his arms and pushed his way in through swing doors that were in desperate need of some tender loving care. He advanced towards the bar and waited. A man with long grey hair pulled into an untidy ponytail glanced up.

'Yeah?'

'I'm looking for a man called Bates. Ex-army.'

'Are you?' The words were little more than a grunt.

'He was my sergeant major.'

'Lucky you.'

'I owe him a pint. Is he in today?'

'Not yet.'

The man turned away and for a moment or two, Mullen was tempted to grab him by his rope of greasy hair and yank hard. But of course he didn't.

'I need to see him. It's my day off and I've driven a long way.'

The man turned round and folded his arms ostentatiously across his chest. 'People who come here normally start by buying a drink.'

Mullen nodded. 'A pint of bitter, then.'

Only when Mullen had paid his money did the barman open up. 'The sergeant major comes in much later. He's probably out fishing now. Just downriver from the bridge up the other end of the high street.'

'Thank you.'

'You can take your dog into the garden, but make sure you don't leave any shit on the premises. I get very angry when that happens.'

'Don't worry. He's a good little chap and I've got bags.'

'That's what they all bloody say.'

Mullen made his way out the back. *Garden* was a very generous way of describing the area behind the pub. It was full tarmac and not a blade of grass to be seen. There were four pots with half-dead plants in them and four picnic-style tables. He and Rex sat at one. They were alone. Mullen was glad of that and he put his mind to rehearsing the questions he wanted to ask Bates when he finally tracked him down. Bates wouldn't be expecting him, probably wouldn't even recognise him at first, so the challenge was to take advantage of that before his guard went up and shutters went down.

Mullen was halfway through his pint when his peace was interrupted: enter left a couple of young women who were smoking, chewing and chatting all at the same time. They sat down at the next table and looked over.

'Cute little dog, mister.' It was the one with short red hair and round John Lennon glasses who spoke. 'My nan's got one like that. Only he farts like nobody's business.' The girls burst into laughter.

Mullen smiled as he sipped his pint. He could take a joke.

'And he tries to impregnate anything that moves,' said the other girl. Cue more laughter. She had a black bob, wore a violet T-shirt and denim dungarees, and had a Liverpool accent.

'Better watch yourselves, then,' Mullen said, getting into the spirit of things. Yet more laughter.

'Gonna buy us a drink, mate?'

He shrugged. 'Another time.' And with that, Mullen beat a retreat, leaving half a glass of warm weak beer behind. 'See you around.'

A string of Scouse invective formed the reply.

* * *

Mullen made his way on foot back along the high street. Twice he was stopped, first by an old lady and then by a girl who ought to have been at school. They both wanted to stroke Rex. Part of Mullen wanted to ignore them. After all, he hadn't come all this way to talk dogs with random strangers, but he didn't have the heart to walk on by. He worried about the woman, who looked as though a light breeze might knock her over. He worried more about the girl: was she skiving or had she been excluded for being a troublemaker? In either case, what was going on at home? Mullen held the view that trouble on the streets usually stemmed from trouble at home. Maybe that was simplistic, ignoring the fact that all teenagers want to kick over the parental traces, but even so, that was what he thought. After all, he had had plenty of experience of trouble at home: a drunken bastard of a father and a mother who couldn't hold things together. Both those things had consequences, one of which was thinking he could save himself by joining the army.

When he finally reached the bridge, he turned left onto a tarmac track flanking the soft curve of the river. There was a wide strip of grass to the left and Mullen unhooked Rex from the leash. Mullen, however, was focused not on the dog, but on some squat seated figures up ahead who looked like they were serious anglers. He was content to move at Rex's preferred pace, which was intermittent and unpredictable — slow, slow, quick, quick, stop, then repeated in any order that took his fancy. The first guy had two rods and was enormous with red face and blotched hands. Mullen walked on.

The next guy was not a guy, but a woman. Mullen liked to think he wasn't sexist, but even so he was taken by surprise. Fishing had to him always seemed a distinctly male activity, and pretty pointless unless you were planning to eat the wretched fish after you had yanked it out of the river attached to your vicious barbed hook. Mullen nodded and moved on until he drew near to another figure crouched in a fisherman's pose — and a shockingly familiar figure it was, too. Sergeant Major Bates sat on a large square fishing basket.

He was rocking slightly but perceptibly, backwards and forwards, hunched over his long pole rod. His concentration on the water was absolute. Mullen stood still, watching him, taking in the pallid smoker's skin, bulbous nose and occasional twitch.

'Caught anything?' Mullin said.

'No.' His eyes remained fixed on the river.

'Sergeant Major Bates, isn't it?'

He glanced up, his eyes taking in Mullen's face. 'Who are you?'

'Don't you remember?'

He turned his face back to the river and his bobbing red float. 'I can't remember everyone. There were so many.'

'Private Mullen.' He trotted out his service number.

Bates shook his head. He began to wind his fishing line in.

'What about Ben Wright?'

Bates wound his reel a little bit faster.

'He shot himself!' Mullen insisted. 'You must remember him.'

Bates continued to ignore Mullen and began to dismantle his gear. Mullen watched in fascination. Bates's hands moved with smooth, unflustered speed. For a few seconds, Mullen was back in the army, watching the sergeant major demonstrate how to strip down a rifle.

Before Mullen realised, Bates was all packed up. He hoisted the seat and fishing gear onto his back. Only then did he look at Mullen. 'I remember now. You and Private Wright were friends. Extremely close friends, as I recall.' His lips curled into a sneer. Then he turned away and headed back towards the bridge and the town. Mullen watched him go, wondering if he would look back. But Bates marched resolutely away up the slope, without even the hint of a backward glance. Mullen wanted to scream after him, to tell him and the world what a bastard he had been. But he didn't do that. Instead he scooped Rex up into his arms and began walking quickly after him. Inevitably, Bates reached the road and disappeared from sight long before Mullen could close the gap, but Mullen didn't panic. It wasn't a huge town and he knew how to track down people.

On reaching the high street, he turned right and thrust his way through the slow-moving mothers and babies, grand-parents and students who were clogging the pavement. He was confident that he would catch up on Bates, as long as the man didn't deviate. And even if Bates did disappear for a while, Mullen was pretty confident that sooner or later, probably sooner, Bates would turn up at the White Hart.

Mullen pressed on, scanning both sides of the road, but Bates refused to reappear. Soon enough, Mullen was back outside the pub, wondering and hoping he hadn't misread his quarry. Because his quarry was what Bates had become, a man to be hunted down, backed into a corner and forced to tell all, because if anyone knew the full truth about what had happened, it was surely him.

Mullen slipped inside the White Hart and looked around. He checked outside at the back in the so-called garden. No Bates to be seen there either. Perhaps he was in the gents. They were situated out the back, a single-storey brick building tacked onto the main one. Mullen went inside, but there was no one there.

Mullen got himself a beer and two bags of crisps and went back into the garden. It was overcast, but warm enough for sitting out. *Don't panic,* he told himself. Bates would have taken all his fishing gear home first. Given time, he'd turn up. And he was a smoker so, as sure as eggs were eggs, he'd come out soon after he got himself a drink. That was Mullen's line of thinking and he was sticking with it. He sat down at the table in the far corner of the garden so that he had a clear view of everything. He ripped open one of the crisp bags and started to eat, swilling the first mouthful down with a swig of beer. *Calm down. Think. Be prepared. You'll have just one chance. One opportunity to catch him off guard.*

Mullen had just finished the second bag when Bates appeared. He was carrying a pint of dark ale in one hand and a packet of cigarettes in the other. He plonked himself down at the table nearest the loo and lit up. Mullen didn't move and didn't say anything. He just sat very still and stared across the space at him. They were the only two people out there and it didn't take long for Bates to notice Mullen. He looked, Mullen was pleased to notice, somewhat alarmed. He took a long pull at his beer and peered over the rim of the glass at Mullen as he did so. Was he worried that Mullen might rush over and attack him?

He put his glass down and wiped the froth off his upper lip. 'What the fuck are you doing here?'

'Same as you. Having a pint.'

'I don't take kindly to being followed.'

'Is that what you think I'm doing?'

'Just because I'm older than I was, doesn't mean I can't look after myself, Private Mullen.'

'Oh, don't worry. I know that. I read in the newspaper how you beat the shit out of a seventeen-year-old.'

'Bloody fag tried it on with me.' His face was a mask of hatred. 'I taught the bastard a lesson, I can tell you.'

'You got a suspended sentence.'

'Slap on the wrists. It was worth it.'

Mullen got up, beer in hand, and walked over to him. He stared down and Bates stared up. Then he slipped into the seat on the other side of the table, his eyes still fixed on Bates. 'But a suspended sentence means that if you were to get into a fight with me, then it's pretty likely that you'd end up in prison, don't you think?'

Bates's nose flared. 'What the hell do you want, Mullen? Cos much as I would love to punch four bells out of you, I'd much rather sit and drink my beer in peace.'

'I want you to think back to the night Ben Wright died.'

Bates shrugged and sneered in a single movement. Mullen felt his heart jump. It was like the intervening years had never happened. Bates was being and doing exactly what he had always been and done back then. He was being a total and utter bastard.

Mullen continued. 'You remember, I expect. We'd been on exercise. Three nights. Lots of us went to the pub. Only you never joined us. Nor did Ben. He was knackered, I know, but he had told me he would come and he didn't.'

'I expect he was too shagged out. Mind you, you shared a tent with him, didn't you? So I expect you would know.' Another sneer, another twist of the mouth, another display of teeth. Bates was like a wolf. He got up and rounded the table. He stood by Mullen and bent so close to him that Mullen could feel his hot, alcoholic breath. 'Now be a good little chap and bugger off,' he hissed. 'Otherwise I'll tell the landlord that you've been giving me a load of hassle while I've been trying to have a nice quiet drink. He really won't like to hear that because I'm a very good customer here.'

Mullen was tempted, *sorely* tempted, to rise to the challenge in Bates's words. His old *bête noir* might still be physically a bit bigger than him, but muscle had started to turn to fat some time ago. Mullen was confident that if it came to a fight, it would be he who came out on top. But it wasn't a fight he was after, or even revenge. It was the truth.

He waited for Bates to disappear into the loo. Then he stood up, spilling Rex onto the ground, and followed his old sergeant major in. The external door swung shut behind him. Bates was already standing against the urinals, his flies open, pissing his beer onto the porcelain. He half turned and saw that it was Mullen. Alarm flashed across his face.

Mullen said nothing. Instead he put his hand into his pocket, pulled out a garden knife and opened it up. It was a good knife. Mullen had found it useful round the professor's garden, cutting back some of the bushes. It was made of high-quality steel with a sharp blade and a curved hook on its tip, which gave it a distinct hint of menace. Mullen held it up at the level of Bates's eyes.

'This is a pruning knife. Very good for cutting off all the bits you don't need. Dead, diseased, damaged.' He glanced down at Bates's flies, still undone.

Bates fumbled at his zip. 'What the fuck is this all about?' He sounded big but Mullen could see the terror in his eyes.

'It's about what happened to Ben.'

Bates opened his mouth, but the words froze on his lips. Mullen could smell his fear and he was glad. 'He killed himself, didn't he? Couldn't take the army life. Not my fault. My job was to weed out those who couldn't take it. He should have been let go. He should have just walked out. He wasn't any use to me or the army. Stick him in the battle zone and he would have been a danger to his comrades.'

'Was that why you did it?'

'I didn't do anything. He cracked. He took his own life. It happens. If you hadn't been such a good mate, maybe he wouldn't have reached that point. Maybe he would have woken up one morning and jacked it all in. So why didn't he? That's the question. Was it because he hid behind you? Relied on you to make things all right and tuck him up in bed at night? Maybe it was your bloody fault, Mullen. Your fault that he stayed in the army and your fault that he topped himself.' The eyes in Bates's head were like marbles. Glaring at Mullen with a crazed intensity.

Mullen waved the knife slowly from left to right. Bates followed it. Mullen wondered if Bates would make a grab for it. Part of him hoped so, because then it would give him the excuse to cut the bastard right across his nasty leering face.

'Well?' Bates wasn't a man to lie down with a whimper. 'What's it going to be?'

'Just one question.' Mullen looked deep into his eyes. He needed to see Bates's instant reaction. This was the moment. He would never get the opportunity again. 'Tell me, *Sergeant Major* . . . was it your idea to make him put on a dress?'

Bates's eyes opened even wider. His mouth gaped. And in that tiny moment before the bravado and the lies kicked in, before Bates asked him what on earth he was talking about, Mullen knew the truth.

But Bates did not ask him what on earth or, indeed, what the fuck was going on, because he was a feral creature with survival instinct embedded deep in his DNA. He was also at this precise moment the proverbial cornered rat. Milliseconds flashed by as Mullen processed the reality he had seen in Bates's eyes. In those self-same moments Bates sensed his opportunity and he attacked, grabbing Mullen's wrist and twisting savagely. The knife clattered onto the tiled floor and then Bates's other hand, balled into a fist, thudded into Mullen's ribcage. He staggered backwards, colliding with the wall.

That was when Bates made his mistake. He dropped to the floor, desperate to grab the knife and give himself the advantage. But Mullen didn't need the security of a weapon. He wasn't, at heart, a killer and he knew that the man with a knife in his hand usually ends up using it. Just as Bates's fingers closed over the handle, Mullen's foot stamped down hard on it. Bates didn't yell. So Mullen stamped again, harder this time, and there was a crunch of fingers breaking and a grunt of pain. Bates tried to rise to his feet but Mullen's knee was waiting and smacked into his groin. He sank to the floor. Mullen watched him writhe. Bates was doubled up and the moans of pains seemed genuine. Even so, Mullen wasn't going to be caught out again. He kicked the knife well away from Bates before he leaned down and retrieved it. He folded the blade away and slipped it back into his pocket.

'Be seeing you,' he said, without meaning it. He never wanted to see the guy again, although he knew that the bastard would almost certainly creep unbidden into his dreams whenever he dreamt of Ben. He pushed open the door and went outside. Rex was waiting for him, whining. Mullen picked him up. Two smokers in the far corner were staring at him, wondering what it was that had been going on in the toilets, wondering maybe if they should have intervened or called the publican. Mullen nodded at them with a smile and went out via the side gate.

'Let's go home,' he told the dog. He never wanted to see this shitty pub again. Rex licked the back of his hand. Unconditional love and no arguments. No wonder dogs were a man's best friend. Or indeed a woman's, he corrected himself.

He had just got into his car when his mobile rang. It was Becca.

'Yes?' he said. 'Are you all right?'

'Becca is fine.' It wasn't her speaking — it was a man, a man with a familiar voice. 'Dr Leo Francombe here. Becca asked me to ring and tell you that she has gone into labour.'

'But she's OK?'

'The baby is breech. Not ideal. So I think they may give her a Caesarean. That isn't my area of speciality, but that's the most likely option. Anyway, I'm calling because I'm a friend of Becca and she insisted that I tell you what's happening. So I've told you.' Francombe rang off without waiting for a reply.

A friend? Mullen swallowed and felt rather faint. Did that mean Francombe was the baby's father? It felt like a revelation. It wasn't like she ever talked about him. She talked about lots of colleagues, but not Francombe. God, he'd rather not have known. It would have been easier to commit to the child if there wasn't a competing father.

Leo Francombe . . . Mullen had never liked him and he was pretty sure he never would. Hell!

Rex whimpered.

Mullen looked at him and nodded. 'You're right, partner. We need to get to the hospital pronto.'

THE END

ALSO BY PETER TICKLER

DETECTIVE SUSAN HOLDEN SERIES
Book 1: BLOOD ON THE COWLEY ROAD
Book 2: BLOOD IN GRANDPONT
Book 3: BLOOD ON THE MARSH

DETECTIVE DOUG MULLEN SERIES
Book 1: DEAD IN THE WATER
Book 2: WHITE LIES, DEADLY LIES
Book 3: DEAD IN OXFORD

STANDALONE
THE GIRL WHO STOLE THE APPLE

Join our mailing list to be the first to hear about the next book in the series:
www.joffebooks.com/contact/

FREE KINDLE BOOKS

Please join our mailing list for free Kindle books and new releases, including crime thrillers, mysteries, romance and more, as well as news on the next book by Peter Tickler!

www.joffebooks.com

Follow us on Facebook, Twitter and Instagram
@joffebooks

JOFFE BOOKS

Thank you for reading this book. If you enjoyed it please leave feedback on Amazon, and if there is anything we missed or you have a question about then please get in touch. The author and publishing team appreciate your feedback and time reading this book.

We're very grateful to eagle-eyed readers who take the time to contact us. Please send any errors you find to corrections@joffebooks.com

Printed in Great Britain
by Amazon

37380004R00131